BOSSY DEVIL

A Nashville Devils Novel

Book 5

MELISSA IVERS

BOSSY DEVIL

NASHVILLE DEVILS BOOK FIVE

MELISSA IVERS

Bossy Devil

Man Cover Designer: Cassie Chapman at Opulent Swag and Designs

Photographer: Xram Ragde

Cover Model: Lucas Montilla

Illustrator: Concepts by Canea

Discreet Cover Designer: Echo with Wildheart Graphics

Editor: Katy Nielsen

Author Note

Please note that Bossy Devil is a work of fiction and while it is a hockey romance, not all aspects of hockey may be accurate. This is a fictional story and as such will have fictional teams, players, and the rules may might not be exactly the same as they are in the real world.

Thank you so much for taking a chance on Bossy Devil. While this is one of my favorite stories, there is content that may be triggering for some. The following topics might be considered sensitive to some: death of a parent, and alcoholism (from a parent).

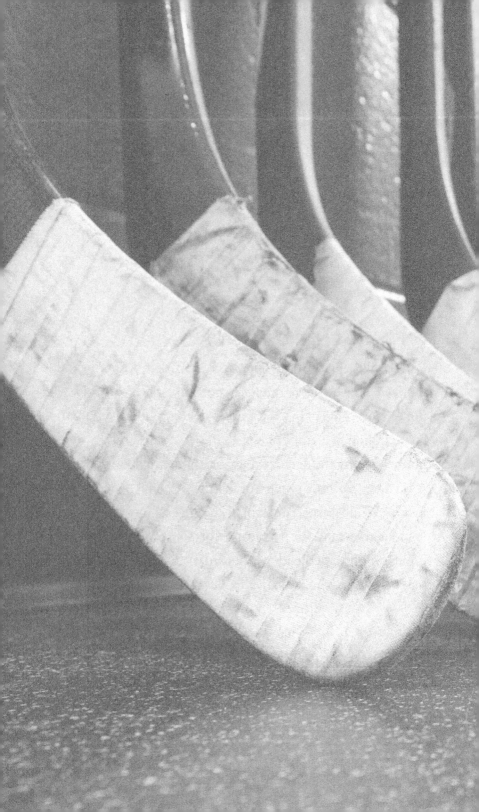

Team Roster

Players
Lincoln Dallas #8 - Right Wing and Captain
Tag Harris #26 - Left Wing
Foster Craig #44 - Center
Ian McIver #9 - Defenseman
Owen McIver #6 - Defenseman
Rhett Remington #28 - Defenseman
Dimitri Kozak #31 - Goalie
Weston Gray #14 - Center
Brad Tavers #3 - Defenseman
Austin Cloutier #29 - Backup Goalie
Thomas Desjardins #11 - Left Wing
Andrei Vasilgev #18 - Right Wing

Coaches
Mick Weller - Head Coach

Chris Miller - Assistant Coach

John Belanger - Goalie Coach

Devils Owners and Support Staff

Gordon Benson - Owner

Jazlyn Benson - Owner

Dean Prescott - General Manager

Krista Irving - Secretary for Head Office

Dan Fraser - Security Guard

Bossy Devil- The Playlist

Bones – Imagine Dragons
Breakeven – The Script
House of Memories – Panic! At The Disco
Against All Odds – Phil Collins
How To Save A Life – The Fray
Somebody To Love – Queen
The Loneliest – Maneskin
Hate That I Love You – Rihanna, Ne-Yo
Over And Over – Nelly, Tim McGraw
Just Give Me A Reason – P!nk, Nate Ruess
Far Away – Nickleback
Story Of My Life – One Direction
Someone You Loved – Lewis Capaldi
Only Human – Ryan Mack
How Do I Say Goodbye – Dean Lewis
Before You Go – Lewis Capaldi

Never Really Over – Katy Perry

Back To You – Selena Gomez

On Bended Knee – Boyz II Men

Back To December – Taylor Swift

Lose Control – Teddy Swims

Black Balloon – The Goo Goo Dolls

I Miss You – Blink 182

Unsteady – X Ambassadors

Sine From Above – Lady Gaga, Elton John

Honey – Maneskin

Come A Little Closer – Dierks Bentley

Last Night – Morgan Wallen

Hanging By A Moment – Lifehouse

Say You Won't Let Go – James Arthur

Dead Don't Die – Shinedown

Radioactive – Imagine Dragons

Fight 'Til The End – Jack Savoretti

I Won't Give Up – Jason Mraz

One – Ed Sheeran

A Sky Full Of Stars – Coldplay

Perfect – Ed Sheeran

The Cure – Lady Laga

Something Just Like This – The Chainsmokers, Coldplay

If your first love is your last. Or if they were the one that got away and all you need is a second chance.

Now sit down and read your hockey smut like the good girl you are.

1

GORDON

I'D LOVE TO SAY I'M NOT STAYING LATE AT THE OFFICE, trying to catch another glimpse of my ex-girlfriend. I really would.

But I fucking cannot.

It doesn't seem to matter that she doesn't deserve a single second of my time. She lost that right over a decade ago, yet here we are. If I didn't already hate myself, I would after the mental gymnastics I've put myself through today trying *not* to think about her, and then berating myself every damn time I did.

Fuck. I lean back in my office chair and blow out a breath, tilting my head toward the ceiling and sending a silent prayer to anyone or anything willing to listen. *Please let me forget.* I don't want to forgive, just fucking forget it all. *Forget her.*

I know she's in this building—she's been here for

hours—down there on the ice, wearing some frilly princess costume I hate, and singing happy songs, which I also hate. Both the singing and the songs, just in case that was a question.

Don't even get me started on the perfectly chiseled Ken dolls putting their hands all over her. I saw the way their sausage fingers wrapped around her waist to raise her up for the lifts. And no, I wasn't spying on her or anything creepy. Jazz and her merry band of hockey idiots tricked me into going to a show last week, and because I'm polite—and was surrounded by said idiots—I stayed.

Surprise, I hate all of it. Everything from the glittery leotards to those handsy motherfuckers. Especially the handsy motherfuckers.

Why?

Not a damn clue.

I shouldn't care. *I don't care.* Fine. I don't *want* to care, but I really think I do. And yes, I hate that, too.

At this point, I'm pretty sure 'grumpy asshole' is my entire personality.

"You're in your office a little late for a Friday night." Jazz, my very loveable but also very annoying little sister, sticks her head into my doorway, a very sweet smile on her face. Just like her, it may appear nice and unassuming, but it can only mean trouble. "No hot date?"

I grunt, shifting forward and moving some papers

around on my desk, trying to look busy. I mean, I am busy. *Very busy.* "I'm always here late. You're the one that's usually off with your... whatever."

"You mean your future brother-in-law?"

"Oh, has he proposed?"

"Not yet. We're enjoying our time—"

"Trust me, I know exactly how you enjoy spending your time with your soft-handed boy toy. I've been an unfortunate witness on several occasions." I hold up a hand and cringe as a mental image of the pose I caught her and Lincoln in last week assaults my brain. With a grumble, I close my eyes, taking a deep breath and reminding myself to google which technique might be safer—eyeball bleaching or a lobotomy.

She smirks, propping herself up against my doorframe and glancing behind her. Presumably at the boy toy in question, who just so happens to be my team's hockey captain. I mostly like him when he's on the ice. Off of it? Well, I'm trying to be *nice*, but it's not exactly my strong suit.

Jazz gestures toward me and the paperwork strewn across my normally very tidy desk. "You're in a mood tonight."

"I'm in a perfectly normal mood."

"Yeah, it's called unapproachable." Lincoln sticks his head around Jazz, pressing a quick kiss to her temple and standing behind her. He's basically blocking the entire fucking doorway so there's no way I can escape from this lovely conversation.

"Doesn't seem to stop you from coming in and talking to me."

"That's because I'm used to your gruff, grumpy bear exterior. You're going to have to learn how to smile if you're going to go down there and talk to your old girlfriend. You'll scare all those poor ice skaters to death if you keep scowling like that."

I grunt, having no intention of continuing this conversation—now or later—and go back to reading whatever these jumbled words are on this paper. Only, I can't concentrate for shit now that I have two sets of eyeballs drilling into the top of my skull.

Waiting.

And waiting.

And then waiting some more.

Why do they have to fuck with me tonight? Literally, any other day would be grand. Any day but fucking today when I know Riley is so close, yet so goddammed untouchable. She's in the same building for Christ's sake. *My building.* I'd be tempted to sneak down there and watch her on the ice if it didn't make me look like a stalker. Not to mention I'd have to listen to all the singing. Hard pass.

She hasn't been this close since…

Since the day she said goodbye and walked away from me.

"I'm not going down to talk to *any* of the figure skaters." My teeth grind together and my jaw tics before I grit out, "And I know how to smile. Thanks."

"Are you doing it right now?" Jazz asks, tilting her head and examining me.

Hate that too.

Lincoln makes a face, and while I think he's trying to look thoughtful; it only makes him look constipated. Hmm. Come to think of it, it's not far off from his usual everyday face.

All I know is that I'd like this conversation to end.

But instead of leaving me in peace, he glances at my sister and opens his mouth. "I don't think he is. You know, I bet he came out of the womb looking like an overpriced lawyer who's late for court."

"Oh, I guarantee it," Jazz laughs. "One of those stuffy lawyers that study for fun and recites the law in normal conversation."

"His face definitely looks like he wants to rain on someone's parade. Probably mine."

"Yeah, you get used to that. I think his eye might be twitching too."

It fucking is. "Are you two idiots done talking about my damn face?"

"See? I was right. It was a frown." Jazz tosses Lincoln a look I can only classify as indecent before she waltzes into my office and leans against the corner of my desk, pointing directly at me. I let out a sigh to rival all sighs. "You better fix yourself before you see Riley."

"I don't remember inviting you in here."

"I don't remember caring. Now, about Riley."

"I'm not going down to see her," I practically growl, tossing around a few random papers on my desk. Are they important? At this point, I don't fucking know. "We have three weeks until the trade deadline and I'm trying to work. If you don't mind, I'd like to get back to it."

"Trade deadline or not, there's more to life than work, you know."

"Not in mine."

"Not much of a life then, is it?"

This time I do growl, running a hand through my hair and gripping the back of my neck. I love my sister, I really do, but sometimes she gets on my last nerve. Like now. "You obviously have something to say to me, so you might as well get it all out."

"Maybe I just wanted to hang out with my big brother tonight. Maybe I wanted to make sure you weren't lonely."

"Okay, let's pretend I believe that." I sigh, glancing toward the door and frowning even harder when Lincoln waves at me. "Then what's Dallas doing here?"

Lincoln crosses his arms and smirks. "Maybe I also wanted to hang out with my future big brother tonight. I hear you're fun at parties."

"You two are perfect for each other, and I despise the both of you."

Jazz tosses her head back with a laugh and pins me with a look, one that says she sees right through me. "You love us. Just like I know you once loved the girl you're trying to avoid."

"That's the key word Jazz—loved. Past tense. As in not anymore." I smooth a hand down my tie and fiddle with the knot at my throat. "Besides, it's not like I ended things. She broke up with me. She made her choice, and it wasn't me." I hang my head with a sigh, ignoring the dull throb in my chest. "I wasn't good enough for her and she proved that very quickly when she moved on to date that dick, Wylder."

"If she's not the one, it doesn't mean there can't be someone else," she shrugs, glancing at Lincoln, a smile pulling at her lips. "There's a whole big, wide world outside this office, and as long as you're sitting in it, you're missing out on life... on love... everything."

"I'll consider it." I put my head down, trying to get back to work, but I can feel the two of them still staring at me. With a huff, I look between Jazz and Linc, so full of life, so full of hope, so full of love. It makes me want to vomit. I don't feel like I'm missing out on any of it, but if I don't give them something, I know they won't be leaving anytime soon. "We can go out after the game next weekend. I'll even smile."

"And you won't dress like an uptight prick?"

"No promises."

"Fine." She lets out a triumphant hum before pushing herself to her feet, giving me a sassy smile, and skipping out of my office... but not before adding, "Good luck with Riley. You know, the girl you're still trying to convince yourself you're not going to see."

I fight the urge to scoff—barely—but I do, and make sure to scowl as I follow Jazz with my gaze until she turns out of sight. Lincoln, however, does not immediately turn to follow like he should. He's still loitering in the doorway, eyeing me expectantly. If he's waiting for me to spew my feelings all over him now that my sister is gone, he's going to be waiting a long time. I no longer have any feelings toward the girl downstairs, pleasant or not, and even if I did, he'd be the last person I would share them with.

Guys like me, we're okay even when we're not okay. We smile while the pain grips our hearts and we don't know if we can get out of bed in the morning; when we're so incapacitated we ingrain ourselves in routine just so we can take a step forward and not dwell the rest of our lives in the past.

It's what I did twelve years ago, and it's what I'm going to do today.

Pain, no matter how excruciating, is tolerable if you find a way to cope.

"Can I help you?" I pick up the antique letter opener my father had in a display case on his desk and twirl it around my fingers. I briefly consider chucking it at him, but with my luck, I'd miss him entirely and end up stabbing the wall. Then I'd have a permanent reminder of not only this conversation, but how Riley's presence in this building affects me, and I don't want that.

Plus, Jazz would kill me if I actually did manage to hit him.

She ruins all my fun.

He cocks his head to the side and smiles, gesturing to the makeshift weapon in my hand. "Thinking about stabbing me?"

"Maybe."

"I'm not sure how that would play out on the local news. Hockey King, Mr. Grumpus, stabs his very innocent, very handsome team captain, for absolutely no reason."

"I have plenty of reasons."

"Maybe someone pissed in his Cheerios. Maybe he wanted to be the best-looking guy here. Or he could've just lost his mind because he spent all day, every day, cooped up in his office. I know you had that injury that keeps you from going back out on the ice, but I don't know how you can spend all day in here." He pauses like he's waiting for me to respond, which I am not. After a few seconds, he sighs and continues. "You deserve a life, Gordon, everyone does. You can have a second chance."

I toss my head back and laugh, despite the pain clutching my chest and squeezing the air out of my lungs. I ignore the way my insides twist and my throat tightens. I ignore it all. I don't deserve happiness. I don't deserve anything. "You know nothing about my past, about everything I had to give up to be where I am."

"Don't I?"

"I imagine, growing up, our lives were very different, Dallas." I steeple my fingers and keep my face impassive as I stare right through him, ignoring the images of my dad's angry face, his insults, his fists, his complete and utter disappointment. "Just because you got your happy ending, don't think the rest of us need or want that shit. Riley wasn't the one that got away. She's not the love of my life, she's nothing but a mistake from my past that I'd like to forget. Now, please leave my office before I toss you out of the building myself."

He nods, shoving his hands in the pockets of his jeans, but doesn't leave. "For a long time, I didn't think I deserved one either." He turns to go, but before he takes the first step, he glances back at me. "You're lying to me —and probably yourself—if you think she's just a mistake. I see you, Benson. You've been different this past week since you saw her. Your sister noticed it, I've noticed it. You use your anger as a shield, a way to keep everyone away, to keep anyone from getting too close. Eventually you're gonna have to let someone in, or you're going to die alone."

Lincoln leaves and I find myself staring after him, into the empty doorway for several minutes before I shake myself off. I put my head down and shift through the paperwork I've tossed everywhere, but nothing makes sense. Not the papers I have no intention of reading. Not my own motherfucking thoughts. Nothing.

Fuck him. Who does he think he is, coming into my fucking office and telling me he sees me? What does that even mean? I fucking see you too, Dallas, and you're nothing but a prick. An asshole who couldn't even come to me like a man and tell me he was screwing my sister.

You're lying to me—and probably yourself—if you think she's just a mistake.

The only mistake I made was staying here way too late and letting my team captain, an employee, get in my head.

You deserve a life, Gordon, everyone does. You can have a second chance.

I lean back in my chair and take a deep breath, only for it to get stuck in my throat. Closing my eyes, I loosen the knot on my tie and run a hand down my face.

Second chances aren't for me.

You get one chance at happiness. One chance to land your dream job. One chance to find love.

One chance.

And it only takes one fucking little thing to topple everything to the ground.

2

RILEY

"HAVE I TOLD YOU TODAY HOW MUCH I LOVE YOU?" GIA frames my face with her hands, squeezes my cheeks together—her hold so tight I might end up with a permanent duck face—and plops a wet kiss to the center of my forehead.

I try to nod, pull away, anything to free myself, but she has a very impressive grip. So instead, I mumble a quick *thank you* that comes out more like *spank you* and hope she flits off to the next person.

"Maybe later, you wicked thing," Gia cackles, jostling me from side to side before releasing me abruptly. I stumble back, catching myself on the wooden bench behind me, but she seems oblivious to my almost fall as she nudges me with her hips and gives me a smile I can't help but return—even though my face hurts. "But seriously. I know you had your reservations getting back on the ice like this, but you saved my ass."

Sure, I had reservations, but they had nothing to do with figure skating and everything to do with the man who owns this arena. I may have given up on my dreams to go all the way to the Olympics, but I never stopped skating. I just made sure to practice somewhere else. This arena, including the practice rink, has been completely off limits. Until now.

Because of him.

Gordon "Asshole" Benson—the one person I'd have been happy to never see again. Except fate thinks she's funny and likes to torture me.

Here I was, executing a perfect lutz jump and getting ready for a lift when I see *him* in the audience. I shouldn't have. It was crowded as hell, and he should've been another faceless person watching the show. Should've been, but wasn't. My gaze was drawn to him instantly. The energy that had always flowed between us immediate, and I had to remind myself of all the reasons I hated him, all the things he's done.

And sitting right there at the top of the list—his ability to draw me in after all these years. After all the reasons I shouldn't even look in his direction, he had me trapped with those dark green eyes of his. I could feel them on me all night.

I could feel *him*.

I fucking *hated* it.

He wasn't supposed to be here. Sure, this is his arena, and technically he can be wherever he wants, but a kids' show? I never thought I'd see him in the audience with a bag of popcorn and a suit that probably costs more than a month's rent. And I sure as hell figured he'd never recognize me in a bright red wig and mermaid costume. Wrong.

I can only hope to get out of here quietly and never come back to his ice palace again.

It's been a week since I saw him at the show and he hasn't hunted me down yet, so there's a good chance I can get the hell out of here without crossing his tracks, and then reaffirm my vow to never come back. I'll burn sage, light candles, carry around whatever crystal my sister says I need to rid myself of evil spirits, because I do not need to run into him.

Like ever.

There's nothing left to say, and nothing he can tell me that will make a damn bit of difference.

Not after how he left things.

For years, I thought about what I would say if I saw him again, if I had the chance to confront him. At first it was a lot of obscenities, and I imagined any possible conversation would end with me walking away after telling him how much I hope his dick rots and falls off. However, as the years crawled by, the narrative changed. Instead of telling him off, what I really wanted to know was how he could tell me he loved me, beg me to stay with him, and shatter my heart in a matter of weeks? How he could be that callous, cold, detached?

One of his biggest fears was becoming his father, and while he was an asshole, I can't imagine his father treating any woman like Gordon treated me.

Maybe I didn't really know him at all. Hell, if he could say those things to me, I really didn't.

"It's not a problem. I'm always willing to help out." This time when I smile at Gia, it's tight, a little forced. It's not her fault. I didn't tell her about my past, about Gordon.

I've never told anyone but my sister, and even then, she had to force it out of me.

"I don't know why you stopped skating and took a boring-ass desk job, but you're better than most of my girls. What's it going to take to convince you to travel with us? I bet I could pay you more than what you make filing paperwork and making copies. You're way too good to be in an office all day."

Heat creeps up my neck and spreads across my cheeks. Her offer is flattering, it really is, especially since I've been figure skating since I could walk, and in my younger years, dreamed about doing it as a career. I'm tempted, I really am, but there are two very big reasons why I won't leave the city. "Well, I don't know, Gia. It gets really exciting when the printer collates and staples for you."

"Oh, come on, Riley. Let me steal you."

I take a deep breath, glancing at the floor as my heart hammers against my ribcage. There are so many reasons why this would be a dream come true, and the little girl inside me is ecstatic. But for every reason urging me to go, there are two more telling me it's impossible.

Figure skating was once my passion, my life, but I have other things—more important things—like my girls. "I'm sorry. You know I can't leave Nashville."

"You sure? I don't give up that easily. I can be very persuasive."

"Do your worst. I don't give up that easily either."

She shakes her head and pulls me in for a tight hug, wiping my forehead before releasing me fully. "Got a little lipstick on you. I guess I'll just have to be content with your friendship. For now."

I huff a laugh, picking up my silver sequin duffle bag and slinging it over my shoulder. "If you'd like, I can give you a picture of me to take on your travels. You can think of me when you're fighting that LA traffic."

"I'll be spanking you if you don't watch yourself."

"Don't threaten me with a good time."

She shakes her head and chuckles, but as she opens her mouth to respond, one of the other skaters—one of the new princes on the tour—waves her over. "Alright, I'll let you be. Go home. Go to bed. Think about traveling the world with me."

With one last hug, she's off, leaving me standing alone amidst the crowd of skaters. They're putting away their costumes and chatting excitedly about their next city. They're all so young and full of life. They have big dreams, and some of them even bigger egos. They live for the spotlight, the recognition. That was once my life, my dream, but now I couldn't be more different. My life isn't full of excitement and I'm more than content practicing when I can at the smaller ice centers around town.

The only reason I'm here is because Gia is one of the nicest people I've ever met and she was so desperate for replacements after several girls came down with the flu, she called me. I almost didn't do it, but let me tell you, that girl is not above begging. And trust me, she needed to beg to get me to agree to work here for a few nights. There was no way I wanted to put myself in the same building as my ex-boyfriend, and had she not offered me a hefty sum of money, she'd have been one princess short.

With a deep breath and one last glance around the locker room, I head out, pushing through the large door, but pause when my phone vibrates in my back pocket. I pull it out, briefly considering ignoring my baby sister, but move my duffel bag to the other side before I answer, holding the phone up to my ear.

"Hey, Harper. Are you bored or hungry?"

"Oh, come on." I may not be able to see her, but I can guarantee she's rolling her eyes right about now. "There are other times when I call you. Maybe I just wanted to say hello to my favorite sister."

I huff a laugh, leaning against the wall outside the visitors' locker room and let my bag fall to the floor. "I'm your only sister."

"See? Automatic favorite. How was your last show? Was it awesome? Did that hottie, Prince David, ask you out yet? He's got a very sizable bulge in those tights of his."

"No, and since he's very happily married, I don't see him asking me out anytime soon." Not that I have the time, nor the inclination to date right now. "You know how busy I am with Max and work, plus your high maintenance ass."

"Well, damn. And I'm not high maintenance."

"You are. Since when are you so concerned with my love life?"

"Or lack there-of?" she shoots back, and I can hear the smile in her tone. "Well, I'm loaded with classes this semester and have absolutely no time for dating. Plus, most of the guys in college are well... gross. I was hoping this show was going to help you get a life and allow me to live vicariously through you, but it seems like your love life is one big dumpster fire."

"Gee, thanks." I glance around the hallway, but aside from a few arena employees, it's relatively empty. "It's not that bad."

"Oh, please. When was the last time you had a date? Actually, don't answer that. When was the last time you had sex?"

"Harper!" I'm pretty sure my voice echoed down the hallway, and after getting a cutting glance from one of the concession guys, I grab my bag and make my way down the hall.

"What? It's a fair question."

"Harper!" This time I whisper-yell to avoid any more bad looks.

"I'm going to assume it's been a while since you've been *serviced*." She says the last word with extra emphasis, and then pauses for a second before gasping. "Oh, God. Was Dan the last one? Has it really been that long? Oh, shit, I bet he had a small dick too. Was it a micro? I bet it was a micro."

"Jesus, Harper, lower your voice. He was perfectly nice."

"Which means *boring*. Wow. I'm so sorry, I've been so busy with school, I didn't realize how dire this situation is. Don't worry, I'm here to help. Every woman needs to get her pipes cleaned out every so often."

"How did we get on this conversation?" I make a turn, one I'm not sure I was supposed to make because this area of the arena doesn't look familiar. Oh well, the damn thing goes in a circle, so if this is the wrong way, I should eventually get back to the right exit. At least I hope so. "I don't need help finding a date—or getting laid."

Harper responds but I don't hear a thing. I can't, not when Gordon Benson himself is standing less than two feet away, towering over me in a black suit that looks like it's molded to his muscular frame. Those dark green eyes of his are narrowed on me like I'm in his way, and if I am, I couldn't care less.

His mouth is quirked up and as his fingers dance along the length of his tie, I get a small flash of what it used to feel like when he used those fingers on me, when they danced up my spine, down my thighs...

He doesn't look much different than how he did twelve years ago. Obviously, he's more filled out than an eighteen-year-old kid, a little taller, and has more scruff. But he still looks similar enough that I have to remind myself he's not the same man I once knew.

Not even close.

"Good to know." Gordon clears his throat, tugging at that damn tie, and suddenly I'd like to choke him with it. You know, after I figure out what in the hell he's talking about. I'm about to ask too when it dawns on me... he must have heard me telling Harper I don't need help getting laid.

Oh, fuck my life.

Fuck it with a rusty butter knife.

The longer I stare at him, not speaking, the more my cheeks heat.

"Riley? You there?" Harper hollers into the phone, and I'm so startled I almost drop it. "Who is that? Is he hot? He sounds hot."

The corner of Gordon's mouth twitches, and as

reality comes crashing down on me, my blood simmers and years of anger wash over me. My hand grips the phone, the metal digging into my fingers, grounding me, giving me a faint reminder of the pain he's caused. "I'll see you back at home. I've got to go."

"I hope you didn't hang up on my account."

I open my mouth. Close it. Open it again, and ultimately decide to take a breath before I tear him a new asshole. "Don't think you have any bearing on how I live my life. You lost that right years ago."

"Funny." He leans forward, crowding my space, and I have to fight the urge to punch him. "I don't remember having much of a choice years ago either."

Shots fired.

3

GORDON

I CAN'T HELP MY GROWING SMILE AS I PEER DOWN AT Riley. She huffs a breath, flipping a curtain of dark red hair over her shoulder, her green eyes narrowing on me.

If Riley could demolish me on the spot with the hatred simmering in her gaze, I'm sure she would. Her entire face is turning a light shade of red, and the more she glares at me, the brighter it gets.

She's fucking pissed, and damn if I don't want to push all her buttons, see how mad I can get her.

Am I playing with fire?

Absolutely. And I can't wait to feel the burn, to feel the flames lick up my skin and consume me. Even if it's with rage it's better than the self-deprecation that usually swims around my head.

"I… What?" She points at me, her dark green fingernail digging into the center of my chest, and I know I should

25

turn around and walk away. I should let her go home and forget all about me. There are so many things I should do, but I don't do a single fucking one of them. Instead, I take a step toward her, and her whole hand curls against me.

It's a simple touch, but it's one that sends an electric current down my spine and makes me feel more alive than I have in years. I let it seep into my veins, let it feed my anger, and I fucking love it.

Her eyes widen and she takes two steps back, her hand dropping into a fist at her sides.

"What's that?" I cock my head to the side and take another step toward her. "I couldn't hear you over whatever bullshit was about to spew out of your mouth."

"Bullshit?" Her voice raises a few octaves as she takes another step backwards, stopping when she comes into contact with the wall behind her.

"That's what I said, little princess. I distinctly remember you being full of *bullshit*."

Her lips curl into a sneer and she growls at me, like full-on growls like a wild animal. "Don't fucking call me that. I may have ended things between us, but I remember some of the stuff you said, and you're no saint."

"Oh, I remember everything I said." I close the distance between us, crowding her against the brick wall.

I'm so close I can see the light scattering of freckles across the bridge of her nose, the rings of light blue and green around her pupils, the way her lips part with every breath. It's been over a goddamn decade, and she looks more beautiful than I remember.

Stunning.

Right now, I'd love nothing more than to ignore all the animosity between us and explore all the curves she didn't have when we were eighteen-year-old kids. Just for a second, I let myself inhale her intoxicating peach scent; let myself imagine what life would be like if she were still mine. If she curled her arms around my neck like she used to and sighed my name.

But then I get a sharp twinge in my chest, a painful reminder of the things *she* said to *me* before she ripped out my beating heart and stomped on it.

She inhales sharply as I lean down, her eyes fluttering closed briefly before they pin me in place. "Do you really?"

I slap the wall beside her head, loving how she jumps, how her eyes flick away and she bites her bottom lip to stop it from trembling. "I begged you to come with me to Boston. I told you how much I loved you, how I didn't want to live without you. I told you that being apart from you would absolutely break me."

Riley opens her mouth to respond, but I don't have a single desire to hear whatever excuse is ready to tumble out. I tear away from her and back up, running a hand down my face and straightening my tie.

Giving myself the space I need to get her out of my head, to fucking breathe.

Her hand reaches out toward me, but before it comes in contact with my arm, she stops and lets it fall to her side.

The second she opens her mouth to speak, I slip my hands in my pockets and let a mask of indifference slide across my face. She doesn't need to see the full extent of how she affects me. The hurt she's caused. "The way out is behind you. Goodbye, Riley."

I don't wait for her to respond, I don't dare. I spin on my heel and walk down the hallway, every step I take sending a new wave of fury through my veins. Twelve years since the day she said goodbye, and her mere presence burrows underneath my skin like a virus.

There are so many things I could say—hell, would love to say—but there's no turning back now. She doesn't deserve another word from me.

So tell me why I'm stomping over to one of the glass doors facing the back parking lot, and watching Riley stalk to her car. She turns around several times, glancing back at the arena with a frown, and I can only imagine she's looking for me, watching the door she came out of to see if I'm going to follow her.

Not this time, Riley. Never fucking again.

4

GORDON – TWELVE YEARS AGO

"THERE'S MY VIP." COACH MORGAN SLAPS MY BACK AS I join him and the rest of the team for a post-game break-down. Normally it would sting a bit without the bulk of the pads, but I can barely feel a thing. "Proud of you, son. That hat trick was a hell of a way to end a season."

I nod, joining the rest of the guys who are vibrating with the same excitement I am. We just won the fucking state championship, and this last season, we blew all the old high school records out of the water.

This was the year of legends, and I was their king.

But that doesn't matter as much to me as it does to my dad. Not really. While hockey is important, there's one thing—one person who trumps everything else, who makes everything around her pale in comparison. Riley Adams.

And I can't wait to give her a different kind of hat

trick. I won't be happy until she comes all over my fingers, my face, and finally my cock. I can't seem to get enough of her and I don't want to.

"You coming out to McNally's tonight?" Jerry asks as he pulls me to him for a quick hug, his smile so damn big it's infectious.

My teammates are all going out to party while their parents look the other way and pretend their eighteen-year-old kids aren't drinking and fucking the night away. Not me. I have somewhere better to be.

I shake my head and squeeze his shoulders. "Sorry, man, I'm taking Riley out, and Hunter doing keg stands doesn't exactly create a romantic backdrop."

"Romantic," he snorts, rolling his eyes. "If I didn't see it, there's no way I'd believe you, Mr. Romance, checked Roger Smith so hard he lost both his front teeth in the first period."

"Hockey players can be both tough and romantic. You just haven't found the one."

"And you have? In high school?"

"Yep. I'm one lucky bastard." I nudge him with my elbow and lower my voice as the coach joins our circle. "When you know, you know. She's it for me, I knew it the instant I saw her."

He makes a gagging sound and laughs. "You guys make me sick, but since you can kick my ass in two seconds flat, I'll allow it."

"You're both idiots," Adrian Wylder spits and curls

his lips into a sneer, sliding into place next to me and running a hand through his perfectly styled hair.

He's such a fucker, and of course, he's my assistant captain and a center, giving me the pleasure of facing off against him all damn season at practice. Fuck, almost my whole damn hockey career. And he's been a pain in my ass since day one.

I wouldn't piss on him if he were on fire. "Fuck off."

"I'll just be waiting for Riley to realize I'm the better choice." He looks me up and down, his smug expression never leaving his face. "Don't know what she sees in you."

I snap my jaw shut, refusing to engage with him. Any other day, I'd be ready to plant my foot up his ass, but not today. Not after winning the championship. And certainly not after knowing that I'm going to be buried in Riley's sweet pussy tonight. In fact, I'm the only one that's ever been there, and that gives me a sense of satisfaction that even Asshole Adrian can't destroy.

He may want everything I have, but that's one thing he'll never get.

Coach Morgan jumps into his speech, and I can still feel Wylder glaring at me. No sweat off my nuts. I stand here, looking like I'm giving him my full attention while my mind wanders to what I have in store for Riley tonight. Her parents are out of town, and this will be one of the few nights I'll get her all to myself. As much as I can't wait to bury myself inside her, what I really want is to wake up with her curled around me, her head resting on my chest.

I want the first moments of the start of her day, and I want the last.

As soon as Coach is done, I shoulder into Wylder, lowering my voice to a whisper. "I'd say let the better man win, but he already has."

I smirk, grabbing my gear bag and hustling out of the locker room as he curses behind me.

The hallway outside is crowded as hell, and I can barely make out Riley's dark red ponytail at the edge of the crowd. I start shouldering my way through the parents and a few students who like to hang with the team after the games, shaking hands and accepting hugs from my teammates' families as I make my way to her.

But I don't get far before my father's hand clamps down on my shoulder.

"You were slow on the drop tonight." He peers at me, his mouth in a permanent frown. "We need to work on that before you leave for Boston. Show them that they weren't wrong when they offered you a full ride."

"We will. Just not tonight." I give him a tight smile, trying to placate him, but it never works. He's a hard man to please. If he got his way, I would live hockey and let nothing—not even homework—distract me. I've dedicated plenty of time to the sport. It doesn't get all of me.

He takes a deep breath, a bright red crawling up his

neck. He can get pissed all he wants, but I know he won't make a scene, not here. Not in front of all these people. "Please tell me you're not going out with *her* tonight."

"Her name is Riley, and yes, I am."

"You're on the edge of greatness, Gordon." He leans down, and I know it's his way of making sure I don't miss a single word, but it's nothing I haven't heard before. "Don't throw it all away for some bitch. It's not worth your career. You've worked way too hard to let that little temptress distract you."

"I'll be ready for drills in the morning," I grit out and push past him, not letting him get in another word. He'll be ready to let me have it, and that's okay. Nothing is going to distract me from getting to Riley. I'll take whatever punishment he has for me, and it'll be worth it.

It always is.

Every interaction with my father leaves me with a heavy weight pressing down on my shoulders, and it lightens the closer I get to her. The seconds feel like hours as I make my way to the edge of the crowd.

Riley's leaning against the wall, texting on her phone, her ponytail swishing back and forth as she hums to herself, and I can't wait to pull it loose. She's wearing my jersey, like she does every game, and a pair of tight-fitting jeans that highlight every one of her sinful curves.

As soon as she looks up from her phone, her face lights up and she gives me a sweet smile that almost knocks me to my knees.

I let my gear bag drop to the floor as I close the distance between us, never letting my eyes leave hers, despite the loud conversations behind us. She lets out a small sigh and I frame her face with my hands, resting my forehead to hers. I lose myself in her peach scent, letting it wash away all the bullshit from my father and that dick, Wylder.

"That was a good game, Benson."

She wraps her arms around my neck, and I answer with a grunt, pressing my lips to hers and crowding her against the wall. The world falls away, and in this moment, nothing else matters. Nothing but her and me.

I sweep my tongue into her mouth, letting myself have a quick taste of her before I pull back slightly. "Hey, firefly."

She laughs softly, pressing a quick kiss to the corner of my lips "Hey, baby. That was one of your best games yet." I glance away from her for just a second, but she's right there, pulling me back to her. "Don't listen to your dad. He's so full of shit. You're already halfway to a billion-dollar NHL contract."

"They don't do billion-dollar contracts."

"They might for you." She sighs, sliding her hands along my shoulders and I mine down the length of her ponytail, tugging on the silky strands. "Are we going out to the party tonight?"

"Nope."

"No?" Her brows draw together, and her light green

eyes examine my face. "You don't want to celebrate with the team?"

"Nope," I repeat, brushing my lips across her temple. "I want to celebrate with you, and I'm not willing to give up our alone time for anyone else."

Her eyes fill with unshed tears, and she nods before whispering. "I love you."

"I love you. I'll love you until the day I die."

5

RILEY

BY THE TIME I TREK UP TWO FLIGHTS OF STAIRS TO GET to my apartment, I'm fuming. Absolutely fuming.

Does he think I don't remember? I mean seriously, who the fuck does he think he is. *I told you that being apart from you would absolutely break me*. It obviously didn't, because he looks pretty fucking fine to me.

More than fine.

Goddamn. The way he made my heart flutter when he leaned into me. When he enveloped me in his cedar cologne and made me forget that I was supposed to be mad at him. That's right, *me*. Not him.

He knew what he was doing, but fuck, after all this time, he shouldn't affect me like he did. He shouldn't affect me at all.

I should've been immune.

I should've been calm, cool, and collected, but just

seeing him made my temper spike. Normally I'd blame it on my red hair, but not this time. This time it was Gordon and his fucking irritating smirk.

Just thinking about that damn smirk has me growling as I open the front door.

"Oh my God, I've been waiting for you to get home for hours." The words rush out of Harper's mouth, and she practically tackles me. "What happened? Why did you have to go? You never told me if the guy was hot. Did he offer to dust the cobwebs out of your lady cave?"

"It only took me twenty minutes to get here. It has *not* been hours." I hold up a hand, effectively silencing her as I walk into the kitchen, tossing my duffel bag on the small island and filling a glass with water from the fridge.

Harper moves my stuff to the floor and slides onto the barstool, her entire body vibrating as she stares at me. "You gotta give me something. Come on."

I drain my glass, giving myself the much-needed time to calm down. "No one is going to be dusting the cobwebs out of my lady cave." *Especially not Gordon Benson.* "I'm actually thinking about swearing off men all together."

"Okay… What brought that on?"

"The guy you heard me talking to was… Gordon."

I get a bit more water and chug it down as Harper stares at me, her brows drawn together as I let that name hang heavy between us. It takes her a few seconds, but I can see the exact moment the dots connect because her eyes widen, and her jaw literally drops. "Gordon, your ex-boyfriend? High school sweetheart? Big, sexy, hockey player?"

"That's the one. Thanks for the reminder."

She gasps, clutching her chest in the most dramatic way ever. "But we hate him." Then she leans across the island, eying me warily and lowers her voice. "We do still hate him, right?"

"Of course, we still hate him. He's... he's just...."

"He's just? What?"

I set the glass in the sink and rinse it out before gripping the edge of the counter and hanging my head. Gordon brings out so many conflicting emotions, I don't know what to say. I barely know what to think.

He was my first everything, and for a long time, I thought he'd be my last.

I take a deep breath as my throat clogs with emotion and I choke it down like a bitter pill. The last thing I needed was a stark reminder of the past, of a time where I was both optimistically happy and then absolutely miserable. As the memories bubble to the surface, I stare down the drain, watching the small streams of water gather and then disappear.

Harper shifts behind me, running her hands up my back, and hugs me from behind. Her warmth spreads through me, and it isn't until she's holding me that I realize I'm shaking. "Are you okay?"

"I…" This time when the emotions swell within my chest, threatening to consume me, I can't swallow them down, I can't hold them at bay. They're suffocating, all encompassing. They'll swallow me whole if I let them. I nod, but as the first tear falls, I quickly change course and shake my head. "He didn't…"

My fingers curl around the counter, gripping it tight as a sob wracks through my body, and I'm afraid I might collapse. I thought I was fine, I thought I was over it, but… fuck. The wound still feels as fresh as it did over a decade ago.

Harper squeezes me tighter and rubs her hands across my shoulders and down my arms. "What didn't he do?"

"He didn't ask about Max. About the pregnancy. He looked at me like I'm the bad guy when he…" I swipe at the tears rolling down my cheeks, and as my legs weaken, I sink to the floor. She sits down with me, sliding her arm back around me, and I rest my head on hers. "I used to love him so much, Harper. He used to be my everything. And when… when he looked at me tonight… it was like I was nothing."

"Well, fuck him," she whispers, letting those three simple words permeate into my brain for several seconds before speaking again. "He really didn't ask about Max?"

I shake my head, taking a deep breath. "Not at all. He may not care about me anymore, but you'd think he'd want to know about his own kid."

While I was the one that ended things between us, I regretted breaking up with Gordon the second those fatal words left my mouth. I didn't want to do it, but I had to. I felt sick to my stomach and I wanted nothing more than to go back in time and take it back. He was hurt, confused, and I was a chicken. Instead of giving him the explanation he deserved, I took the easy way out and lied. I told him I didn't love him anymore. I hurt him because I knew it was the only way he'd let me go.

It was the only way I could ensure he'd leave for Boston and not insist on staying with me in Ohio. He'd give up his dreams for me, and I refused to let him. I took his choice away.

It was something I had to live with every single day after.

He had no idea that my mom was diagnosed with terminal breast cancer the week before and only had six months to live. He didn't know how hard it was to say goodbye, how I told myself I'd love him forever, but I didn't want to hold him back from achieving everything he's ever wanted.

Then a month later I found out I was pregnant.

I cried myself to sleep that night and called Gordon the next day. He didn't answer, but he sent me a series of texts. Texts that made me glad he was out of my life for good.

"What an asshole. Seriously. He doesn't deserve either of you."

I nod, because, yeah, but it doesn't make me feel any better—especially for Max who has to grow up with only one parent. She'll never have a dad to dust her off and tell her she's okay, to make her laugh during the tough times, to chase off all the boys who aren't worth her time.

Sure, she has me, but we all know moms are never cool, especially during the preteen and teen years.

I know firsthand how hard it is knowing you have a dad who doesn't give a single fuck about you. The only time my dad showed up was when he needed money, and once he swindled my mom into giving him everything she had, he'd disappear for another couple of years.

Harper is too young to remember a time before he left our family, not that we were particularly happy even back then. It didn't take long for him to realize he wasn't cut out to be a dad and a husband. He left shortly after I turned eleven, and has been a constant disappointment in our lives since.

He never checked on us when our mom had cancer, and only reached out once after she died. He didn't care that I was nineteen with a baby and sole custodian of my ten-year-old sister. He didn't care that I could barely manage to get through a normal day, that I had to get a fulltime job, that I had to give up on all my damn dreams.

In a sense, Max is lucky. Having no dad is better than him being a deadbeat.

I don't wish that hurt on anyone.

Harper holds me tighter to her, rubbing her hand across my back, and I wallow in the small modicum of comfort it brings. It's a ray of sun peeking out from behind the turbulent storm clouds. She holds me together, she keeps me sane, she reminds me that there are still genuine people out there, and tonight I need that.

Once the tears dry and the past is packed back up in a box where it belongs, I push myself up from the cool floor, say goodnight to Harper, and make my way to Max's room.

The door is slightly ajar, the glow from the hockey nightlight I got for her last year spilling into the hallway. I try to keep my steps light as I walk into her room, even though I know there's no way I'll wake her. Max snores as loud as a grown man and sleeps like the dead. A meteor could land right outside the apartment complex, and she wouldn't even bat an eye.

Her vibrant red hair is barely visible under the mounds of blankets covering her, but I run a hand through it anyway, pressing a kiss to the top of her head. "Goodnight, my little superstar. I love you."

She flips over, her arm swinging out, and I narrowly avoid getting slapped in the face.

I may not have been ready to be a mom when I found out I was pregnant, but I wouldn't trade it for anything in the world. Gordon may have given me this gift, but that's where it ends.

And now that I'm done with the ice show and they're moving on to a new city, I should never have to see him again. Come Monday, I'll be back behind my desk at Hawkins Investments, and all will be right with the world.

Harper's right. He doesn't deserve me, and he sure as hell doesn't deserve Max.

If I see him again, I'll hold my head high as I strut right on by. It'll be my turn to pretend he doesn't exist.

6

GORDON

"YOU LOOK LIKE SHIT. ROUGH NIGHT?" RYAN ASKS AS he smirks at me and stands up from his spot on my front porch, a six pack of his fancy locally brewed beer hanging from his fingers.

Gunner stays sitting, his gaze sweeping over me, and as soon as he takes in my undone tie and my disheveled hair, he gives me a knowing smirk. "Did you finally discover what it means to have a good time? I've never seen you with a hair out of place, so you must've been doing something better than counting your millions or whatever else you do in that fancy office of yours."

"Jesus. Sitting in my office and counting millions my ass," I mumble, raking a hand through my hair for the thousandth time tonight. "Who do you think I am? Scrooge McDuck? Fucking football players. Don't know why I hang out with you assholes."

My hair really does look like shit, so I'll give them that, but in my defense, I had a lot going through my mind on the way home. You know, like the past fifteen years of my life, every memory from the day I met Riley in English class our sophomore year, to the day I finally asked her out. And let's not forget when we lost our virginity to each other, the first time we whispered those three little words, *I love you*, and when she broke my heart.

I didn't have much time to grieve, to wonder what the hell happened between us that she suddenly fell out of love with me before I had to leave for Boston.

To an outsider, my life from there looked like a dream. Two years playing hockey in college, drafted to the NHL at twenty, and had my first cup at twenty-two. Up until two and a half years ago, I had everything most guys dream of.

A fancy car. Millions in the bank. Women dropping themselves at my feet.

But not what I *really* wanted. What I *needed*.

"I think I'm offended," Gunner whines and places a hand over his chest, glancing up at Ryan. "Are you offended?"

"Nah." Ryan slaps a hand on my shoulder and gives it a squeeze, not hard enough to rip off my shoulder blade, but enough I know he can. "Just means this asshole is going to pay for pizza and then tell us why he made us hang out for an extra hour outside his bougie guest house."

I let out an exaggerated sigh, one that turns into a groan, but neither one of them bats an eye. They just shake their heads and laugh like I'm telling them one of those Dad jokes Ryan likes so much.

Normal people would be afraid of my exasperation—or at least a little wary, not them though. They don't even flinch. Maybe I'm getting soft at my old age. I will be turning thirty-one in a couple of weeks... maybe I'm losing my resolve, my edge. It could also be the monthly poker games Ryan Devlin and Gunner Rose—football players for the Nashville Aces—insisted I host after being arrested with a few of my players.

They called it mandatory bonding. I thought they were full of shit, but I liked the idea of taking their money and knocking them down a few pegs. Athletes can be notoriously self-centered. I would know, I was one.

"Technically, I'm not late." I glance behind me to the dark mansion monstrosity that used to be my dad's house, a place I stayed while I was recovering from surgery and spent more time alone than I did with the one person who was supposed to be there for me. The person who lectured me almost daily on tossing away my career instead of making sure I was okay with losing the only thing I had. The day he died, I moved out here. "You fuckers just like to be early."

"Well, duh," Ryan quips and follows me in, crossing the living room to put his beer in the fridge. However, instead of flopping himself across my very expensive couch like he usually does, he hovers in the kitchen. "When else are we going to get our two on one Gordon time?"

"I hate it when you call it that," I grumble, making sure he sees my frown.

Gunner closes the door behind us, and once we get in the kitchen, gives me a pointed look and crosses his arms —which I'm sure, for a football player, is a great accomplishment. "Speaking of... what's got your perfectly styled hair all jacked up? I believe you owe us a story."

"You guys are worse than my sister, and that's saying something." I pull the tie from around my neck and drape it, along with my suit jacket, on the back of one of the barstools. "I ran into my ex on my way out of the arena."

Ryan points to the island and I obediently sit, running both my hands through my hair and unbuttoning the top two buttons on my black dress shirt. Ryan glances at Gunner while he pours two fingers of Angel's Envy in a glass tumbler and slides it in front of me. "Is this the princess girl from the ice show?"

I nearly choke on my bourbon. "How the fuck do you know about that?"

There's no way it's a lucky guess. I swear these athletes are the biggest gossips I've ever encountered. Instead, he hands Gunner a bottle of water and grabs a beer for himself. He takes a small sip and then gives me his signature smirk, one that works wonders on the ladies and pisses me off—both of which he knows. "I'll give you one guess."

"Fucking Foster Craig." I shake my head with a groan, glancing over at Gunner as he slides on the stool next to mine, grinning like an idiot. These two, I swear. They're two peas in a pod. "Knew it. That man can't keep a secret to save his life."

"So..." Ryan drags out the word, gesturing for me to continue. "Please continue. You were about to tell us all about the mermaid who stole your heart and your virginity."

Motherfucker.

They want their story and I'm really not in the mood to talk about her, not when I'm feeling so damn raw, so exposed. I may have been the one to walk away with the upper hand tonight, but it didn't feel good.

Not really.

They're both staring at me, waiting, and I know they're not going to let it go. They never do. So, I drain half my bourbon and give a curt nod. "Yeah, it was the one from the ice show. We dated the last two years of high school. She was—is—a figure skater."

She's obviously still skating, but when we were in school, she had planned on going to the Olympics—not that I was checking on her or anything, but I might have noticed that she was never on the roster. And had I been paying attention, that would've been surprising because she was a better skater than most of them that made it. That has to mean she didn't try out, and I'd love to know why.

Gunner whistles, spinning the water bottle between his palms. "That's fucking hot." Slowly, very slowly, I turn and pin him with a glare. He lets out a noise that sounds like he's dying and holds his hands up before continuing. "Obviously, I mean in general. They've got to be pretty damn flexible, and I've always been a sucker for a girl on skates."

My jaw tightens and I force myself to take a breath, finish my bourbon, and try to relax. It's not like he's talking about Riley, and even if he were, it shouldn't concern me. My feelings for her were buried long ago, and I made peace with her moving on with her life.

Or at least I thought I did.

"Yeah." I huff a laugh, unbuttoning the cuffs of my dress shirt and rolling up the sleeves. "We spent a lot of time on the ice together. She'd help me with my skating technique and I'd… well, I'd watch her when she practiced. She was a hell of a skater. It was pretty fucking hot; I'll give you that."

"And what happened?"

"I don't know. Life?" I sigh, resting my elbows on the island and dropping my head in my hands. "One minute everything was great—I was getting ready to head to Boston College to play hockey and she was going to come with me, take some undergrad, and train for the Olympics. And then… it was done. She told me she wasn't in love with me anymore and was going to stay in Ohio."

"Ouch. That hurts."

"Yeah, it fucking sucked."

Ryan takes my glass, pouring me another two fingers of bourbon, and nods. "And that was it? You didn't hear from her again?"

"Nothing. I meant to call, text, show up at her doorstep—I don't know." I squeeze my eyes shut for a second, and when I open them, stare at my glass. My throat clogs, and my heart, the one thing that has betrayed me the most, stutters in my chest. "I spent days trying to come up with something to say, something that would convince her to give us a chance."

"Did you?"

"Never got a chance. I lost my fucking phone right before I left for Boston and had a full-on panic attack. It took my dad a couple days to get me a replacement, and then when I got on my socials, I saw a few pictures of her with that dickhead, Adrian Wylder, who plays for Vegas. Her and I just weren't meant to be. That's it. I haven't seen her since the day she broke up with me. I wasn't who she wanted."

The three of us descended into silence.

Gunner's picking at the label on his water bottle; Ryan is sipping his beer, his gaze cast down on the floor.

And me? I'm trying to block out some of the pain so I don't let it consume me, let it turn me into someone I don't want to be. I'm already so full of hurt and disappointment, I don't need more.

Yeah, I think it's safe to say I'm not over my ex like I should be.

Ryan drains his beer and jams his hands in his pockets. "You know how I am with all my rules for dating—"

"Fucking," Gunner interrupts, coughing into his hand. "There's nothing date-like about what you do with any of these women."

Ryan tosses him a petulant look and the middle finger. "And there was a girl I thought was special. She almost made me consider breaking every single one of those damn rules to see her again, but then she disappeared before the sheets cooled. Didn't even get a chance to get her number."

"Or her last name, cause you're a dumbass. It's a good thing I don't have time for dating or drama. No thank you. I'd rather be single and alone the rest of my life."

I huff a quick laugh. "I forgot. The big, bad, quarterback is too good for a girlfriend. He prefers to spend all his time on the field—or posing for underwear ads."

"That was one time!" He smacks my arm as his cheeks turn a light shade of pink.

Ryan tosses his head back and laughs. "Yeah, but it was for a banana hammock."

"You know they gave me a box full of those things? I don't know how women walk around in thongs all day. That shit was super uncomfortable."

"I'll take your word for it."

"As much as I'd love to sit here for the next half hour and talk about Gunner in a thong, we should maybe set up for this poker game before everyone shows up." I wrap my knuckles on the island and muster up the best smile I can. "And if either of you try to make me talk about my feelings again, I'm going to punch the both of you."

"I was definitely ready to talk about my feelings. Damn, you really know how to kill the mood. I was even going to let you hug me." Gunner slides off the barstool and I show him my middle finger too. "Guess we should set up though. Foster and Rhett are on their way, and Theo said he and Hudson will be here in ten."

I nod, because that's all I can do. I could really use the distraction from my life.

Seeing Riley tonight really threw me off, and I'm going to have a hell of a time focusing on poker—especially when all I can picture is the hurt and anger swirling in the depths of her gaze.

But really, she's the least of my problems.

If the Devils don't make the playoffs this year, Jazz and I will be forced to sell the team to an anonymous buyer. Probably one of my dad's asshole friends. It was the one damn stipulation in his will when Jazz and I inherited the hockey team. It's his way of fucking me over and controlling me from the grave. For him, it was as easy as breathing. He's been gone for over a year, and his ghost still haunts me.

He liked me under his thumb, and the only time I had a sense of freedom was when I played in the NHL. *Following in his footsteps like I was born to do.*

Then all it took was one cheap shot—one fucking guy to ram his knee into mine and bounce me off the boards in a hit that ended my career—and I was back under my father's control, living the life he wanted me to live. Even in death, he's the one pulling the strings, and fuck, I don't know how to cut myself loose.

There's never been a part of my life he didn't touch, didn't taint.

Except Riley—and maybe that's why she's always been so damn special.

7

RILEY

"WHOA, WATCH THE HEAD." I MANAGE TO DUCK SECONDS before being slapped in the face with a hockey stick.

I'd love to say it's some kind of cool maneuver, maybe something out of the Matrix, but no. I jerk back, pull a muscle in my neck, and almost lose my footing. It makes me look real cool in the very bright afternoon sun. You know, right out in the open where anyone could see me—including Mrs. Cunningham who's two cars down, glaring at me. To clarify—a woman who smells like cheese is glaring at me like I'm the offensive one.

Great.

Max barely spares me a glance, just enough to roll her eyes in my general direction and toss her gear bag in the back of my poor thirteen-year-old Honda CR-V. I manage the barest of flinches as everything crashes to the bottom of the trunk and politely wave at Mrs. Cunning-ham, who's still glaring at me instead of going on her merry way. Must be my lucky morning. Or maybe she really doesn't like my supermom coffee cup and ice-skating is always the answer t-shirt.

Eh, her loss. Both those things are awesome.

I pull the hatch closed, and by the time I toss my purse, ice skates, and hoodie in the back, Max is already buckled in the front seat, her nose glued to the phone. Her bright red hair has fallen forward, partially obstructing her face, and she's gnawing on her bottom lip as she types out a text.

I clear my throat, but it doesn't get her attention. Not that I'm surprised, she's been attached at the hip to her best friend, Madylin, and I'm a little concerned I'm going to have to surgically separate them. "Excuse you, little miss sassy pants, you almost took my head off."

She doesn't look over at me, just switches the radio to her 'angry' music as soon as I start the car and turns up the volume. Apparently, rock music is her new favorite.

I'm pretty sure she's listening to it so much because she thinks it annoys me, but what she doesn't know is that rock music, especially nineties rock, is a weakness of mine. But I'm not going to tell her jack shit. The second I do she'll change the station, and I guarantee this time she'll pick something I don't like for real.

"Maybe I'd be less sassy if you let me actually play hockey." She mumbles something that sounds a lot like *cause you're a jerk,* which I ignore. "And hitting a puck around the ice by yourself doesn't count."

"You know exactly why I don't want you playing hockey."

"Yeah, yeah. Because of my…" she pauses to do air quotes, *"condition.* I'm well aware."

I toss her a look, one she doesn't see because she's still texting, and pull out of the apartment parking lot. "I think you missed the whole point of the conversation; one you might have gotten if your face wasn't buried in your phone."

Her response is a grunt.

Lovely. The teenage years are going to be a blast. It's going to be great when she's all hopped up on hormones and doesn't know what to do with herself.

I can't wait.

"And you know exactly how dangerous playing a contact sport can be. It's not like you have asthma or a bunion the size of a peach like your third-grade teacher. We just got your epilepsy under control. I don't think you understand how dangerous it would be if you had a seizure in the middle of a game. Figure skating may not be your favorite, but it's safe."

For both her and my piece of mind. If I let her play hockey and she had a seizure in the middle of a play and was injured by the puck or another player, I'd never forgive myself.

"No, thanks."

"Oh, come on. Figure skating is way better than hockey anyway. You don't have all those pads. No one is trying to hip check you into the boards. You don't have to worry about being hit in the face with the puck." *And the possibility of losing all your teeth.* Can't forget that.

"Yeah." She huffs a quiet laugh and shakes her head, her hair flitting around her shoulders. "Boring."

"It's not boring. You know how hard it is to perfect some of those jumps? It's a big deal when you finally land your first axel. Don't even get me started on the quadruple lutz."

"Please don't. This conversation already has way too much figure skating in it. I want to play hockey, not skate around in a glittery leotard. That's your dream, Mom, not mine."

"You used to have so much fun out there. You loved ice skating with me." And it's true, she did.

We would go through my old routines almost every weekend, and Max used to have a blast. Most of the time she watched, but when she did skate, she was a natural. Then a few months after she turned four, she had her first seizure, and my entire world shifted. We were on the ice and she was going through a small turn when she fell. I thought she lost her footing. No big deal. I figured she'd get right back up.

She didn't.

By the time I got to her, she was alert but tired. I had no idea what happened, and our family doctor at the time thought I was being dramatic and needed to relax. He said kids fall down, but deep down, I knew something wasn't right. We didn't skate as much after that, and I successfully turned into a hover parent. She had two more seizures in the span of a day a few weeks later, and I finally found a doctor who didn't think this was all a figment of my imagination.

It's been manageable since she started taking medication, but I'm really not enthused about her playing any kind of contact sports. Or really anything that might trigger an episode. That's a risk I'm not willing to take.

And for some damn reason, she fell in love with hockey after catching a game on TV. She's wanted to play ever since, and there's nothing I can say to talk her out of it. The sport is in her blood, but as the years moved by and she got older, I hoped she'd outgrow the desire to play.

I hoped she'd be content watching from the couch.

She has not outgrown it, and even if she didn't have a serious medical condition, I'd be wary of letting her play.

After how things ended with Gordon, I hated hockey so much—or at least I tried to. But then I'd catch myself lingering around conversations at work, hoping to overhear even the tiniest detail about the

Devils. Not that I needed them. Once Max was addicted, she watched every game on TV, and every now and then I'd pretend to clean the kitchen so I could watch along, silently cheering on a team I had no business liking.

Not since Gordon took over.

Hockey was such a big part of my life while I was in high school, and once Gordon and I split up, it was such a stark reminder of everything I lost. I didn't watch a game for years. Not until he started playing for Chicago.

Then I couldn't help myself. It was my salvation as much as it was my greatest punishment.

It was a way I could still feel close to him. A way to torture myself with the harsh reality of his betrayal.

And then there's Maxine. His double in so many ways. Sometimes it hurts to look at her; to meet her eyes and see his staring back at me as she asked me the questions I thought I was ready to answer, but I fucking wasn't. *Why don't I have a dad like the other kids? He doesn't love me? He doesn't want me? Is it because I'm defective? Because I'm damaged?*

I thought *I* was broken, but that day, I fell apart. I completely lost myself.

But it wasn't her fault he turned out to be such a damn disappointment. Wasn't mine either.

I know what it's like to have a dad who doesn't care, who won't be there when you need him, who's selfish and unreliable. I know what it's like to watch your mom struggle to work two jobs, sacrifice everything she had just to support you. I fucking know.

And I'll do anything to keep her safe.

She finally puts down the phone and leans her head back, crossing her arms over her tight, black athletic shirt, and closes her eyes. "Used to, mom. Past tense. You know I don't like figure skating. I. Want. To. Play. Hockey."

Now it's my turn to sigh.

"Max, it's dangerous for you. You could get hurt."

"Yeah, just like everything else fun." She turns to me and flashes me a fake smile before unbuckling her seat belt and practically jumping out of the vehicle as soon as I pull into a spot outside the hockey complex and shift the car into park. "I'm going to hit some pucks with Cassidy. Hopefully that's not *too dangerous* for me."

The door slams shut behind her, and with a groan, I run my hands around the steering wheel. "Good chat. Good chat."

If she hears me, she doesn't acknowledge it as she grabs her gear from the back and hustles to catch up with her friend and her family.

I don't get out right away. Hell, she probably won't even notice if I don't come in for a while. Her and Cassidy have been working on their puck handling which basically means balancing it on their sticks and hitting it back and forth to themselves over a very short distance. It's the only thing she's allowed to do right now.

She's been on me more and more about hockey lately and I wish things were different for her. I wish she could stay up late and not have to worry about having a seizure the next day because she's exhausted. I wish she could load up on all the carbs she wanted without a care in the world. I wish we didn't have to worry about adjusting her meds every time she hit a growth spurt, but we do.

And sometimes... sometimes when it's late at night and I'm haunted by my thoughts, I wish she had two parents, two people that love her as much as I do, so she doesn't ever have to feel incomplete or unloved.

Or unwanted, like I did growing up.

After a few minutes, I take a few deep breaths, and as I move to get out of the car, my phone rings.

I glance down at the screen and see a picture I'd taken of Lexie, a coworker of mine, shoving a twinkie in her face in the lunchroom. It's odd she's calling me on a weekend, so I immediately answer. "Hey, Lexie. How's it going?"

"Well, it's before noon on a Sunday and I'm wide awake and out of bed. But Riley... shit." She takes a deep breath, blowing it out slowly. "We have a problem."

My fingers tighten around the phone as all the possibilities swirl around in my head. Her abusive ex-boyfriend could have shown back up on her doorstep. She's been having problems with this asshole in the apartment next door. And she has a cat that's older than dirt. "What kind of problem? What happened? Are you okay? Is it your cat?"

"Lilith is under my bed plotting the end of the world and taking a nap. I'm fine. At least physically. Mentally? The jury is still out."

"Lexi, what is it?"

"Shit. There's no good way to say this, and you know I'm not great with sugar coating things." She doesn't say anything for a few seconds and that only makes me more anxious, makes my heart race a little more. Makes me think of all the damn things in the entire world that could be wrong. "Hawkins Investments is closed. Like immediately and permanently."

I open my mouth and snap it shut and then repeat a few more times. "Closed? What do you mean closed? We're supposed to go to work tomorrow!"

"I'm afraid not. Mr. Shaffer called me this morning and said we're shutting down, effective immediately. They're bankrupt. He's trying to figure out if he can even pay us for the last couple of weeks, but it doesn't sound good. There's nothing left."

"What?! There's nothing left? How can that be, Lex? We were just there on Friday and everything was normal!" This has to be some kind of mistake. I need my job... a paycheck... health insurance. Maxine's medicine is affordable with insurance, but without? "No, I can't lose my job. Did Mr. Shaffer know about this?"

"He's devastated. The owners didn't tell him a thing.

Poor guy thought it was business as usual. That company was his life, Riley. I don't know what I'm going to do, but I feel bad for him. He's probably going to call you later, but I couldn't not warn you. You're my work wife. Fuck. This sucks."

I struggle to take a breath, to talk… to do anything. It's like all the oxygen has been sucked out of my lungs and I'm frozen in place as the world crumbles around me. Rent is due in two weeks—along with the phone bill. I've got to pay for water, electric, internet. Hell, we need groceries.

I've got four hundred dollars in the bank, and that's not nearly enough to cover everything. I'm fucked. I'm so fucked. That job at Hawkins Investments wasn't perfect, but I'm a single parent with a high school diploma, and in a world full of jobs that require a college degree, my choices are limited.

Lexi and I say our goodbyes, and I sit here with my phone clutched in my hand for several seconds before I force myself to toss it in my purse.

I need to get inside the rink. I need to see Max. I need to skate. The feel of the ice beneath my feet, the cool air whipping through my hair, the way my mind clears the second I lace up my skates—I need it. Even if it's just for an hour, I need to escape the anxiety crawling up my spine and threatening to suffocate me.

Then I can look for jobs. Figure out a plan. Everything will be fine.

It has to be and even if it's not, I'll figure it out. Maxine, my sister... they depend on me. I'm all they have. I can't fall apart.

I'm on autopilot as I make my way toward the building, the bag holding my skates clutched tightly in my hand. I'm so consumed with my thoughts I almost don't hear my name being called, and I sure as shit don't know who's trying to get my attention until I'm being pulled into a tight hug, and I'm too stunned to enjoy the tiny bit of comfort if offers.

"Riley, holy shit. I thought it was you."

My skates almost fall to the concrete as a woman who looks so much like her brother steps back with a smile. Jazlyn Benson. What are the odds of running into her right after I lost my job? The universe must be having a laugh at my expense.

Did I do something terrible in a past life? Did I really piss off Karma this much?

I haven't seen either of the Bensons in years, and now I've crossed paths with both of them in the same weekend.

The same weekend I lost my job. This can't be happening.

"Oh, wow, didn't think I'd run into you here." *Or ever.* "It's been a long time."

She doesn't hesitate to drop her duffel bag on the ground and pull me into another quick hug, one I can't help but return. "The women's team lets me play with them when I can. There's no way I can sit in an office all day and not get my hands dirty every so often. How are you? Still figure skating, right?"

I nod because I can't seem to find any words. Surely she knows I stopped skating competitively, that I never made it to the Olympics, but does she know why? Does she know what her brother did?

Does she know she has a niece?

"How have you been?"

I open my mouth to lie, to tell her I'm fine, but before I can stop myself, the words tumble out. "The company I worked for suddenly closed and I just lost my job like five minutes ago. I'm not sure what I'm going to do. I don't have a college degree and can't afford to work my way up from the bottom again. I'm so fucked." As her brows raise, I hold up my hands. "Shit. I'm so sorry. I didn't mean to vomit my problems all over you. I haven't seen you in over ten years and I'm sure you were being polite. I should really let you get going. Again, I'm so sorry. It was great to see you."

"You don't have to apologize to me," Jazz says and waves me off with a laugh. "What kind of work do you do? Are you not skating with the princess show full time?"

I blow out a breath, glancing down to the ground before answering. "No. They had a couple of girls come down with the flu and I filled in at the last minute. I usually only skate for fun these days. I've been an executive assistant at an investment firm for several years, but please don't worry about me. I'll be fine. I'll find another job. How are you?"

"Honestly, I can't complain." Jazz studies me for a few seconds, tapping her bottom lip with an index finger as she assesses me. "I actually might know of a few job openings."

"You do?"

She nods, getting out her phone and bringing up the contacts. "Give me your phone number and I'll send a few things your way."

"Gordon can't know about this." The words are out of my mouth before I can help myself, and once they're hanging in the air between us, there's no way to snatch them back. I should be grateful for the help, but I can't stomach the thought of him knowing his family helped me with anything; of him somehow being attached to a favor I'll never be able to repay. "Sorry," I mumble, "I know you're only trying to help."

She huffs a laugh and leans toward me, her voice lowering slightly. "There are a lot of things I don't tell Gordon. He doesn't know I'm playing with the women's rec league yet, but if he's lucky, I might drag him to a game."

Jazz gives me a playful wink, and I can practically feel my stomach sinking to my knees. I can never come here again. There's no way. I'd have to move, simple as that. There's no way I could keep my mouth shut, watching him pretend to be a human being while ignoring the daughter he fathered and walked away from. I know I can't. Sooner or later, I'd say something nasty, be forced to make a snide comment, and we'd get in such a big fight someone would film it and it would be on the internet forever.

And what if he said something to Max?

Dammit.

There's no way Jazz knows that Gordon and I have a kid together. None. She's way too nice, too casual, to know I'm harboring a niece she's never met. Jazz and I were never close when Gordon and I dated, but I'd think she'd ask about Max. Maybe even want to meet her— which is why I need to end this conversation and get the hell out of here.

"Yeah... great. I bet he'd love that." With a forced smile, I give Jazz my number. She can text me a few options, and if I let her stay unread long enough, she'll forget about me and maybe I can move out without the possibility of seeing a Benson ever again.

"Thanks. I'll touch base with you sometime this week. I can't believe you live here in Nashville," she chuckles, picking up her gear bag and slinging it back over her shoulder. "Small world."

It's an innocent enough statement, but it has my heart racing and my insides twisting into knots. Small world doesn't even cover the half of it.

The best I can do is nod my head. ""It was great running into you."

"You too." Her smile is bright and mildly contagious as she lays a light hand on my shoulder. "I'm sure we'll run into each other again soon."

Yeah, that's what I'm afraid of.

8

GORDON

I LET OUT AN EXASPERATED SIGH AND RUN BOTH HANDS down my face. This has been a long fucking week already and it's only Tuesday. *Valentine's Day*. Stupidest day of the goddamned year if you ask me.

A worthless holiday made popular by the candy companies to capitalize on people's misery—sorry, I mean love.

My office trashcan has been lined with more paper hearts than I ever wanted to see in my lifetime, and on top of that, there's a half-naked baby holding an arrow someone thought would be cute to tape to my door. It wasn't.

The last time I celebrated a Valentine's Day, I was eighteen. I was young, naive, and so fucking in love I almost believed unicorns farted rainbows. I was also stupid. It didn't take long for life to slap me across the face and tell me to open my damn eyes.

"Happy Valentine's Day, Gordo." Jazz plucks a rose from the menagerie on her desk and tries to hand it to me as I walk by.

My eyes narrow on her as I take in her bright red dress with matching shoes, the white rose in her hand, and the dreamy smile on her face. Instead of taking the flower, I growl at her as I pass. Maybe it makes me a dick, but this damn day is really grating on my nerves.

I manage to put on my blinders but only make it a few more steps before I stop, back up, and rip down the glittery hearts hanging across the top of her door frame.

"Hey!" She gestures to the hearts dangling from my fingers, shaking her head in disbelief. "I liked those. They were cute."

I snort and hold up the hearts. "They're going to look real cute in my trash. Are you coming to this meeting or are you going to stay in your office all afternoon huffing those flowers until you pass out?"

"It's called taking the time to smell the roses. You should try it sometime. I bet if you asked nicely, Lincoln would send you a dozen too."

"No thanks. He'd just be disappointed when I don't put out. Besides," I nod to her desk and the multitude of vases covering it, "it looks like your boy toy bought out the entire store."

"Probably not the whole store." She leans against the doorframe, that damn wistful smile back on her face.

"Lovely."

"Thanks. We should probably get to the meeting, though. I'm leaving early."

"Of course you are."

"Linc is making me dinner."

"Of course he is." I huff a laugh. "Although I have to say, I'm surprised he knows how to use kitchen utensils."

Jazz gives me a light shove as she heads out of her office and follows me down the hallway. "Is that because you think he's a dumb hockey player? If I remember correctly, you played hockey for a pretty long time."

"Well, I'm not a dumbass."

Jazz gives me some serious side-eye, her lips curling into a smirk. "Valentine's Day really makes you extra grumpy."

"Gordon's always extra grumpy. That's nothing new," Dean Prescott, our new GM, chimes in as he breezes past us and into the conference room. He makes a show of sitting down at the head of the table, spreading his files out in front of him and rearranging some of the stacks. "Are you two coming in or is this the first time you're seeing someone actually work?" He glances up, a rueful smile sliding across his face, and winks. "Happy Valentine's Day, Grumpy Gordo."

"Fuck you guys," I mumble, walking into the room

and tossing the glittery hearts in the trash can by the door. "Don't tell me you're leaving early today too."

"Most definitely not. I don't date, and I especially don't date on a day like today. You take a woman out on Valentine's Day and she's going to expect you to propose before dessert. This holiday is for suckers."

I nod, taking a seat to Dean's right, rifling through the files, and completely ignoring the glare he's shooting my way. He might be in charge of a lot of things, but I'm in charge of him, and I refuse to be one of those owners who rolls over and only shows up for occasional games to peacock for the press.

This is my team. My life. Hockey is everything I know, and even though I might not be able to play, I'm not taking a backseat.

Jazz laughs, taking a seat across from me and pushing the folders back to Dean who looks like he's about to have an aneurysm. "You're going to give the poor man a heart attack. Leave his stuff alone."

Dean glances at me, the corner of his eye twitching. Hell, maybe the whole half of his face. "Your brother clearly has no manners. Without a secretary, it took me way too long to put this stuff together."

I open my mouth to give him a witty reply when Mick Weller, the best coach the Devils have ever seen, runs into the office, slamming the door behind him and doing his best to make as much noise as possible as he makes his way around the table and takes a seat next to me.

"Sorry I'm late, I got hung up in my office. Didn't realize what time it was."

We all turn to look at him as he pushes his heart shaped glasses on the top of his head. Glasses which match an absolutely horrendous black Hawaiian shirt covered in red hearts. Jesus Christ.

"Nice shirt. Do they match your crocs?" Dean asks as he steeples his fingers, a smirk working its way across his face as he continues to stare at Mick.

"Ha. Ha." Mick smoothes his hands down the front of his shirt. He really should consider taking it off and setting it on fire. "It was a gift from Tessa. We match."

"See what I mean? Sucker."

"It's called being happy. You two should try it sometime."

"Alright." Jazz slaps her hands on the table, shooting them a look that has both of them sitting back in their chairs and giving her their undivided attention. "I have somewhere to be in…" she makes a show of checking her watch, "two hours, so let's get this meeting underway."

Dean smiles, and it's quite possible it's even more disturbing than Mick's Hawaiian shirt. He passes a few of his meticulously organized files around the table and launches into a forty-minute dissertation, updating us on trades, contracts, injured players, and I'm pretty sure he poked at Mick and his coaching staff a few times.

I take a few notes, Jazz asks a few questions, but ultimately, I don't see how this gets us to where we need to be—the playoffs.

At this point, I'm pretty sure we need a miracle.

When I played for Chicago, going to the playoffs was a given. We were one of the top teams. We had drive. We had grit. And we worked our asses off year after year to be the best. They may not have drafted me out of college, but it's where I ended up before my injury, and I owe them everything.

They're the team that gave me two cup wins. The only ones I may ever have.

I miss playing hockey; the thrill it gave me every single damn time I stepped on the ice before a game. The energy that thrummed through the air, settling in my bones, and pushed me to win.

Now, the only high I get comes from beating the guys at cards during our poker games once a month.

"This is great and all, but if we're going to make the playoffs," I glance around the table, adjusting my tie and tossing the papers back at Dean, loving how annoyed he looks when they scatter in front of him, "we need to get some more depth. The first two lines are great, but the others—"

"They're slow, and there are some guys who seem

like it's their first time with a puck." Jazz crosses her arms and nods to Mick. "I'm sorry, but it's true."

Mick blows out a breath and tosses his glasses on the table. "You're not wrong. I think we need to do more skating drills, get these younger guys to move faster, more efficiently. I think we should look at hiring a trainer specifically to help with that."

"I might have a few ideas. There are some teams recruiting retired figure skaters and Olympic speed skaters. I can get in touch with a few people and see who I can get lined up for interviews, maybe see if we can find a good fit." The guys murmur their agreement and Jazz's gaze meets mine, her eyes softening ever so slightly before they swing to Dean. "I also ran into an old acquaintance at the Nashville Ice Complex and think she'd be perfect for the secretary position. I know you'd like to have someone up here ASAP."

Dean nods, raising a brow and running a hand across his chin. "Does she have experience?"

"Yep. She's been working as an executive assistant for an investment company."

"That's a little far removed from professional sports. I'd really love to have someone who can follow along in a conversation without making me stop to explain what a term means every five minutes."

"Totally understand." Jazz glances toward me again. It's quick but leaves me feeling uneasy. "But if it makes you feel better, she used to figure skate and she was pretty involved with hockey for a while."

There's no way she means who I think she means... right? No... she wouldn't... would she?

Dean leans forward, glancing at Mick before his gaze swings back to Jazz. "What do you mean, involved with hockey? Did she play?"

"She dated someone who did."

My pulse quickens and I try to get my sister to glance back my way but she won't, cause she's doing exactly what I think she is. She doesn't have many friends outside the team, and I doubt she ran into Lucy at the skating rink. There's only one other woman I can think of that would have a reason to be on the ice over the weekend—someone who used to be a figure skater and dated a hockey player.

Riley Fucking Adams.

And she can hire her over my cold, dead body.

"Absolutely not!" My fist slams down on the table, and as irritating as it is, no one seems surprised at my outburst.

Mick clears his throat, his lips twitching. "Are you offended by the thought of a new secretary, or—"

"The answer is no, Jazlyn." I point a finger at her, and as soon as I notice a tremble, let my hand fall back to the table. "You can literally pick anyone else. Anyone. I'd even take Avery's quirky-ass neighbor, Gloria."

Jazz scoffs, and I'm pretty sure she rolls her eyes at

me. "As much as I love Gloria, she knows nothing about hockey. This girl is perfect for the job."

"You don't know her."

"And neither do you," she snaps and blows out a breath, lowering her voice as she continues, her gaze drilling into me. "Not anymore."

There's no way in hell I can have Riley here, in my damn arena—no, my fucking office—day after day when the stakes are so high. I won't be able to concentrate. I won't be able to get a damn bit of work done, and I sure as shit won't give two fucks about keeping my distance.

It wouldn't take long for me to be pulled back into her orbit, and I have no desire to let anyone get that close to me ever again.

"Am I missing something here? I trust Jazz's judgment, and you all have needed help up here for a few weeks now. Maybe we should give this woman a chance. You know, bring her in for an interview." Mick tries to interrupt our stare down, but neither of us even look his way.

"Nope," I grit and shake my head. "This is a terrible idea. Not happening."

"I think she'd be a great fit. And it's not like we've had a line of applicants. We've had three. The first two declined when they realized they wouldn't be working directly with any of the hockey players, and the other one had zero experience. We need someone who knows the game and doesn't want this job just to sleep with a player. Besides, it would be good to shake things up around here. We could use a change." She raises her brows and pins me with one of those looks I hate. One that says she knows she's right.

"I don't like change," I grumble.

"Yeah, well, it's part of life."

I blow out a breath and tug on my tie, loosening the knot and swallowing the lump growing in my throat. I glance to Dean and Mick who are starting at me expectantly.

Fuck.

If I insist that we pass over Riley, I'm an asshole. If we hire her, I'm going to be an asshole. There's no winning here for me. None.

Motherfucker.

"There's no way she'll say yes." I'm grasping at straws and I know it. I close my eyes and let out an exasperated sigh, running a hand through my hair. "She hates me. And how do you know she even lives in Nashville? Maybe she was using the rink before she left town."

"Wait." Dean throws his hand up, his eyes bouncing between Jazz and I. "Is this the girl from the princess ice skating show?"

"Jesus Christ." I mutter, shaking my head. "Does everyone know about that?"

This time it's Mick that answers. "Yes. Literally everyone knows. Just embrace it."

"I ran into her this weekend, just FYI, and trust me,

she lives here. She might say no, at first, but don't worry, I'll get her to accept a job so long as the rest of you agree that this is a good idea… and Gordon can manage to be a professional." Jazz stacks her hands in front of her and looks around the table.

Dean laughs while reorganizing his files, and I want to slap them out of his hands. "It's a terrible idea, but I really want to see how this plays out. I'm in."

"Mick?"

"Oh, yeah." He picks his glasses up from the table and slides them back on the top of his head, the heart lenses mocking me. I'd like to slap them straight off his face. "I'd pay good money to see the shitshow this is sure to be. So, please—pretty please—hire his ex-girl-friend to help us out and torture him at every turn."

Jazz smiles and it looks downright menacing. "Don't worry, I can be very convincing when I want to be."

That's what I'm afraid of.

Can I really ignore my ex when everything is on the line? When we either make the playoffs or have to sell the team to one of my dad's sleazeball friends? I need to be on. Dedicated. I need to do everything I can to keep the team.

Even if it means seeing Riley every day and dealing with my feelings.

Fuck my life.

9

RILEY

I STARE AT MY PHONE IN COMPLETE DISBELIEF BECAUSE what the hell just happened? I'm shocked. Stunned. Shooketh.

"Well, that was interesting," Harper comments as she walks into the living room, drops her backpack to the floor, and sits down next to me on the couch. "I don't think I've ever heard you say no so many times in one conversation, and that's saying something. Remember the time I talked you into trying squid?"

"Not just any squid, *raw* squid. And let's not forget what happened after I tried it—I immediately vomited and continued to do so for the next three days." I shiver just thinking about all those slimy tentacles. I swear I felt them move around in my mouth before I was able to swallow it down. And then throwing them up? I had nightmares for months. Those three days were almost worse than childbirth.

"So, what's worse than the raw squid?"

"Working for Gordon Benson." I don't add anything. I don't think I need to. The statement says everything, and my tone conveys the horror I feel at having him as a potential boss.

The only time I'd let that happen would be a big, fat never.

Harper hums her agreement, her gaze scanning my face for a few seconds before her eyes widen. "You're serious? Holy fuck. He offered you a job after your run-in last Friday?"

"Unfortunately. Well, not him personally, but his sister, Jazz. She's the one who just called me. We ran into each other last weekend outside the ice center while Max and I went in for open skate."

"Oh, shit. She didn't see Maxine, did she?"

"No. You know Max. She was gone before I put the car into park, thank God. Could you imagine how awkward that conversation would be?" Before I can set my phone down it vibrates, and Harper watches with a raised brow as I check the text.

> Unknown: Let me know if you change your mind. And don't forget the sign-on bonus.

> Unknown: Text me anytime - day or night.

Harper leans over, peeking at my phone. "What kind of job is this?"

I shrug and set my phone on the table in front of me. "I'd be the executive assistant to the owners and the GM. It's really similar to what I've been doing."

"Okay... and you didn't say yes? It doesn't sound like you've had any luck finding a job that would come close to what you were making at Hawkins."

I rear back, my eyes widening as I take in her words... and then the time to process them as waves of shock flood my system. "Of course not. I don't need any job that bad! Are you out of your fucking mind?"

"Don't take this the wrong way..." she says slowly, her tone light, like she's afraid anything more will push me over the ledge. It might. With a shake of her head, she crosses her arms and gives me a pointed look. "But why not?"

I stare at her for several seconds. I blink. And then I blink again. "What do you mean, why? I don't want to see Gordon again, let alone work for him. He. Would. Be. My. Boss. And there's no way I can handle that. I don't care how much money they're willing to throw at me, it's not worth sacrificing my dignity. It's not."

"Just out of curiosity, how much money are they offering?"

"Double what I was making before."

"And the sign-on bonus?"

I sigh. "Five thousand."

"What?!" She sits straight up, her hand flying my way and smacking my arm. "Are you serious? Double your salary and five thousand dollars? Am I hearing that right? Talk to me like I'm five. Why would you pass up this opportunity? It's not like you're going to be giving Gordon lap dances every day. I bet you'll be so busy you won't even see him most days."

I groan, setting my phone face down on the coffee table in front of us. "There's only three of them in the executive suite, so I highly doubt I'll be able to avoid Gordon every day, and after our last conversation, I'm surprised he's even allowing this. I don't know, Harper. The job feels too good to be true. The money is great, and I'd have immediate health insurance for Max and I. They'd give me tickets to any home game if I want them —all I have to do is sell my soul. No big deal. There has to be a catch. Why would they want me when they probably have hundreds of résumés?"

"And you submitted yours?"

I sigh, my shoulders falling as my entire being deflates. "Yes. And I had a video interview with Dean, the GM. I couldn't not see what they would offer, and I sure as hell didn't expect it to beat what I was making before."

"And you're not going to do it? That's a lot of money, Riley. Gordon aside, this seems like a no-brainer. It's not like you couldn't take this job and quit when something better comes along."

"There's no Gordon aside; he's a huge factor in this decision. If this was for literally anywhere else, I'd take the job. But it's not. It's for the Devils, and he's the biggest Devil of them all."

"Did you say Devils? Are we finally going to a game because I want to go to one so bad?"

"Holy fu...dge sticks." I nearly jump out of my skin as Max appears at my side, shrugging off her backpack, and looking between us with a wide smile on her face. Fuck, I was so deep in my own head, stewing in my own anger, I didn't hear her come in.

This is exactly why I cannot work with that man. Ever.

He makes me lose sight of what is important, and that's something that can't happen. I've worked so hard to make my life... well, safe, and I'll be damned if I let him rip apart everything I've worked so hard to build.

The job offer has already thrown me for a loop, and I turned it down. Imagine seeing him every damn day? My life would be like riding a roller coaster—an old, rickety, wooden one that makes you want to vomit.

She leans across the arm of the couch, looking at me expectantly. "So... a hockey game?"

I can feel everything turning into slow motion as my head swivels from her to Harper. What do I say? I can't tell her about the job, and I sure as hell can't imagine taking her to a game. Not when there's a chance we could run into one of the owners.

Harper meets my gaze quickly before shrugging at Max. "I don't know about a game, but your mom..."

"Has horrible diarrhea," I say at the same time Harper blurts out, "Got a job offer to work for the Devils."

Max squeals, holding onto my shoulder and jumping up and down. The look on her face is so damn ecstatic, so contagious, I can't help but smile back, even though I am anything but happy.

I'd love to blame Harper for spilling the beans and putting me in this position, but it all comes back to Gordon. If I hadn't run into him after the show last week, we'd never be having this conversation. My life would be normal, and I wouldn't feel the crushing weight of the entire world pressing down on my shoulders.

Obviously, I still wouldn't have a job, but I'd figure something out.

"Sorry," Harper leans toward me and whispers. "You know how I'm a terrible liar. I'm not good under pressure, and she was looking at me."

I huff my agreement, turning back to Max who's now pointing to the t-shirt she wore to school, specifically a Nashville Devils t-shirt.

"You could have left out the part with the diarrhea, but, Mom, The Devils? Really?" Max rests her elbows on the arm of the couch, her dark green eyes reflecting so much hope as she looks up at me. "They offered you a job? Please tell me you're taking it. That would make you the coolest mom in the school. Maybe the whole state of Tennessee."

"Gee, thanks. I thought I was already the coolest mom in the state."

She rolls her eyes and scoffs. "Please. Sadie's mom brings the entire class homemade cookies every month. You can't even make us boxed Macaroni and Cheese, and you're still burning pancakes after making them every weekend for years." She picks up her backpack, balancing it between her and the couch as she digs through it for a minute and pulls out a stack of mail and tosses it at me. "I grabbed the mail. You're welcome."

"You're welcome to keep some of these bills and pay for them yourself."

"No money," she sings out, a huge smile on her face. "Oh, and I'm getting low on my medicine, I only have five left. But, Mom... The Devils."

I sort through the bills as Max drops herself between Harper and I, and the two of them launch into a conversation about how cool it would be to work with actual hockey players. *Not very if your ex is going to be your boss.* She's going to be so disappointed when I tell her I'm not taking the job. You know, the job I wasn't going to tell her about because I knew how excited she'd get.

Freaking Harper. She's the worst liar on the planet.

I should've known better than to mention it to my sister in the first place. I should have told her I had diarrhea when she overheard my phone call and hid in the bathroom for an hour.

At least then I wouldn't have the two of them going back and forth about their favorite Devils players. Harper doesn't even like hockey.

Traitor.

As I mentally add up the rent, electric, water, and cable bills, along with what it might cost for a medication refill without insurance, my gut sinks. The money I have left in the bank won't even cover rent.

Not that there's a great time to lose your job, but this is the worst. I don't know how I'm going to get through till next month, and there is absolutely no way I can let Max's pills run out.

Dammit.

Harper's right, I haven't had any luck on the job search. I found a few secretary positions, but one was part-time, and the others were almost half of what I made at my old job. I bet the benefits aren't half as good either.

"I'm going to go tell Cassidy and Patricia your good news. I'm so excited for you! I hope they give you free tickets to every game and I can go with you. This is awesome!" Max pulls me in for a quick hug, and before I can let her down and tell her that I will not be working for any hockey team, she runs off to her room.

I curse under my breath. "I am not taking this job. I know money is super tight, but I'll find something. I'll get two jobs. I'll wait tables, make coffee, hell, I'll even clean toilets if I have to. It'll be fine. It's all fine."

Harper eyes me speculatively, pulling her bottom lip between her teeth. "So… is this a bad time to remind you we still need to pay for the books I had to get for organic chemistry?"

Fuck. Me.

I hang my head and think about my mom, about what she would do if she were in this situation, and it only takes me seconds to get the answer. She'd take the job regardless of how it might make her feel. She'd deal with the Devil every day if it meant she could give my sister and me a good life. She'd sacrifice everything for us.

With a sigh, I grab my phone off the table and fire off a text I instantly regret.

> Me: I'll take the job, but I have a few conditions.

10

GORDON

OH LOOK, ANOTHER DAY WHERE I CAN'T SEEM TO GET shit done. Great. *I love it.*

With a sigh, I push away from my desk and lean back in my chair, staring at the ceiling like I don't have fifty things I'd like to get done today. I haven't been able to concentrate all damn week, and I only have myself to blame. I can't get out of my own head, and I can't stop analyzing the small interaction I had with Riley a week ago.

Seven days.

That is how ridiculous I am right now.

Like a damn brokenhearted kid, I had my heart pinned to my sleeve and I didn't hesitate to vomit my emotions all over her, which is not something I do. Fucking *ever.*

I feel like I'm ripping apart at the seams, like I'm

falling off a ledge, and there's nothing to break my fall. Nothing to hold on to. Like I have a damn war going on inside my head and there is no winner, no loser, nothing but chaos and pain.

Some days I feel like I'm drowning in my own misery, and though the sun is clearly shining, I can't feel its warmth.

But I sure as shit don't tell anyone about it.

I don't get attached, and I definitely don't open up and let anyone in, don't let anyone see what's really going on inside my head.

So why did I show her a part of myself I haven't shared with anyone? The answer is right in front of my face—there's a part of me that still belongs to her, always has—but I push it away. *Mind over matter.* If I don't acknowledge it, it's not true. And if my sister managed to talk her into working for us—for me—I can push her away, keep her at arm's length until I can shut her out of my mind for good, and can go back to being alone without all these thoughts haunting me.

They've been here since I was a little boy, since my dad took away my childhood and held me captive to a sport that demanded all of my attention, took my life away from me before it even started. A sport, a career, that I pissed away when I let myself get hit like I did, and lost everything I've worked so hard for.

Including her.

But fuck. What if Jazz did get her to agree to work

here? There's a small part of me, a very small, insignificant part, that wants to see her again. That wants to get to know her. That really wants to know what she's been doing for the past twelve years. And I really want to know how long she's been living in the same damn city.

Why?

Because it seems like I want to torture myself when I know I should leave it alone, which is why I haven't followed up with anyone after our meeting on Wednesday. I don't *need* to know what happened. I don't *need* to know if she took the job.

I shake my head with a scoff. And what a meeting it was. That was where everyone decided to throw me in the middle of the street and run me over with a metaphorical bus—multiple times.

"Are you angry with your ceiling? Has it personally offended you, or is it the color? Too boring? Too textured?" Dean teases as he lets himself in my office and sits down in one of the brown leather chairs on the other side of the desk. He props his black Prada dress shoes right next to my lamp, and gives me a smile most people probably find charming.

"Is it too early in the day to tell you to go fuck yourself?" I growl out and scoot my chair up to my desk, running a hand down my tie.

Dean chuckles, giving his head a shake, his eyes never leaving my face. It's unnerving, and I can't say I like it. "It's past eight am so I think you're okay, even if it is a touch unprofessional."

"Like you coming in here and putting your feet on my desk?"

"Something like that."

He continues to watch me and I tug on my tie, needing something to do with my hands, and tap my more expensive Tom Ford loafers against the wood floor. The silence stretches between us, and dammit, I don't have time for this shit today. I'm too busy beating myself up.

With a deep sigh, I run a hand through my hair and slap it down on the desk. "You obviously want something."

"Do I?" His smile widens as he adjusts his posture, sinking down in the chair and crossing his legs at the ankles, his feet still on my damn desk.

"Don't you?"

"Maybe I want to hang out with you this morning. Maybe I want to see if you're in here absolutely losing your shit."

I take a deep breath, and then another. "And why would I be losing my shit?"

"Your ex-girlfriend." Dean lifts up his silk tie, running a finger along the black and red stripe pattern. "Does this line look crooked to you?"

"Dean," I grit out, my jaw clenched so hard I can

practically hear my teeth grinding together. "Put down your tie before I choke you with it."

"*Tsk Tsk.* Is that any way to talk to your best employee and dear friend?"

I raise a brow and rest my elbows on the edge of my desk, leaning forward enough to put him within reach. My heart hammers in my chest and my stomach dips like the floor has been pulled out from under me, but I ignore it all. "What about my ex-girlfriend? Did she take the job?"

He doesn't answer me right away, because of course not. Instead, he sits up straight, finally taking his feet off my desk and scooting the chair closer so he can mimic my position. This close, I can see every speck of amusement in his eyes, and I'm so close to personally wiping that smile right off his face. "You don't know."

"Know what? For Christ's sake, Dean, spit it out."

"She accepted the offer yesterday. Came in this morning to get everything all signed and official."

"Okay, she came in this morning. That's hardly a big deal."

It is a fucking big deal, and I should have been notified the second she walked in my fucking building. I should have been there to... what? Piss us both off? I blow out a breath and force myself to relax.

"She's cute. I see why you're still hung up on her."

Before I can stop myself, I growl, like a full-on chest rumbling growl at my general manager. Cute? He thinks she's cute? I'm not sure if I should be pissed because he doesn't realize how gorgeous she is, or because he's looking at her at all. Obviously, the correct answer is neither, and I need to get a fucking grip.

"I didn't notice when I ran into her last week," I lie and take a deep breath, avoiding looking directly at Dean. "And I'm not hung up on her."

He laughs, and I take back all the good things I've said about him. "She's still here. Jazz thought it would be a good idea for her to meet the team and sit in on a practice. The McIver brothers seem to be warming up to her quite quickly."

I jump up and pace the small area behind my desk, running my hands through my hair and flinging off my damn suit jacket. My heart is hammering against my ribcage like it's trying to break free, my damn palms are sweating, and any calm I thought I had is completely out the window.

"I thought it wasn't a big deal?" Dean taunts as he leans back, continuing to watch me with a smirk on his face. "Doesn't look like you're over her to me."

Her being here, working for me, shouldn't be a big deal. Logically, I know this. Jazz is already showing her around, and going down there, interfering with their tour, would single her out and probably look bad on me.

Okay, it would definitely look bad on me. It would make me look like a huge jackass.

But the more I pace, the more I think about it, the

more I convince myself it'll be fine. I'll simply go down to the practice rink and see how things are going. That's it. I won't talk to her, I won't interfere. I'm just checking on my new employee and the team I own in the arena I own. No big deal.

Yeah, right.

"Judging by that look on your face, I'd say you're going down there. Does it matter if I tell you it's a bad idea?"

"Trust me, Dean, I know it's a horrible idea. Don't pretend like you didn't know the end result when you came in here. You knew what you were doing." I grab my jacket and put it back on, smoothing out any wrinkles, real or imagined.

"I might have," he shrugs, pushing himself to his feet and slipping his hands in his pockets. "And I think I should go with you. It's only appropriate you have a chaperone."

"To keep me from making an ass out of myself?"

His lip twitches, but at least this time, he stops himself from smirking at me. "I feel like that's fairly obvious."

With a curt nod, I let him lead the way out of the office suite.

As the two of us descend the stairs to the practice rink, we settle into a comfortable silence. Well, I'm comfortable, but I can tell Dean has more to say. He keeps glancing at me like he's waiting for me to spill my guts, let him in on the history I share with Riley.

Maybe I should, but I won't.

Before we can exit the stairwell, Dean blocks the doorway, and this time when he turns around to glance at me, his face is stoic. "Your history with Riley is none of my business, but it's obvious there are some unresolved issues here, aka your feelings. You might want to consider distancing yourself from her if the two of you are going to be working together on a daily basis. Either that, or you can, you know, talk it out with her and move on from whatever this is that has your panties all twisted up."

I grunt in reply, simply because I don't think I'm going to do either one of those things. Would it be logical? Yes, but I feel anything but as I push past Dean and make my way to the ice.

The closer I get, the more I feel that deep ache in my chest that never seems to go away.

The more I feel a buzz of energy beneath my skin.

I can feel Dean at my back as I step into the practice rink, and it takes me about two seconds to find Riley on the other side of the ice, standing next to Jazz and watching the team run through drills. The two of them are deep in conversation, and every now and then, Riley glances toward the team, toward the ice I know she used to love.

Her eyes are full of longing, and there's a sadness

surrounding her that wasn't there before. Is she thinking of me? Of the countless times she watched me practice? Of that time I snuck her into the locker room after everyone had gone home and fucked her so hard she couldn't stand afterward?

Probably not.

After how she ended things, after telling me she didn't *love* me, and after moving on so quickly to someone else, there's no way she thought about me before running into me last week.

Probably not even close to how often I think about her.

Dean clears his throat, and as he comes to a stop next to me, digs his elbow right below my ribs. I'm sure he'd like me to stop staring at her, but I can't help myself. She's fucking beautiful, and I hate that I can't pull my eyes away.

Her deep red hair is pulled into a high ponytail, the bottom of it curled slightly and swishes across her shoulders as she talks to Jazz. She's wearing a tight knee-length gray skirt that has my imagination going exactly where it shouldn't, and a white button-up blouse I'm itching to toss on my office floor.

Which is exactly why her working here is such a big mistake. It's been five seconds, and I've already lost all my focus.

I should've ignored Dean and stayed in my office, far, far away from the only woman who tempts me by just existing. I'm supposed to hate her for how badly she broke my heart, but for some reason, all I want to do is put on a pair of skates and ask her to skate with me.

An idea that's absurd for multiple reasons. I haven't put on a pair of skates since I was smashed into the boards and needed a multi-ligament reconstruction on my knee. The trainers encouraged me to get back out there after my surgery, but I knew there was no point. I was done. Plus, this really isn't the place to see if I can still skate, or if I'd look like a baby giraffe on the ice. The entire team is out there, and they're clearly in the middle of practice.

I wasn't—I'm not going to interfere, so I'm really not sure why I'm making my way around the rink toward her and my sister.

Maybe I'm possessed.

My brain is telling me to turn around, yet my feet keep carrying me forward.

"What is it you're planning on doing?" Dean mumbles as he leans toward me.

I shake my head, running a hand through my hair and down the side of my neck. "No idea."

"Maybe try not to scare her off before her first day. I like her."

I barely contain the growl threatening to rumble across my chest... well, at least I managed to keep it mostly quiet. What's wrong with me?

Dean stares at me for a few seconds before he chuckles. "You really should get that under control."

I brush him off and come to a very casual stop a few feet from where Jazz and Riley are standing.

Jazz notices me almost immediately, pursing her lips and making it abundantly clear that I'm intruding on their conversation. It takes a few seconds—seconds that feel like hours—and Riley finally glances toward me. Her back stiffens and a mask of indifference slips over her face before she turns and tries her damnedest to look in the opposite direction.

She can pretend to be indifferent, pretend I don't affect her, but I'm close enough to see the pretty pink blush crawl up her neck.

I lean toward her just for a moment, just long enough to smell her intoxicating peach perfume, to feel the soft rumble of laughter hit me square in the chest.

I used to love her laugh. It's been so fucking long since I've heard it, my chest tightens and I can't breathe. I'm drowning in a sea of painful nostalgia and longing, but I try to ignore it, just like Riley is trying to ignore me.

I shouldn't want her.

I shouldn't feel anything when I see her.

But fuck if my heart didn't get the memo.

The longer I stand here looking at her, watching her pretend like I don't exist, watching her laugh at something Weston Gray says as he skates by, the more pissed I get. The buzzing under my skin has turned me into a livewire, and I feel like I could snap at any given moment.

She laughs again and my jaw clamps shut.

I hate it.

I hate all of it.

I thought this would be fine. I thought I could be a grown-up. I thought I could have Riley working here and I'd be completely unaffected, but it's bullshit.

Just like how she smiles at everyone but me.

"You doing okay there, boss?" Mick stops in front of me, glancing warily between Dean and me, his face etched with concern.

Dean laughs and bumps Mick's fist with his own. "I'm not sure if he's about to combust on the spot or stomp back out there on the ice and punch someone. Is it bad that I wish I'd have been here to see that?"

"It was epic. I wish I'd have gotten some video footage. That was a fail on my part. The way he was slipping and sliding yet so determined to get to Dallas… it was great."

"I hate both of you," I mumble, my hands fisting at my sides, my gaze fixed on the ice.

Dean knocks me with his shoulder, and if he's not careful, I might punch him. Don't even have to chase him out on the ice. "Are you having any luck pulling that stick out of your ass?"

I ignore him and it's not like it matters; they continue

talking, but I don't pay them any attention, not when Riley turns, this time meeting my gaze and holding it. Her eyes narrow as she assesses me, and this time, I glare right back.

She's so angry, so full of hate, it throws me off balance. I'm the one that deserves to be angry. Not her.

"I'm surprised to hear you took the job." I rake a hand through my hair as Mick and Dean turn to stare at me with wide eyes. I'm painstakingly aware I shouldn't be talking to her, but I can't help myself, I can't stop.

Her mouth falls open for a second, brows furrowed, before she huffs a breath and crosses her arms. "Don't worry, it has nothing to do with wanting to see you again. In fact, knowing you'd be here almost made me reconsider your sister's offer."

"Maybe you should have." The words are out of my mouth before I can stop them, and Jazz gives me a sharp look. I should be asking her why she took the offer. If she despises me this much, why would she agree to work in a place she has to see me, day in and day out? I should, but I don't. "This isn't the fucking Ice Capades."

"Oh, really? I didn't notice the lack of leotards and glitter. Thanks for pointing it out. Would have never noticed without you."

"Anytime. I'm here to help."

"Doubt it."

Mick clears his throat and shoots me a look, mumbling under his breath. "I really wish you'd shut the fuck up." He slaps my arm and smiles at Riley and Jazz. "We're lucky to have you, Riley. Jazz, I'm sure I'll be seeing you tonight."

"Yeah. Lucky," I scoff, immediately regretting my words as a flash of hurt crosses her face. It's quick, but I catch it.

And it makes me feel like shit.

I don't wait for a response before I promptly turn and stomp back to my office. I can't do this. There's no way I can ignore her presence in this building any more than I can pretend she doesn't affect me.

But fuck.

I need to try to do both before I throw every ounce of my professionalism straight out the window and allow Riley to distract me from what's important—doing whatever I can to make sure my team makes the playoffs.

Riley might be my past, but this team is my future, and there's no way I'm giving it up without a fight.

Even if the only person I'm fighting is myself.

11

RILEY

THE SECOND GORDON DISAPPEARS FROM THE PRACTICE rink, my hands ball into fists and I barely hold back a slew of insults. I can practically feel the anger rising through my body, causing my blood to boil and my face to heat. The longer I stand here, staring at the exit, the hotter I get, and since I'm a ginger, I'm sure that means my face is currently bright red.

That asshole gets under my skin like no one else, and seeing as how he's going to be my new boss, I should've kept my mouth shut, but I couldn't help but fight back. It seems every time he's around, my hackles rise and I go on the defensive. Which is bad, very bad, considering my first day of work here is Monday.

Which is exactly why I didn't want to take this job in the first place.

I knew he'd cause problems, just like I knew seeing

him would affect me, throw me off my game and make me forget how much I need this job right now. After a conference call with the owners of Hawkins Investments, the chances of reopening seem slim to none, and I can't afford to be out of a paycheck or health insurance.

Unless I want to take a significant pay cut, this job is my only chance.

And it seems I've already made quite the impression on everyone around here.

Jazz is appraising me, her brows nearly in her hairline. Mick and Dean are looking at me with what I can only assume is pity. Then there's the entire hockey team who aren't that far away and probably heard some of that exchange. I don't know how many of them are staring my way, but I don't dare look out there. I don't really want to know.

Fucking Benson and his big mouth.

I can't believe he came all the way down here to start shit with me. There's no way he wanted to actually watch practice—none—or he would've pulled the ridiculously large stick from his ass and played nice in the sandbox.

Or maybe even just kept his mouth shut and acted like the professional he's supposed to be.

Jazz nods after Gordon, laying a soft hand on my shoulder. "Sorry about my brother, he's just... well he's…"

"A jackass." My teeth clench so hard I'm surprised she understands me, but she nods again.

Mick shakes his head, chuckling as he skates back out to join the team while Dean smiles. "He's a huge jackass and no one would blame you if you followed him and put him in his place. Maybe let him know you won't tolerate being pushed around."

Jazz murmurs her agreement, glancing at Dean, the two of them sharing a look I can't decipher. "Besides, you don't work here yet."

I take a deep breath and then three more. This has bad idea written all over it. Even more so than taking this job in the first damn place. I can't go chasing after Gordon just to give him a piece of my mind.

Can I?

"He usually takes the stairs across from the exit," Dean adds, his tone casual as he pulls out his phone and taps away. "If you hurry you should be able to catch him before he makes it back to his office."

You know what? I sure as hell can.

I don't start till Monday and he needs to know that I refuse to be pushed around, not by him. It's going to be hard enough coming to a place where I know I have to see him every day, to have a daily reminder of who he once was to me... and the monster he turned out to be. To have to look him in the eyes and pretend I'm okay, pretend we both don't know about the child we had together because I'm sure as shit not bringing it up, and if he hasn't yet, I don't think he will either.

He's been so apathetic, so indifferent, it's like there's

no part of his past self that remains. It's sad really, and if I didn't hate his face, his very essence, I'd feel bad for him.

Fueled by my anger and the ghosts of my past, I stomp across the practice arena. I don't turn around and I sure as hell don't look back at the people behind me, or I'm afraid I'll lose my nerve.

The stairwell is easy to find and I fling open the door expecting it to be empty, but Gordon is standing in the middle of the staircase, unmoving, almost like he's frozen in place. His back is to me, his shoulders slumped, and his head is hung down like he's completely and utterly defeated.

I almost feel bad for him, almost turn around and walk back to the rink, but I don't. I just stand in the doorway and stare at him, waiting for him to change position, to turn around... something.

He doesn't move an inch, and the only sound between us is his heavy sigh.

The longer I stand here, the thicker the air grows around me, wrapping around my throat, choking me. I wonder if he feels it, if he's affected by me at all, but in reality, he's probably not.

"If you're going to stand there judging me, don't bother. I already know I was an asshole."

"Yeah," I whisper, pausing to finally let the door close behind me. "You were."

"Riley." He's said my name a thousand times, but

never like this. Never so full of anguish, longing, despair... and just for a second, I can pretend he's the man I once knew, the man I loved with my entire being. But that illusion shatters as soon as he turns around, his mask of indifference already in place.

He doesn't say anything more, and for a second, neither do I. We simply stare at each other, and I'm not sure how to break the silence any more than I know how to talk to this new, grumpy, I-hate-everything, Gordon.

His green eyes pierce through me, and where they used to make my knees quiver and my panties damp, only simmering resentment remains. His gaze softens for a moment, and he opens his mouth, but quickly snaps it shut and glares at me instead.

I don't know if he's angry because he felt something in that cold, dead heart of his or if it's taken over his entire personality, but it shakes me out of my stupor and reminds me why I'm here.

"I think it goes without saying we're going to be seeing a lot of each other." I cross my arms and do my best to ignore his strangled groan. "I don't like it either, but I need this job and you need an executive assistant. We're going to have to learn how to be professional if this is going to work."

His mouth flattens and his hands go to his tie. I'm sure he has something to say, but he just nods.

"You can't follow me around, pelting me with insults because it makes you feel better about yourself." My arms fall down to my sides and my gaze lowers to the ground. "It's embarrassing."

My throat clogs with emotion and as tears prick at the corners of my eyes, I turn around. I'm sure I should run back out the door, tail tucked between my legs, and go the hell home, but I don't want him to know he gets to me. I can't.

The last thing I want is to give him the upper hand. And because of my history with Gordon, I'm already at a disadvantage with anyone who knows about our past. And even worse—the whole team knows he thinks I'm an idiot... an idiot who doesn't belong here.

I'm so stupid.

I don't know why I thought this was a good idea. Well, okay, a decent idea that would help pad my savings account until I can find a viable long-term job.

I just... I can't do this.

Not right now.

Not when the walls are closing in on me and I'm suddenly feeling so damn raw.

I place my hand on top of the door handle, intent on getting the hell out of here before I have a breakdown in front of Gordon, but freeze when I feel him behind me.

He doesn't touch me. He doesn't speak.

But he doesn't need to.

I know he's there.

He's so close, I could lean back and press my body against his. Let him wrap his arms around me and pretend we're still naïve eighteen-year-olds who love each other. Pretend we're both not so full of hurt and jagged edges that all we can do is make the other bleed.

It would be so easy to pretend... but sooner or later, the illusion would end and I know I'd be more broken than before. So, instead of giving in, I turn around and meet his softened gaze.

"I'm sorry." His voice sounds strangled, and his mask is nowhere in place, giving me a glimpse of the vulnerability he buries away. "I didn't mean to embarrass you. I don't... I don't know how to act around you."

My throat clogs and my legs tremble. I have so much to say, so many questions to ask, but I can't force myself to say a single word.

It's like his proximity has sucked all the air out of my lungs, all the thoughts from my brain.

He lifts a hand, but pauses halfway to my face, anguish marring his. His fingers curl toward me, sweeping gently across my cheekbone. A shiver works its way down my spine, and I can't hold back the sigh that escapes from my lips.

Gordon's eyes close as he leans forward, his forehead touching mine. His fingers travel down my neck and I swear my heart is going to beat out of my chest.

His lips are so close to mine. Every breath is like a light caress, a plea for forgiveness.

I'm so lost, so confused. I don't know if I want to push him away or drag his body against mine.

I hate this.

I hate him.

I really hate that it all feels like a fragile lie.

"Riley." His voice lowers to a whisper and he wraps his hand around the back of my neck. "Firefly."

Hearing my old nickname is like being doused with a bucket of cold water and I take a quick step back, ramming myself into the door behind me. His eyes snap open and flash with anger. His hand hangs between us for just a moment before it flexes into a fist and falls down by his side.

"Gordon." I take a step forward as he sneers, glaring at me with unabashed hostility.

He shakes his head and takes a step back, his voice curt as he says, "I'll see you Monday. Please dress appropriately."

As soon as he finishes the last word, he turns around and stomps up the stairs, leaving me staring at his back and wondering what the fuck just happened.

Was he…?

Was he going to kiss me?

Was I going to let him?

One thing is for sure, I need to find a new job by Monday. It seems Gordon is still a weakness of mine, and when it comes to my life, to Max, I can't afford to be weak.

12

RILEY

I THINK IT'S SAFE TO SAY I DIDN'T FIND A NEW JOB OVER
the weekend. Well, unless you count the frazzled mother
of four who asked me to hold her dog's leash while she
wrangled her kids in her van outside the apartments.
Sadly, I don't think the position was full time, nor do I
think she'd be willing to pay very much.

At least the dog was cute and didn't try to kiss me,
unlike my new boss.

I still can't believe he did that. I spent the entirety of
the weekend going over that moment in the stairwell and
dissecting every little detail. The way he leaned into me,
the scant distance between our lips, the annoying flutter I
felt in the pit of my stomach, and the way every single
breath felt like it was shared between us.

I tried to rationalize what in the hell he was thinking,

tried to come up with some other reason he was touching me, but came up blank. It didn't seem like he was having a medical episode, but I can't rule it out.

Why else would he have done *that*?

He hates me, I hate him.

It's pretty cut and dry.

Yet he tried to kiss me.

And I've been waiting all morning for him to come out of his office and give me some clue as to what he's thinking, of how our work relationship is going to go. I can only hope he's going to take the high road and be a professional.

At least one of us needs to be.

I took his last parting shot to heart—*please dress appropriately*—and decided to do the opposite. I have no idea what's wrong with me but Gordon makes me very irrational, which is a terrible realization for me to have. It's why I'm stationed at the front desk of the office wing, in a short skirt that could barely pass as office appropriate. A skirt that had Harper watching me leave the apartment with wide eyes and a slack jaw.

At least Dean didn't seem to notice. Either that or he decided to politely keep his mouth shut and his eyes on my face.

After the almost kiss that most definitely shouldn't have happened, I'd be better off wearing a dress that covers every inch of skin. And a puffy jacket. And maybe a hat.

I click a few buttons and send the newly compiled stats to Dean and pull out my phone from the desk drawer. It's buzzed a few times already, and I know I shouldn't be on my phone during my first day at work, but it could be Max, and I need to make sure everything is okay. But it's not Max, it's Harper.

Harper: Have you seen the Devil yet?

Harper: Is he why you wore the scandalous skirt?

Harper: I'm assuming since you're not answering, the answer is yes, and you two are boning in his office right now.

Me: OMG no!! Calm your tits, woman. I'm at work. Just in case you forgot, this is my first day, and I'm trying to make a good impression.

Harper: Pretty sure one of your bosses already has an opinion. <eggplant emoji> <peach emoji>

Me: Funny. Very funny.

Harper: Well, duh. So, about the office boning...

Me: Jesus. No one is boning anyone in any office. I'd rather die.

Harper: Boring.

> Me: And no one says boning. Are you five?

> Harper: Would you prefer fuck?

> Harper: For example, are you fucking your ex/current boss in his office?

Apparently, my sister thinks she's hilarious, and just as I am about to type out a reply, a throat clears behind me.

"Holy motherfucker!" I jump about two feet in the air and my phone slips out of my hand, hitting the desk and clattering to the floor. "I mean fudgesticks."

I say a silent prayer that it's Dean or Jazz coming back out to check on me, but I know it's not. Gordon's presence is like an electric shock straight down my spine. And here I am, phone on the floor, in the shortest skirt I own and I'm not ready to face him.

To buy myself a little time, I inch the chair around as slowly as humanly possible. Maybe if I take until Tuesday, he'll get frustrated and leave.

No such luck. It's only been about twenty-five seconds, and he's still here.

Looming.

Gordon is standing a few feet away, a smirk on his face, his intense gaze raking over me, and I really try not to feel anything at the sight of him, I really do, but I fail. My stomach is in knots, and my heart is already working overtime. What is it about him that affects me so much? I wish I knew so I could figure out a way to circumvent said feelings.

He cocks his head to the side and undoes the buttons on his suit jacket. A move that shouldn't be sexy, but it is. I need help. Professional help. "I feel like it's too late to correct yourself when the whole motherfucker is already out of your mouth."

"Debatable." My response is quick, and as he crosses his arms, my entire argument goes right out the window —and much to my utter dismay, I find my eyes traveling the length of his entire damn body.

Not only was he checking me out, but now I'm making it so much worse. No matter how much I want to, I can't seem to look away. It's like I've been hypnotized by all his muscles, which is ridiculous, because I've seen muscles before.

Not like his, and he still has all his clothes on.

He's wearing a black suit that's molded around his broad shoulders and really highlights his powerful frame. It makes him look imposing, domineering, and if the little flutter that's back in my stomach is any indication, very dangerous for my indifference. I can almost imagine him lifting me up, bending me over this desk, and fucking me so good I forget how to walk. Almost, but I don't. Because as I remind myself for what seems like the hundredth time, I hate him.

And I'm going to at least pretend I'm a professional. Even if my skirt and blatant ogling say otherwise.

"You gonna get that?"

"Huh?" My eyes are stuck between his chest and his very large biceps but after he clears his throat again, I manage to tear them away and meet his.

He points to the floor behind me, the smirk on his face growing, and holy mother of God, it hits me exactly where it shouldn't. I like him a whole lot better when he's frowning at me. It's safer. "Your phone. Are you going to get that?"

I stretch backward, but as soon as I feel the skirt inching up my thighs, I freeze. My face heats and I try to pull the fabric back down, but it doesn't budge. "I think it's good. It looks nice on the floor."

Gordon's response is a grunt and his disarming smile morphs into a frown as his gaze settles on my exposed legs. "Is that a figure skating skirt or is this your idea of dressing professional?"

"Dean didn't seem to have a problem with it."

The words are out of my mouth, and I don't quite realize what I implied until he takes a step toward me and growls. His hands flex into fists at his side and it looks like he's struggling to maintain control.

"Excuse me?"

I grip the sides of the chair and take a deep breath, his signature spicy yet woody scent washing over me, and I fight against my entire being to stay in the present and not lose myself in the past. It would be so easy to give myself over to the memories, to pretend he's someone else, but I can't. I can't lose myself. "I mean, he didn't say anything about my attire when he was out here earlier. He was polite."

"And I'm not?"

"Not right now."

He doesn't respond right away; he just openly glares at me, and I force myself to fold my hands across my lap and not fidget. Let me tell you, that's easier said than done. Especially when I'd love nothing more than to shift back and forth so I can pull this stupid ass skirt down.

Not that I get much time to worry about that when Ian and Owen McIver push their way into the office space moments later and stop right in front of my desk, huge smiles plastered on their faces. They look like trouble, especially when they're together like this.

I turn away from Gordon and greet the brothers. Hopefully, he'll take the hint and go back to his office and leave me and my skirt in peace. "Good morning, gentleman. Is there something I can do for you? Do you need to set up a meeting with Dean?"

"We came here to see you, actually," Ian replies and leans over my desk, completely ignoring Gordon, who has gone rigid at my side. "Owen and I are having a joint birthday bash and wanted to make sure you were invited. The team would love to get to know you more."

Gordon scoffs, uncrossing and recrossing his arms as he grumbles, "Yeah, the team. Real original."

I raise my brows and toss him a look, but he doesn't even spare me a glance. He's too busy staring a hole straight through Ian's chest.

There's one thing I promised myself when I walked through the doors this morning—I'm not going to let him or his dickish attitude dictate my life. If—and that's a big if—I'm going to keep this job, it would be nice to have some friendly faces on the team. Especially if I'm going to be stuck up here with Captain Grump most days. "That sounds fun. I'll have to check my schedule, but—"

"You're busy."

"Excuse me?"

"You heard me," Gordon grits out, gesturing to Ian and Owen and laying a possessive hand on the back of my chair. "Whatever kind of sex party these two are inviting you to, you're busy."

My spine straightens and suddenly, I wish I'd worn a shorter skirt. Who the fuck is he to tell me what I'm allowed to do? He's nothing to me, not anymore, and even if he was, he has no right to dictate what I do on any given night. I'm my own person, and right now, I really want to know more about what kind of sex party these two are throwing.

Especially if it pisses off Gordon.

My gaze volleys between the brothers as I do my best

to completely ignore him. "Sex party? That's got to be an exaggeration, right?"

Ian's smile seems to get bigger as he winks, his hands curling over the raised edge of the desk. He leans over, his fingers inches from mine, and while normally I'd casually scoot back, I don't. It's clear he's trying to get under Gordon's skin, and I'd hate to miss an opportunity to join in. Although if the steam coming out of his ears is any indication, Ian is doing a fine job on his own.

"There's an actual birthday party," Owen laughs. "It'll be Friday night. We're meeting at Whiskey and Rye around seven for drinks, and those of us that are..." He pauses, glancing between his brother and Gordon, "a little more adventurous, will be going to Onyx later on."

Onyx?

I haven't gone to a single bar since coming to Nashville, so I don't know any of the local hotspots, but there's something about the way he finished that sentence that makes me think this isn't a normal dance club, but before I can open my mouth to ask, Gordon practically pushes me out of the way, slams his hands on the desk, and leans toward Ian. A lesser man would probably run.

"She's not interested," Gordon growls and nods to Ian's hands. "And if you don't get your hands away from her, you're going to lose them."

Ian remains unfazed, although Owen takes a small step back. It's clear that I'm no longer involved in this conversation, but this seems like a good opportunity to let Gordon know he is not the boss of me outside this place.

"I'm actually very interested." I stand shoulder to shoulder with Gordon, giving Ian what I hope is a shy smile.

"She's not."

"I am." I turn to Gordon, eyes narrowed, and stare at him for several beats before I swing back around, knocking my elbow into his. "I don't believe any of us were talking to you."

He stands up straight, adjusting his tie, his face turning a lovely shade of red. "Unless this is work related, you two need to fuck off."

Ian strums his fingers on the edge of my desk and goes to turn, but not before sending me a wink and another one of his smiles. "I hope to see you Friday, beautiful."

Gordon growls again and I give them both a wave. He really needs to get himself under control, but he continues to stand there seething, even after they're gone. So I sit down and quickly grab my phone. My skirt travels dangerously far up my thigh, but he's too busy glaring at the elevator door to notice a damn thing. I put my phone in the drawer, adjust my clothes, and pull up my email.

"Is there something I can help you with, Mr. Benson?

Unless this is work related, you really should—what is it you said? Fuck off?"

He spins me around, lowering until we're eye to eye, and grips the armrests, caging me in. I should hate this with every fiber of my being—and believe me, I'm trying—but it's hard to keep my head straight when he's this close.

He closes his eyes for a second, his nose brushing along the length of mine, and I swear he mumbles something before he pins me with his piercing green eyes. "Just to be clear, you're not going."

"Just to be clear," I lean forward letting my lips graze his. I know I'm playing with fire. I know we're both about to get burned, but I can't seem to stop myself. "I'm a grown-ass woman and can do whatever I want. I'm single, and don't think that because I work for you, you can dictate what I do in my personal life."

"Riley." This time when he says my name, it's filled with heat, a dangerous mixture of anger and desire.

"Gordon."

"You're not going."

I heave out a sigh and glance toward the heavens. His domineering attitude is making it a lot easier to ignore the feelings churning around my chest. He's an asshole— an asshole who left me and our daughter on our own for years. "I know this may come as a shock, but I've been taking care of myself for a while now. You're not *my* dad, so unless you have something work related you need to tell me, I think this conversation is done."

He continues to stare at me for several seconds before uttering a curse under his breath and pushing away from me. He curses several more times as he stomps down the hallway and slams the door to what I can only assume is his office.

As far as first days go, I think this went well.

Maybe tomorrow I won't want to kill my boss.

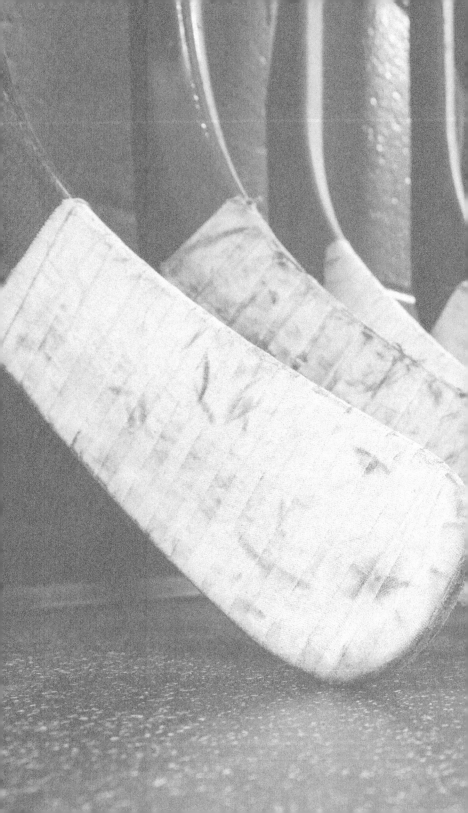

13

To: RAdams@NashvilleDevils.com
From: GBenson@NashvilleDevils.com

Subject: New Policies

Miss Adams,

First of all, I want to apologize for my very unprofessional behavior this morning. It seems I'm not myself when you're around. Please see the attached policy revisions to the employee handbook. You'll see that the dress code has been expanded to include an acceptable length for all skirts and shorts as well as an amended fraternization policy.

Best,

Gordon Benson

(Final)

. . .

To: GBenson@NashvilleDevils.com
From: RAdams@NashvilleDevils.com
CC:JBenson@NashvilleDevils.com,
DPrescott@NashvilleDevils.com

Subject: Re: New Policies

Mr. Benson,

Since you admitted in your previous email that you cannot find your best self, I've taken the liberty of adding Jazlyn and Dean to this email as it appears you've forgotten them. I'm sure they would love to know of any policy changes as it affects the organization as a whole. On a personal note, I appreciate your concern with both my extracurricular activities and my choice in attire. Not every boss would go to such great lengths to assure I don't get chilly. Perhaps you can adjust the thermostat to the offices instead of instituting an entire revision in order to cover my legs.

Thanks,
Riley

To: GBenson@NashvilleDevils.com

From: JBenson@NashvilleDevils.com
CC:RAdams@NashvilleDevils.com,
DPrescott@NashvilleDevils.com

Subject: Re: Re: New Policies

Really Gordon? This is ridiculous. We're not amending company policy because you want to be a dick.

Get ahold of yourself,

Jazz.

To: GBenson@NashvilleDevils.com
From: DPrescott@NashvilleDevils.com
CC:JBenson@NashvilleDevils.com,
RAdams@NashvilleDevils.com

Subject: Re: Re: Re: New Policies

Jesus. It's her first day.

Riley, I'm so sorry. Let me take you out to lunch tomorrow and we can go over expectations. Alone.

Dean

To: DPrescott@NashvilleDevils.com
   From: RAdams@NashvilleDevils.com
   CC:JBenson@NashvilleDevils.com,GBen-
son@NashvilleDevils.com

Subject: Re: Re: Re: Re: New Policies

Thank you, Dean. That's very kind of you. I'd love to go to lunch tomorrow and discuss what this job does and does not entail.
   Thanks again,
   Riley

To: GBenson@NashvilleDevils.com
   From: RAdams@NashvilleDevils.com

Subject: Suck it

I think the title of the email says it all.
   Best,
   Riley

14

GORDON

I had every intention of crashing Riley and Dean's lunch today, but I ended up spending all morning on a conference call for a new charity foundation I'm a part of. It's for a good cause, I know it is, but I missed my opportunity to insert myself right in the middle of their conversation, one I've convinced myself is all about me.

Why else would Dean want to take her out to lunch alone?

Unless he's also noticed the particularly short skirts she's been wearing.

If she had just read the email like a normal person and not CC'd Jazz and Dean, those policies would be in effect, and I wouldn't have to see her and her creamy legs every damn morning when she comes in. I wouldn't be distracted during the day, imagining those legs wrapped around my head while I feast on her pussy. And I sure as hell wouldn't be walking out to the reception area so fucking much with a dick that's half hard.

Wouldn't be out here now either, making copies of shit for our meeting today, when I have a perfectly good printer in my office.

Yeah, I know. I have a problem—and her name is Riley Adams.

Also, this goddamn copy machine that literally just jammed.

Fuck my luck.

I say a few choice curse words, pull on the paper to no avail, and curse some more. It's beeping, I'm close to yelling, and as I'm flipping up several compartments to make the damn thing shut up, someone lays a soft hand in the middle of my back. No. Not someone. Riley.

"You know, if you're a little nicer, you'll probably get what you need a little faster."

I don't know if she's talking about her or the copy machine, but I'm itching to find out. Well, I was, but then Dean clears his throat and points to the machine. "What did it ever do to you?"

I grunt, slapping one of the compartments, and forcing the door to close. "It's jammed."

"Is the printer in your office broken?"

"No."

He chuckles and I whirl around, intent on telling him where he can shove his printer, but then see Riley, and everything vacates my brain. She's dressed in a gray skirt —and yes, it's shorter than yesterday—light pink heels that make her legs look a mile long, and a matching blouse with a little neck tie. It shouldn't look so fucking sexy, but the only thing I can think about is pushing her to her knees and grabbing that damn tie while I feed her my cock.

Jesus.

I'm a walking sexual harassment lawsuit.

I'd say I need to rub one out and get over it, but I fucked my fist once last night and twice this morning.

It hasn't helped.

"I hope you're not making more copies of the stats for our meeting," Dean says and jams his hands in his pockets, rocking back on his heels, a small smirk growing on his face. "I've already got everything handled."

"I wasn't." I was, even though I knew he already had everything done, but I don't need to tell him that.

Riley pushes me out of the way and in two seconds, she has the jammed paper—the one Dean already has copies of—out of the copy machine and the alarm stops. She glances down at it with a frown, and just when I think she's going to call me out, she balls up the paper and tosses it in the trash can under her desk.

"Did you guys have a nice lunch?" I try not to sound like a dick, but the look Dean tosses me tells me I failed.

Riley grabs a pad of paper, several red folders, and a

laptop from her work bag. "It was nice talking to someone who isn't trying to attack you every five seconds. I found it refreshing."

"I'm sure it was." I grab the stack from her and tuck it under my arm, gesturing down the hall to the conference room. "If Jazz continues to attack you while you're at work, just let me know and I'll speak with her."

"How generous of you." Her sarcasm is clear, and I can picture her teenage-self rolling her eyes and giving me a playful nudge with her elbow. "I'm going to use the restroom; I'll meet you guys there."

She flips her red waves over her shoulder, and I don't even try to pretend I'm not staring at her ass as she walks away.

"Real subtle," Dean grumbles, shaking his head and giving me a hard shove down the hallway. "Just like you waiting behind her desk for us to come back. Next time, why don't you follow us there and hide in the bushes outside the restaurant like a complete stalker?"

"If you tell me where you're going, I might." Dean stops dead in his tracks and turns to stare at me. I hold my hands up with a laugh, I'm not entirely serious. "I'm kidding. Relax. I'm too big to hide in the bushes."

"Fucking hell." Dean runs a hand down his face and blows out a breath. "I really thought watching you crash and burn would be funny, but I want to keep Riley. And before you get your tight panties in a bunch, that's entirely work related. She's smart, and even though she's only been here a day, she's already anticipating what I need."

"Well, good for you." My chest swells with an odd mixture of pride and jealousy. It's very annoying.

"You should have her help you with your new charity project. I'm sure she'd be more than willing to set up some meetings for you."

I scoff and continue down the hallway.

This isn't a project I want or need help with, but before I can tell him that, Riley appears at Dean's side. She peers around him, her bright blue eyes piercing right through me. "What's the charity?"

I lead them into the conference room and take my seat at the head of the table. "It's a children's charity. We want to help provide hockey gear, special clinics, and scholarships to kids from lower income families. It's an expensive sport, and we don't want a child left behind simply because their family cannot afford it."

"I didn't think you liked kids."

Riley's comment throws me off guard, but my answer is instant. "I don't."

Her face falls, and where she usually looks at me with anger or indifference, she looks disappointed. It's not something I like seeing on her face when she's looking at me, but it's really not my problem. Or at least it shouldn't be.

There was a time my answer would have been different. A time when I imagined Riley and I having a family and being fucking happy. But we all see what happened there, and I haven't been in any type of actual relationship since. I'm going to be thirty-one next month. Kids just aren't in the cards for me.

Really, it's for the best. What kind of legacy would I be able to leave anyway?

I'd probably be a terrible father.

My dad was an abusive alcoholic and a narcissist, and my mom was barely more than a statue in the background. There's no way I'd know what to do or what to say. With Riley it was different. *We* were different.

But that dream crashed and burned just like all the others. A family. My hockey career. And pretty soon, this damn team. I'll have nothing left.

I'll be nothing.

No one.

A washed up has been who had everything, and now has nothing left. No identity, no hopes, no dreams. Not even a single person to share dinner with.

My legacy is laced with failure.

I'm better off alone.

Which is why my eyes narrow and I stare at Riley until she looks away, and I'm sure she won't look back. I'm no good for her. I'd only drag her down. Only tarnish everything good about her.

"Hey, guys," Jazz greets as her and Mick walk into the office, my sister looking between Dean, Riley, and me with raised brows. "I see the three of you have settled right in."

"Something like that," Dean mutters, snagging the folders from me and passing them around the table. "Here you'll find all our current stats, where we rank in the conference, as well as profiles on the players I'd like to try to get before the trade deadline in about ten days."

Mick flips through the folder and tosses it in front of him. "The team is doing good, the coaches and I are doing the best we can, but I think we need to bring someone else on the coaching staff. Someone who can specifically work with some of these guys on speed and skating techniques. The top lines are great, but the bottom... well, that's where we're falling flat. And we're playing against some teams with great depth."

"Anyone in mind?"

"Jazz reached out to a few of her friends, and we have a few people coming in for interviews," Mick states and blows out a breath. "With as much change as this organization's had, both up top and the players, this would normally be a rebuild year. Your dad is an asshole."

I nod, glancing through the trades, and frown. Don't get me wrong, there are a few good players in here, but we need more. "We need to get someone disruptive, but we also need a team player. A lot of these guys you like are good, but none are great. We need someone like St.

Claire, Henriksson, or Volkov. We've got a month and a half to be great, or…"

"Or what?" Riley asks and glances up from her laptop, where I'm assuming she's been taking notes.

"Or the Benson's will be forced to sell the team to one of their dad's dick friends," Mick grits with a scowl and shoves his folder away with a huff. "I really don't like that guy."

"Yeah, well, he's dead now." I slam a hand down on the table and all eyes fall on me. "What's done is done."

Jazz's sharp intake of breath fills the room, and she's the first one to break the silence. "Jesus, Gordon."

"It's the truth. Shit, it's the whole reason we're here. It's not like anyone in this room misses him."

"That's hardly the point."

Riley stays quiet, but that damn disappointed look is back on her face and I hate it. I hate everything.

"Sorry," I mumble, sinking down in my chair and tugging on my tie, and for the first time, wish I could skip out on the rest of this meeting. The damn thing could be an email, anyway.

No amount of talking will make a shit-ton of a difference when it comes to the playoffs. We either make it— or we don't. We can talk about it until we're all blue in the face, but it's not gonna change a damn thing.

I'm sure my dad, the great Oliver Benson, is down in Hell, laughing at us right now. He's been dead for over a year, and here we are, still playing his games. It's how he operated when I was a child, and I really can't be surprised that he never changed.

He wanted me to be miserable. Pliable. Easy to use and control.

I catch Riley's gaze and hold it. I want to tell her I'm different, that I'm better than my father… that I deserve her and her forgiveness for how I've acted. And maybe there's a chance that I can forgive her too, for breaking my heart, for leaving me alone, for taking away the life I wanted. But I'm not sure if any of it's true—if I'm capable of forgiveness, or being better. At the end of the day, I am my father's son, and there's a good chance I'm just as toxic.

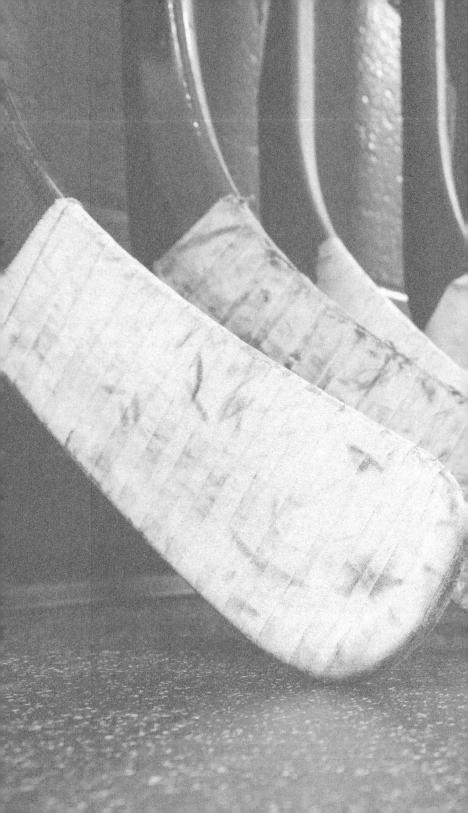

15

Dean: How's your week going, boss?
Are things more or less awkward than
they were on Monday?

Gordon: Why are you texting me?
We're on the same plane.

Dean: Yeah, but you're all the way in
the front all by yourself. Are you
wishing you had your assistant?

Gordon: And why would I need my
assistant to fly? I'm a big boy. I can fly
all by myself.

Jazz: You want her here so you can
make googly eyes at her.

Gordon: The two of you are absurd.
For the record, I have never and will
never make googly eyes.

Jazz: Are we? I don't feel like I am.

Jazz: Lincoln says I'm not absurd.

Gordon: He has to say that. Also, he's the kind of guy that makes googly eyes. Not me. He's probably making them at you right now.

Dean: I feel like that's true. But you seem extra grumpy today. Maria said you growled at her when she leaned over to check your seat belt.

Gordon: Maria wants to check more than my seatbelt, and I'm not at all interested.

Jazz: I bet you'd let Riley check your seatbelt.

Dean: Among other things.

Jazz: He might be a whole lot more pleasant if he had his 'seatbelt checked'.

Dean: He might even smile.

Jazz: I don't know if I'd go that far. It's a bit of a stretch.

Dean: Depends on how long it's been. He might skip up and down the hall outside the office.

Gordon: I don't skip, and I'll smile if it gets the two of you to shut the fuck up. My sex life is none of your business—either of you. Some of us are actually trying to work.

Jazz: Dad scolded us. How rude.

Dean: I feel no shame.

Gordon: I hate the both of you.

Dean: Hey, Riley! I'm hoping you can clear something up for us. Has Gordon always been a dick, or is this a relatively new development? Jazz says no, and he growled at me which I'm taking as a yes.

Gordon: You are under no obligation to answer that question, and the fact that Dean even asked, is highly unprofessional.

Dean: What? I'm just asking her a very innocent question. She can tell me that she'd rather not answer.

Gordon: She'd rather not answer.

Riley: I'll gladly answer. And sadly, no. Jazz is correct.

Jazz: In your face!

Riley: I don't know if he told you, but he was prom king our senior year. Everyone loved him. Well, most everyone. Our English teacher didn't like him very much, but to be fair, Gordon told him to shove the Grapes of Wrath up his ass.

Jazz: He didn't! <Shocked face emoji> He never told me about that.

Riley: Oh, but he did. Landed him in after school suspension too. He had to miss practice and got a huge lecture from his coach.

Dean: Please tell us more about teenage Gordon.

Gordon: I think we've taken up enough of Riley's time. I'm sure she has plenty of work to keep her busy.

Dean: One more thing, Riley. I need one more thing.

Riley: Ask him about the time the guys put itching powder in the cup of his jock strap.

Gordon: Thanks for that.

Riley: You're welcome.

Jazz: You should see his face right now. It's the best.

Riley: Congratulations on your win tonight. I know how much it means to you.

Gordon: Thanks.

Riley: Sorry if this is weird. I watched the game and my sister said I should text. And now I'm making it worse. Have a good night. See you tomorrow at work.

Gordon: It's not weird.

Gordon: You watched the game?

Riley: I might have caught some of it. I had some trouble falling asleep and thought it might help. Probably be exhausted tomorrow.

Gordon: Very funny. It wasn't that boring. Are you still planning on going out to the bar?

Riley: Isn't that what normal people do on a Friday night?

Gordon: I wouldn't know.

Riley: Are you going?

Gordon: I wasn't invited. And you haven't answered. Are you going?

Riley: I haven't decided.

Riley: Goodnight, Gordon.

Gordon. See you in the morning.

Riley: What's Onyx? I couldn't find anything about it.

Gordon: Goodnight, Riley.

16

RILEY

"Nope. Boring. Boring. Too professional. Too frumpy." Harper scrunches up her nose as she rifles through my closet, frowning at whatever shirt is on the next hanger. "This looks like something Nana would wear."

"Oh, come on. None of my stuff is that bad." I push my way in front of the closet door to see what shirt she's talking about, but she pulls it out, holding it up in front of my face.

She shakes it for emphasis and quirks a brow. "This is that bad."

"Okay so it's a little old looking."

"Extra frumpy."

"Hey." I snatch the offending shirt from her hand and clutch the poor thing to my chest before casually putting it at the back of the closet. It's yellow and floral. Oh, and it has ruffles. It's the definition of frumpy, but I like it. I'm just not going to wear it to go to a bar with a bunch of hockey players.

Not that I would know what to wear to a bar per say. When all my friends were turning twenty-one and drinking at least three days a week, I was sitting at home dealing with a toddler who didn't like the word no. She was cute and I wouldn't trade her for the world, but it was hell on my social life.

Meaning I had none.

Harper flips through the rest of the closet quickly, so quick I don't think she's fully appreciating some of the gems that are in there. "This is hopeless. You are a disaster."

"Well, that's just mean. You didn't even look at the stuff on that side." I point to the far end of the closet and Harper just sighs, flopping her arms down very dramatically.

"Because I don't need to."

I reach behind her, blindly grabbing something, and pulling out a burnt orange sweater dress. See? This side of the closet is good. "But you missed this. This would be really cute, especially with some high boots."

She scoffs, snatching the dress from my hands, and tossing it over her shoulder. It lands on the floor and I toss her an irritated look, one she ignores. "It's cute if you're a pumpkin."

My mouth drops open, and I stare at her in disbelief.

Rude. I like that dress. Well, maybe not so much now. But I do have other things. Non-orange things. I reach over her shoulder to grab something else, but she snags my hand and drags me away from my closet and out of my room.

She continues pulling me through the living room, only slowing down when Max gets up to follow us. "Nothing good in mom's closet?"

"Please." I wave my free hand her way and gesture at my work clothes. "I have good stuff in there. Harper here just didn't like anything."

Harper makes a gagging sound and directs me to sit down on the edge of her bed.

Max flops down, resting her head on her hands, and eyes my blouse. "Your clothes are good if you're going to do someone's taxes."

"Are you saying I'm boring?" I fake a gasp, but neither of them are laughing. Also, rude.

Harper dives into her closet, taking a few things out, inspecting them way longer than necessary and shoves them back in. "Neither of us are going to dignify that with an answer."

She resumes her search, taking out a very skimpy top that has me shaking my head and Max nodding. Nope.

No way am I wearing something that dips halfway down between my breasts. That shirt is going to give off all the wrong signals, and I don't need anyone thinking I want to go home with them.

Especially Gordon.

He claims he wasn't invited, but I wouldn't put it past him to show up. And then there's this whole Onyx thing. I'm still not sure if it's a nightclub or something more, but I'm also not sure I want to find out. That shirt sends all the wrong vibes.

"Put that right back in there." I shake my head, looking at my sister like she lost her damn mind. "I'm not wearing something where the girls are millimeters from falling out."

Max rolls her eyes and shakes her head like I'm the one being ridiculous. "Hockey players like that, Mom."

"I'm not going there to impress any hockey players. Maybe I shouldn't go."

Maybe I shouldn't. I'm thirty, not in my early twenties. I'm too old to go out and drink and party. If it weren't for Gordon going all caveman on the McIver brothers, I'd have politely declined and would be wearing my sweats right about now.

Reason number one hundred and forty-five of why Gordon is the Devil.

He makes me irrational. And when I'm irrational, I make bad decisions. You know, like borrowing Harper's skirts this week to make sure he was irritated every time he saw me.

"Mom." Max pins me with a look, the same one my sister is giving me. One that's telling me to get real. "You never go anywhere. You work and go to the ice rink. You need a life, and I don't mean one that involves you sitting in your sweatpants on the couch, eating popcorn, and watching lifetime movies that only make you cry."

That is what I do. "I don't do that every night."

"No." Max pauses for a second, and just when I think she's going to drop it, she says, "Work nights, you're in bed by nine. I stay up later than you, and I'm only eleven."

"Maxine Stella Adams!"

"You know, if you let me play hockey, I'd be so tired I bet I'd fall asleep by eight. They're having tryouts this weekend for the spring rec league. It's not travel, so it's not as intense. Only one or two games a week. That's nothing."

I glance to Harper for help, and the little traitor simply shrugs before she turns back around and continues looking through her clothes. Not that she'd really be any help anyway. She doesn't understand why I won't let Max play, the anxiety I feel squeezing my heart at the thought of her being out there on the ice like that.

What if she had a seizure? What if she got hit with the puck as she went down? Or a skate? Or another player? She'd be vulnerable, completely unprotected.

But then I have this little voice in the back of my head, one that tells me I'm making a mistake, that I'm holding her back… and one day she might resent me for it. She's got a natural talent for the sport—thanks to her dad—and I'd be letting it go to waste, making her suffer because of my own insecurities.

This is a battle I fight every freaking time she brings it up, and it's getting harder and harder to say no.

If my mom were alive, she'd agree with Harper. She'd understand my perspective, but tell me I'm being too protective. *Let the girl live, Riley.*

"I don't know, Max, I—"

Max sits up and pulls out her phone, furiously typing across the screen and mine pings several times in succession. "I sent you articles on nine players in the NHL who have epilepsy. They can do it, why can't I? Just let me try, Mom. If I get hurt, I'll quit." The tears in her eyes break my heart wide open. And after a few seconds of silence she whispers, "I promise. I'll be careful."

Fuck.

Harper sits down next to me for a moment and throws her arm around my shoulders. "You can't protect her her whole life. You're a good mom, Riley. She'll be okay. She's got the both of us in her corner."

What she's really saying is that I'll be okay, and if I ever doubt myself or Max, she'll be there to kick my ass and set me straight. But this... hockey... I just...

I glance down at my phone and pull up the first link. One of the highlighted quotes at the top of the page has me holding back my own tears. *I wouldn't be here if it wasn't for the support of my family. They believed in me so much, I believed in me too.*

If I can't be there for her, if I can't be the one to believe in her and encourage her, who will be?

And she's right; if something happens, we can reassess and I can pull her out. I just... I'm going to need some moral support to get through the first few games if she makes the team.

I take a deep breath, letting it out slowly as I look between the two of them. "Fine. But the instant something happens, I'm yanking you off the ice. You hear me? The instant."

"OhMyGodThankYouSoMuch!" Max flings her arms around me, and I don't think she's hugged me this tight in years. "You're the best mom ever."

Harper's arms come around me from the other side, and I close my eyes. Tears sting the corners of my eyes and I take a shaky breath to steady myself. These girls are my life, and I love them with everything I am. They're the only family I have left, and they're all I need. These moments don't come often, especially from Max, and I soak it up as long as she'll let me.

But eventually she disengages, detangling herself from us, and gives me the biggest smile. "Have fun tonight. I'm going to brush my teeth and text Cassidy. She's going to flip." She runs out of the room, but seconds later, sticks her head in the doorway. "Have her try on your green dress."

"I almost forgot about that dress." Harper jumps up from the bed and claps her hands. "Your daughter is a genius! I almost forgot about that one. It's going to be perfect. *All* the guys are going to want to take you home."

"I don't know, Harper."

"Trust me. Those hockey players aren't going to know what's hit them."

That's what I'm afraid of.

This is going to be… something.

17

GORDON

ANOTHER FRIDAY NIGHT, AND HERE I AM IN MY OFFICE, convincing myself to go the fuck home, but I just can't force myself to leave. The reason? My damn executive assistant.

I don't know if she went to Whiskey and Rye for the McIver birthday bullshit, and I'm too fucking chicken-shit to text her and ask. I'm half tempted to go over and see for myself, but then she'll know I'm checking up on her. Not only that, but Ian was clearly baiting me. I'm sure he'd love to see me charging in there, riled the fuck up, and ready for a fight.

What I did to Dallas's face would look like child's play.

I'd beat the shit out of anyone that laid a finger on what's mine—and Riley Adams most definitely belongs to me.

Neither one of us may like it, but it's a fact we both need to accept.

So, I'm obviously thinking straight.

I scoff and run both hands through my hair. I haven't been thinking straight since I saw her that night on the ice. She's... magic. That's what she is.

She made me want more for my life all those years ago, and now? Now, she's starting to beat down the wall around my heart, brick by brick. Every barbed insult, every heated look. It's all embedded in my soul, in my very core, and I don't know how to get her out.

I don't know if I want to get her out.

I don't know what's up, what's down, and I certainly don't know if I like who I am any more. And you know, I was just fucking fine being miserable before she showed up, twisting me in all these knots, making me second guess every damn thing.

And you know the funny part? She's got no idea. She thinks I hate her, and yeah, some dark corner of me still does, but the rest of me is still... I don't know what I'm feeling, but it's not hate.

Has it ever been?

But the thing is, she was too good for me back then, and she's too good for me now. The only difference is that I'm smarter now, and there's no way I'd stand a chance when there are probably thousands of guys that are better for her.

Yeah, thousands. I scoot back and toss a pen onto my

desk. Just let me see a single one of those motherfuckers touch her. Just fucking one of them, and God help him if it's one of my players.

Maybe I need to get laid, get her off my mind and out from under my skin, but the thought of another woman putting her hands on me makes me physically ill.

My body and my brain are clearly in a war that neither of them stands a chance of winning.

"What are you still doing here?" Dean asks as he pokes his head through my doorway, typing on his phone for several seconds before raising his head and assessing me with a quirked brow.

I cross my arms and meet his gaze. "I could ask you the same thing."

"Well, I'm actually working. I've been on the phone all day with the pro scouts and agents instead of sitting in my office and sulking."

"I'm not sulking." I roll my shoulders and glance down at my crossed arms, the miscellaneous paperwork strewn across my desk, and the screen saver that popped up on my computer at least thirty minutes ago.

Fine, maybe I am sulking, but in my defense, I don't know what to do with myself.

Do I stay here? Do I go home? Do I casually stop by the bar?

Dean leans against the doorframe, shoving his hands in his pockets and nodding toward me. "Isn't there a birthday party or something over at Whiskey and Rye?"

He pauses, looking me over with that damned annoying smirk. "Did she go?"

I blow out a frustrated breath and loosen my tie. "I don't fucking know. Ian and Owen stopped by earlier this week to invite her. Used some cheesy ass pickup line too. She didn't say and I didn't ask, although, trust me, she knows how I feel about her hanging out with the two of them."

Dean laughs, his smirk turning into a full-blown grin. "Were you a complete dick and told her she couldn't go?"

"Basically."

"Then she's definitely going to be there. Obviously I don't know her that well, but she seems like the type to do something just to spite you. Not anyone else, but you?" he gives me a pointed look, "Abso-fucking-lutely."

A low growl rumbles deep in my chest, surprising the both of us. The biggest thing she could do to spite me would be going to Onyx with the two of them, and there's no way I'm allowing that shit to happen. I don't care if I look like the biggest dick on the planet, I cannot, in any context, let her go to a sex club with those two assholes.

Not only do I not want her to even know a place like that exists, but I'd lose both my best defensemen if either of them lay even a single fucking finger on her.

"Motherfucker," I manage to grind out before snapping my jaw shut, and dammit, I wish I hadn't tossed my pen across the desk earlier because I'd like to throw something right about now.

Dean chuckles, shaking his head as he invites himself into my office. "Exactly. And from what I've seen, the McIvers can be quite charming when they want to be."

"Fuck."

"If you're going over there, you might want to consider leaving your suit jacket and tie in the car. I'd suggest changing into some jeans, but I don't think you own any."

"I own jeans," I grumble, pulling off my tie and tossing it on my desk. "You're not going?"

Dean shrugs, checking something on his phone before sliding it back into his pocket. "I wasn't invited. And I have plans."

I narrow my eyes, looking at him expectantly. "What kind of plans? I didn't know you had friends."

"That's only because you don't have any," Dean points out with a laugh. "Have fun tonight. Don't do anything I wouldn't do."

"I feel like I should be saying the same to you."

"Maybe." Dean gives me a quick wink and heads out of my office, leaving me with way too many thoughts swirling around in my brain.

This is why I didn't want her working here in the first place. She's too much of a damn distraction. I should be helping Dean, reaching out to potential trades, and doing what I can to make sure we make the playoffs. I should... but I'm not. Instead, I'm so worried about Riley hooking up with one of my hockey players I can barely see straight.

And really, it's none of my business. Like she said, she's a grown-ass woman who can do what she wants. So why do I care so much? Why does any of it matter? And why the hell do I get this deep ache in my chest when I think about her?

Either way, Dean's right. I can't sit here all night stewing in my own feelings. I need to stop by the bar for a few minutes and make sure everything is okay. A quick in and out, and then I can go home with a clear head.

She's probably not even there and I'm overreacting.

There's a chance that's true. Right?

18

RILEY

Harper: Are you at the bar? How many hockey players are there?

Harper: Are they hot?

Harper: One more question and then I think I'm done. Any of them single and ready to mingle? Backing away from the crowd and ready to throw down?

Me: Did you get into the rum again?

Harper: Nope. Just thinking about what it would be like to have a hockey player wear my thighs as earmuffs. You know, no big deal. I'd hate for one of them to catch a cold. <winking face emoji>

Me: Harper!

Harper: Just saying. <woman shrugging emoji>

Me: You're ridiculous. These guys are super sweet.

Harper: How do you know? You're sitting here talking to me instead of actually talking to any of them.

Me: Well, you're texting me! And don't worry, a couple of the guys invited me out to this swanky club and we are on the way now.

Harper: You don't have to answer me as soon as I text you. Go have fun. Figure out how to relax. Let them see how sexy you look in that dress.

Harper: Maybe make that boss of yours jealous.

Me: He's not here, Harper. <eye rolling emoji>

Harper: Like I said, go have fun. And if you find me a hot hockey playing boyfriend, I won't complain.

WITH A CHUCKLE, I MOVE TO SLIDE MY PHONE INTO MY clutch but stop when it vibrates with another text. Damn, Harper isn't going to give it up. If she wasn't at home with Max, I'd have invited her out to this Onyx night club. She's been studying hard this year and could use a break. But I frown when I open up my phone and see the messages aren't from Harper.

> Bossy Ex: Where are you? I'm at the bar and can't find you anywhere.
>
> Bossy Ex: Please tell me you went home and didn't leave with Ian and Owen. Those guys are bad news.
>
> Bossy Ex: Riley?

"Miss? I'm going to need your phone and I can take your purse as well." The beautiful blonde smiles at me from the other side of the immaculate reception desk, extending a perfectly manicured hand my way.

I have a moment, a small one, where I briefly consider telling Gordon where I am. Which, of course, is quickly followed by the desire to tell him to fuck off. He doesn't get my time while I'm not at work, nor does he need to be privy to my every move—especially when I'm not even sure where the fuck I am, or why I can't have my phone and clutch.

But you know, there's some sort of satisfaction in that, in the knowledge that not only can he *not* find me, but that, for the first time in my adult life, I'm finally doing something for myself. Ian and Owen haven't told me what kind of club this is, so I have no idea if it's going to be something I like, but I'm here. I'm trying something new. I'm stepping out of my comfort zone, which is something I really haven't done in a very, very long time.

If Gordon has a problem with anything I'm doing, he can suck it. He's not going to ruin the only night out I've had in well... ever.

He doesn't have to stay at Whiskey and Rye, but I sure as hell don't want or need him coming here. So, even though it's strange that this club needs our cell phones and my purse, I hand them over without question.

Let him text me now.

The boys hand over their cells as well, and the blonde, Sylvia if Ian accurately remembered her name, hands Dimitri and me a few papers while two of the rookies head inside. "As non-member guests for tonight's party, the two of you will need to read and sign the NDA and the house rules."

My gaze volleys between Ian and Owen, runs around the reception area which is super fancy, and my brows shoot up to my hairline. "I know I haven't been out much, but... is this a night club?"

"Oh, shit." Owen pulls me to the side, whispering in my ear. "I'm so sorry, I thought you knew where we were going, and if you didn't, my braindead brother would have filled you in. This is ahhh... I don't know how to say it nicely, but this is an exclusive fantasy club."

"Fantasy? As in...?"

He clears his throat and glances at his brother. At

least Ian has the good sense to look slightly apologetic. Also, slightly amused, but we don't need to focus on that part. "Sex."

I guess that explains the basket organized with condoms, lube, and sanitary wipes. Also, explains why Gordon was so damned pissed about the thought of me coming to this place.

Which really begs the question, how the hell does he know a place like this exists?

A tiny—so tiny I shouldn't even worry about mentioning it—sliver of jealousy cuts through me at the thought of Gordon having a membership at some swanky fantasy sex club, at the idea of him coming here with some gorgeous model, a woman who's way more adventurous than me, and doing whatever it is you do here. Fucking in front of an audience? As part of a group?

I don't know exactly, but I sure as hell plan to find out. He's not the only one with a wild side, the only one allowed to move on and live his life.

Owen glances to the ground momentarily before meeting my gaze. "Obviously, you don't have to stay if you don't want to, and you definitely don't have to do anything you're not comfortable with."

I hold up a hand. While I appreciate his concern for me, I've made up my mind and I can't walk away now. I have to know what this place is really like. Plus, we've all read Fifty Shades of Grey, and can't say I'm not a little curious. "I'm in."

"Are you sure?"

"Yeah." I glance down at my dress, smoothing it around my hips. "Do I look okay?"

"You look hot as fuck in that dress," Sylvia says and points toward me with a pen as Ian and Owen nod in agreement. My cheeks heat and damn, I'm glad I let Harper talk me into wearing this. "And don't worry, these guys will take care of you."

She points to the brothers and winks. Wait... Do I want these two to take care of me? Does that mean...?

But before I can ask, she hands over the pen, leaning over the reception desk and giving me a huge smile and an ample view of her cleavage. "If anyone in there makes you feel uncomfortable, let any of the employees or security know right away. We're all about consent and creating a safe environment to live out any of your wildest fantasies." She pauses, twirling a lock of her long blonde hair. "I can think of four you can help me with when I get off shift tonight, red."

It takes me a minute to realize she's not talking to Ian and Owen, and this time when my cheeks heat, they're a full five-alarm fire. If I can't get myself under control, I'm not going to last two minutes when I get inside.

"Umm. Thanks." Yep. Nailed it.

I quickly scan and sign the papers. The NDA is pretty standard, but then there are the rules. Things like consent, boundaries, and cleaning up after a scene stand out in particular. And shit, I'm not completely sure I belong in a place like this. I have a vague idea of what a scene is, and while I understand consent, I've never been in a situation where I've given over any sort of control to a virtual stranger.

My stomach flutters with nervousness, and just when I'm about to back out the door and call for an Uber, I see the bottom of the page. *Have fun, and remember, you don't have to do anything you're not comfortable with.*

Have fun.

It's the same thing Harper's been saying to me since I mentioned this party, and really for the past couple of years. I don't have to do anything. I can just watch.

And that's when something else blooms in my core, a flutter of something that has nothing to do with nerves.

Oh, shit.

I think maybe I'd like to watch some of these fantasies play out, but hell, I don't really know for sure. I really hate to admit that after Gordon, my sexual history is limited. At the beginning, I was learning how to be a new mom and trying to take care of Harper on the heels of our mother's death. I barely had time to breathe, let alone date. Then as time wore on, it became less and less important.

Then I met Dan at work. He seemed nice. Safe. Dependable. He spent months being my friend until I agreed to go on a date with him. Things between us were never hot and heavy. The few times we had sex it was very vanilla. Lights off, minimal foreplay, and a few grunts and thrusts before he'd roll over and go to sleep. I'd inevitably head home and get myself off in the shower while I washed his mediocrity off my skin. There were a few times I wanted more, where I wished he were more adventurous, but I was too scared to ask.

Well, I'm not sure I'm scared anymore.

I hand everything back to Sylvia, her fingers grazing mine as she takes the papers and she tosses me another wink.

I'm not interested in what she has to offer, but I'm not sure what the etiquette is, so I give her a small wave. She shakes her head with a smile, and Owen and I follow Ian and Dimitri—the team's goalie—inside.

"So, I have to ask," I begin and nudge Ian, "you guys don't really know me. Why would you invite me to a…" I glance around and lower my voice, "a sex club?"

Ian laughs, tossing an arm around me and leading me into a very elegant looking sitting room. The lights are low, which drives your attention to the long, lit up bar on the other side of the lounge. There are several leather couches and chairs scattered throughout the space to create a casual yet intimate setting.

I'm surprised to see so many people here, both men and women, and all of them dressed like they're going to a formal event. I'm not sure what I expected, but it involved a whole lot less clothes.

"Why not?" Ian asks and leans toward me, running

his nose along the shell of my ear, and for a moment, I completely forget what I even asked him.

"Come on." I push him away, needing to create a little bit of distance between us. I may have come here with him and his brother, but I will not be doing anything with either of them. It's not that they're unpleasant on the eyes, because it's the complete opposite, but it doesn't feel right. "I'm here now, so you might as well fess up."

"In my defense, we were genuinely coming up to invite you out to the bar. We only mentioned the club after Gordon went full caveman and assumed the worst. Honestly, I didn't think you'd want to hang with us, but I'm not gonna pretend I'm disappointed."

"Thank you?"

"No problem."

"So, you and Gordon..." Owen muses, pulling off his suit jacket and draping it over the back of the high-backed bar chair, an expectant look on his face.

I follow, pulling out a chair and sitting between the two of them, while Dimitri goes to the other end of the bar, sitting next to one of the other guys from the team. "Sorry to disappoint, but there is no me and Gordon."

"That's not what I heard," Ian says and nudges me with a smile, flagging down the bartender. "And let's not forget how berserk he went when you told him you were interested in our b-day bash."

"There used to be an us. In the past. Where it's going to stay." I give him a sideways look as I glance over the wine list. It might as well be Greek, and something tells me their wine is better than the boxed stuff I pick up at the grocery store.

"Let me buy you a drink, and you can tell us all the dirty details while we give you a tour of this place."

"I don't know about the details, but I'd like a tour."

I order a random cabernet from the list as my thoughts drift to Gordon.

Everything with him was in the past, that much is true, but why do I feel like it's not staying there like I want? Maybe it's because we have some unfinished business. Maybe it's because I want to remind him about the family he left behind when he went into the NHL. Hell, maybe it's because I can't get him out of my freaking mind.

One thing is for sure, I'm going to have a slew of new texts waiting for me after leaving him on read for so long. He's going to be pissed on Monday morning, and that makes me a lot happier than it should.

19

GORDON

I'M FUCKING LIVID.

Like I am about to lose my shit on the first person that crosses my path. I can only hope it's Ian or Owen McIver. They're going to be the Bruised Brothers when I get my fucking hands on them.

I can't believe they took Riley to Onyx. To a goddamned sex club.

Who knows what they're doing right now? Or *who* they're doing. It's been an hour since I texted her with no response, and there's so much depravity there that they could have already gotten her into.

Dammit. I should have left the office as soon as I finished talking to Dean, but no. I sat there for at least another hour having a heated debate with myself, and eventually decided to stop by the bar. It was supposed to be a thirty-minute detour, say hello to the team, do my best to make it look like I'm not there to check on Riley, and head home.

But that was squashed the second I walked in and she wasn't there.

I swear to Christ, if they've touched her, I'm going to kill them on the spot. No one gets to see an inch of her perfect body, and they sure as shit can't touch it. No one can, and God help any man that thinks he has any right to.

Including me.

But right now, I don't give a flying fuck if I don't deserve her, if I'm still nursing the hurt from our past. I don't fucking care. I need to see her. Touch her. I need to feel her against me, and more than anything, I need her to know she's mine.

It's irrational, I know, but I can't think clearly where she's concerned. She's a problem I can't seem to solve, an itch I've never been able to scratch—especially when my brain remembers so much of the past, and my damn heart reminds me that she was the one that got away. That she was the only light in my constant darkness, that she was the only damn thing that ever meant more to me than hockey. I lost her, and then I lost everything.

I'm having a hard time separating her from my memories, from the girl I used to love, and fuck, I know I should, but I don't know if I can.

"Mr. Benson, how are you tonight?" Sylvia greets me at the door with a smile I have no intention of returning.

Instead, I grunt, handing over my phone and ignoring the shocked look on her face as I barrel past her into the club. The bar area is crowded, which isn't a surprise this time of night, but I don't see her anywhere. I do, however, see Ian at the bar, chatting with a brunette that is very much not Riley.

I'm torn.

Obviously, I'm fucking ecstatic he's not draped all over her, but if she's not out here, then there's a chance she's in a fantasy room. I can only hope she had the good sense to go home. Otherwise, I may end my evening in jail.

"Tell me she went home." I lean between Ian and the other woman, cutting off their conversation.

It's impolite, I know, but ask me if I care.

Spoiler alert—I don't.

"Who?" Ian gazes at me with a lazy smile, one I'm about to punch off his face.

My teeth clench together and I barely manage to grit out, "You know who."

"Owen?" He cocks his head to the side, quirking a brow as his smile grows. "He went upstairs a little bit ago. Seems he found some agreeable company."

"I clearly said she. Today is not the fucking day."

He rests his arm on the bar, very casual for someone who's about to get his ass handed to him, and nods my way. "Someone's testy."

"That someone is about to drag your ass right out of

here." I swear all I can see is red, and if he doesn't tell me what I need to know, I'll be following through on my promise. He has three seconds.

He sighs, running a quick hand through his hair. "You really know how to spoil all the fun."

I lean toward him, making sure to get right in his space. "If you're about to tell me she went off with your brother, you're about to become an only child."

"It's okay, I have a spare brother back home." This time when he smiles it's halfhearted. "You might find your secretary in the voyeur hall. But, Gordon—"

I don't give a flying fuck what he has to say and stomp away before he can get another word out. He's lucky I haven't completely ruined his night, although there's still time. It all depends on how—and if—I find Riley.

No other woman has ever made me feel this emotional, or hell, really anything at all. After Riley, sex was nothing more than a transaction, a mutual exchange of orgasms and we went our separate ways. I went through the motions, and once the door closed behind them, felt emptier that I did before we fucked.

But Riley? I feel every goddamned thing, including so much hurt, anger, and a possessiveness that I've never felt before. I feel like a wild animal, like my skin is splitting at the seams, and the only thing, the only person, that calms the storm inside me, is her.

One of the doors to the viewing rooms is closed,

which means multiple people are in there putting on a show, and with this place, it could be anything from fantasy play, to a BDSM scene, to a full-on orgy.

The closer I get the more my blood boils, and once I reach the entrance to the viewing area, I'm about to erupt. I hope she's in the hallway between the rooms and not in the one with the closed door. I doubt this place would appreciate me breaking through the glass in the middle of play—doesn't matter how much I pay a year in membership fees.

Before I can bust into the voyeur hall, I take a deep breath. And then fifty more. The last thing I want to do is scare the shit out of Riley—or anyone else that might be in here.

Fuck.

Do I care?

At this point, no.

My heart hammers in my chest, and it feels like all the damn dread and misery in the world is slithering through my body. *What if she's in here? What if she isn't? What if she's found someone who can give her all the things I can't?*

With one last breath, I open the door and slip into the hallway. It's darker here than in the rest of the club, but I can see her standing toward the back, watching whatever's happening on the other side of the glass. She's alone, thank God, and now that I know she's alone and safe, I can finally breathe.

She so focused on what's happening in front of her, she didn't notice me coming in, and I can't help but wonder what she thinks of the two guys railing this woman in the other room.

Is she shocked? Appalled? Or maybe my little Firefly isn't as innocent as I thought.

She hasn't seen me yet, and as I edge closer, I see the dress she's wearing. Dark green, molded to her body, and short enough I could bend her over right here and fuck her against that glass. I wonder how wet she is. I wonder if she'd like the exhilaration of getting caught, the knowledge that someone could come in any minute and see my cock buried in her perfect cunt.

Her presence is intoxicating and I feel myself stepping closer. The need to run my hands all over her is strong, but I manage to resist.

For now.

I take another step and don't stop until I'm right behind her, so close I can smell the light peach scent of her shampoo. It reminds me of the past, of my future, of everything that could be.

Mine. That little voice is there, egging me on, daring me to touch her, to let her know I'm here.

My dick twitches as she lets out a low moan and shifts, rubbing her thighs together and sweeping her hands over the front of her dress.

Fuck. Me.

A better man would turn around and walk the fuck

away. He'd sneak out of here like a gentleman and never let her know he saw her like this. But fuck him. I'm not a better man, and there's no goddamn way I'm walking away right now.

Not when she looks like that.

Not when I feel like this.

There are so many things I want to do to her right now, so many things I want to say, and I think I'm about to short circuit.

She likes to watch.

"Firefly." Her nickname is barely a whisper, and I lean forward, placing my hands on either side of the glass, caging her in my arms. Right where she fucking belongs. "What are you doing here, you naughty little girl? You don't respond to my texts. You come here after I told you not to. You like getting me all riled up, don't you?"

She sucks in a breath, her body stiffening as her hands come to rest on the glass next to mine, her pinky brushing along my thumb. It's a small touch, but one I can feel down my entire body.

"I spent the last hour thinking about nothing but you." I brush my chest across the back of her shoulders, and bury my nose in her hair. "Imagine my surprise finding you here, watching these deplorable things and *liking* it."

Her low whimper almost snaps the modicum of control I have, almost.

"Do you like that, Firefly?" I lean my body into hers, loving how she relaxes against me, how she rubs her ass against my hardening cock. I hold back a groan, trailing a hand slowly up the length of her arm, across her shoulders, and down her back. My touch, a stark contrast to the harshness of my words. "Do you like watching her take a dick in her ass while his friend fucks her mouth?"

This time her whimper has my fingers skimming the curve of her hips, and I love the way her body trembles with every touch, every caress.

"Answer me, Riley."

"Yes." She's practically panting, shifting against me, and I know she can feel my dick twitching between us.

"Are you wet right now?" This time when she doesn't answer I grip her waist, grinding her into the glass. "I don't like repeating myself."

"I... yes."

"Good girl." The words rumble across my chest, and she lets out a soft moan. Jesus Christ, this woman is going to be the death of me. No one has ever felt this good. Never made me this fucking hard. Never felt like *her.* It makes this entire thing so much more dangerous. "Now tell me to leave. Tell me to get the fuck out of here." Her silence damns us both, and I blow out a breath. "Tell me not to touch you."

She tries to turn her head toward me, but I grab her chin and force her to watch the scene in front of us, to keep her eyes on the woman being thoroughly destroyed by those two men; one fucking her ass with reckless abandon, and the other gripping her hair while he thrusts up into her mouth. It's carnal, raw, and so fucking hot to watch.

"Gordon." My name sounds like a plea on her lips, and I can't wait to hear her screaming it.

"Keep your eyes on them, Firefly. Watch how good they fuck her." I slide my hand over her hip and down her thigh. My fingers curl around the hem of her dress, and even though I want to rip this damn thing off her, I pull it higher. "Have you thought about me laying you across my desk and licking your sweet cunt until you come all over my face?" She gives me a hesitant nod, relaxing her head against my chest as she shifts beneath my touch. "Have you imagined me bending you over, filling you with my cock, fucking you so thoroughly you won't be able to walk for days?"

"Fuck," she groans, her hands curling into fists on the glass. Her entire body is vibrating with need, and her breath hitches as I lightly brush my hand across her upper thighs. "Gordon, *please.*"

"Please what?" *Please don't ask me to leave. I can give you anything, but I can't do that.*

"Touch me."

Thank fuck.

The couple in front of us change positions, the woman crawling on top of one of the men and impaling herself on his cock as the other continues to fuck her ass.

She throws her head back, a litany of moans and curses tumbling from her lips as she squeezes her breasts and looks toward the glass. She may not be able to see us, but she's giving one hell of a show.

This may not be my first time standing here and watching, but it is my first with someone else. Someone who shouldn't be seeing this side of me, but I can't help but let her in, just like I can't help but touch her. At least she wants it—wants me, even if it's only right now.

With a barely contained growl, I run my fingers along the hem of her dress, slowly bringing them between her thighs. "Don't forget that anyone can come through that door and see how much you want to fuck my fingers. How bad you need me filling up this greedy pussy."

I sweep my thumb down the center of her panties and a shiver runs down her body as she arches against me and groans. My little dirty girl is fucking dripping with want, desire. It's soaking through the lace fabric, and fuck me, I'm so close to ripping it off her body, but manage to shift it to the side.

The throuple in the other room are moaning in earnest now, the sound of the woman's screams surrounding us, and I wonder if Riley is imagining me making her scream that loud, me pounding into her, and me filling her with my cum.

I sweep a thumb over her clit, and this time, her moan rivals the others. "So wet, so needy. Just watch,

Firefly. Watch them make her come while I play with my pussy."

Lust surges through me, setting my entire body on fire, and for the first time in what feels like forever, I let myself feel everything... every exhale she makes as she leans against my chest, every subtle shift of her hips, every whimper, every moan. They all belong to me. *She* belongs to me.

I need more. I need *her*. She makes me feel so desperate, depraved, and I'd love nothing more than to bury myself inside her and lose control, lose myself. But she's not ready for that, and if I'm honest, neither am I. But this? I can give her this.

I rub her clit again, keeping the pressure light, and dipping down to slide two fingers inside her. She's so slick, so tight around my fingers, and I can only imagine how she'll feel squeezing my cock. It's been too long since I've had her, and the thought of being buried inside her cunt is consuming me. *She's* consuming me.

She arches her back with a moan, forcing me deeper. She's already trembling, her body squeezing around me as I thrust my fingers inside her, making sure to rub a spot I know drives her wild.

I take my other hand off the glass, wrapping it around her neck and giving it a gentle squeeze. "You feel so good, Firefly."

Too good. Between her pussy fluttering around me, her soft whimpers, and all the fucking ten feet away, I'm about to come in my pants. The control I pride myself on having is paper thin.

"Oh, fuck. Gordon. Fuck." She chants my name as I pick up the pace, fucking her with my fingers like I want to fuck her with my cock. Faster. Deeper. Harder.

I squeeze her throat a little tighter as I grind the heel of my hand against her clit, and she falls apart. Her body jerks against mine, her legs wobble, and she lets out a scream that sends the throuple into a frenzy, each of them chasing their own orgasm.

Her cunt tightens around my fingers, pulsing around me and giving me a small glimpse of heaven. She whimpers, moans, and lets out a curse as the waves of her orgasm subside and she sags against me.

I pull out of her slowly, fixing her dress, and then move away so quickly she almost stumbles to the floor. I reach out, steadying her, but as soon as she seems stable, let my hand fall to my side. She felt so good, too good, but as I come back to reality, I am slapped with shame.

Riley was enjoying a private moment. She didn't ask for me to come in and put my hands on her. She didn't ask me to take this experience from her. I'm a dick, and she deserves so much better than someone who can't control himself when she's around.

At least she doesn't say anything, just stares at me, her mouth open slightly, and her eyes full of questions. Questions I can't bring myself to answer.

This shouldn't have happened.

We have too much trauma, too many unresolved issues, and I did nothing but take advantage of her when she was most vulnerable. She showed me a private part of herself, and like an asshole, I took everything and more.

She opens her mouth again, but before she can say anything, I turn and leave the hallway, letting the door slam behind me.

I don't turn around, I don't dare.

She deserves someone better.

Someone who's not me.

20

RILEY

I'M THE WORST MOM IN THE HISTORY OF MOMS. MAX IS out there skating her ass off, trying out for this hockey team, and instead of watching her and being supportive, my damn mind keeps wandering back to last night.

After a very restless night of sleep, I told myself I wouldn't think about it anymore. *About him.* Or at the very least, I'd try to not let it consume every single thought I have.

It's not working.

Last night was… it was… I don't even know how to describe what happened.

It was like I fell into an alternate reality, like if The Twilight Zone and Pornhub had a baby. That's where I was.

At first I thought they were messing with me, and maybe the woman at the front desk was in on it—the bar area didn't look like anything out of the ordinary, and there wasn't a whip or chain in sight. Then after Ian and I fell into a comfortable conversation, I started noticing things.

The waitresses were wearing very high-end lingerie and heels. That was it. Like nothing else.

There were a few men wearing masks, and a few ladies were completely naked.

And then there was the tour.

I'd never seen any place like it, and I spent the entire time being torn between impressed and aroused. They had a classroom, a library, a few very large rooms with multiple beds, and then I found the voyeur hallway. At some point, I was all set to turn around and let Ian lead me to the next space, but then two guys entered the adjoining space, pulling a woman right behind them.

I was mesmerized. It was like I was placed right in the middle of one of my fantasies. Watching porn is one thing, but seeing it live was something else completely. I was so engrossed in the scene in front of me, I didn't hear Ian leave, and I sure as hell didn't hear Gordon come in.

The world was nothing but me and the three people in the room next door. Or at least it was, until Gordon leaned into me, and put his hands next to mine on the one-way glass.

I had so many questions on the tip of my tongue, but they all died the second he whispered his old nickname for me. *Firefly...* something that shouldn't still affect me like this all these years later, but clearly it does.

It's the second time he brought up my old nickname, but they feel so different, and I don't know why.

This time, it knocked down all my defenses and crumbled all my walls. Gordon wormed his way in and burrowed himself deep in the recesses of my heart with one simple word. *Or maybe he never left.*

The version of me from the past used to love hearing that name. He used to tell me I was his light in the darkness—or I was until he became the darkness. But something about the desperate way he called to me last night erased all that, if only for a moment.

I knew I should have told him to leave, and definitely shouldn't have asked him to touch me, but I had to know what he was going to do, how far he would go. And that mouth. The Gordon I knew would never have said those things, and damn if I didn't love that new side of him. I wanted everything he said, and more. I wouldn't have hesitated to bend over and let him fuck me right there.

Feeling his hands on me was like a reckoning—a promise of what was to come. He touched me like he owned me, like my pleasure was his to claim, and I was powerless to stop it.

I didn't want to stop it.

Especially when he slipped his fingers inside me and fucked me like I've dreamed of getting fucked.

Hard. Fast. Deep.

It was so raw. So fucking wild, and out of control.

Between his rough hands and the three people in front of us, I was in a fevered dream. My ability to think rationally fled.

It's why I let him touch me in the first place—or at least that's what I keep telling myself.

Doesn't really matter though. None of it does. Instead of facing me and the line we crossed, he ran out of there like the place was on fire. After how he left Max and I all those years ago, I shouldn't be surprised, but I am. And I'm such a fucking fool for thinking he'd be any different.

But not everything was the same.

The way he touched me, the things he said… When we were younger, he was always gentle with me, like I was something precious, breakable.

"Are you sure you're ready?" Gordon places a gentle kiss to my lips before sinking into the kiss, framing my face with his hands and sweeping his tongue into my mouth.

He takes his time kissing me, with long, lazy strokes of his tongue. He doesn't know how anxious I am to finally feel him inside me. Our virginity has been hanging over our heads for weeks, and everything has come down to tonight. To this moment.

Gordon is nervous, and I'd be lying if I said I wasn't. He wants to last for me, to make it special, and I want to make sure he'll never forget.

I shift underneath him, lifting my hips to meet his. He's hard as a rock, and this time, I've been dreaming about how he'll feel stretching me. Having my hand and mouth on him isn't the same. I need more. I need everything he's willing to give me. And the fact he wanted to wait until the both of us were ready made me fall for him even more.

"Yes," I breathe out, grinding my hips against him again.

He leans his head back with a groan and swears. "You're so damn sexy. I need you to be sure, Firefly, because once I feel your naked body underneath mine, I may not be able to hold back."

I glide my hands up his bare back, loving how his muscles flex under my touch. If he gets me off with his fingers and tucks me into bed one more time, I might scream. We've been together for almost eight months, and I know he's the one. Sure, I'm young and have my whole life ahead of me, but when you meet your other half, you know.

"I need you, Gordon. I need this." I frame his face with my hands and bring his forehead down to mine. His emerald eyes darken with lust as he gazes down at me. He's looking at me with so much reverence, so much love, and I can't wait to embed him on my soul.

He brushes his lips across my jaw, whispering, "I love you so much."

"I love you with my entire heart."

He kisses me with so much passion, desire, and longing. It's full of all the love, the tenderness he possesses, and I melt under his touch. He claims my mouth as his hands peel off the rest of my clothes, and then his own.

He lays over me for several minutes, stroking his hands over my body, kissing up and down my throat. I'm so turned on, so ready for him, and wetter than I've ever been.

I shift, wrapping my legs around his waist and forcing his cock to rub along me. "Please, Gordon."

"Anything for you, Firefly."

His lips are on mine as he pushes into me. He's so big it hurts, but only for a second. He's so gentle, so careful, so damned controlled. It's his first time too, so he has to be losing his mind, but I know he wants to make our first time special. As long as he's here, it is.

"Mom, did you see that shot?" Max skids to a stop on the side of the rink, her arms flying around with every word. "Coach says I'm a natural. He thought I'd been playing for years. Years, Mom."

I was buried so far in the past, I completely missed the shot in question, and dammit, I really need to get my head in the game—no pun intended. Or you know, hover over her from the sidelines and make sure she's fine.

Gordon is a damn distraction and I need to focus on what's important, on the family I have left.

"I'm so proud of you. You're doing great." I meet her smile with one of my own. She's so happy it's infectious, but really, I'm thankful she's not scowling at me like she usually does.

Except that beautiful smile wobbles as she glances at a few of the other moms before her gaze swings back to me. "Are you sure you're okay?"

I lean back trying to maintain my composure, even though that question is a sucker punch to the gut. She's an eleven-year-old with epileptic seizures. I should be asking her that question. Scowls and all, she really is the best daughter I could ever ask for, and I feel like I'm a failure, like I've let her down and been holding her back for years.

In truth I probably have, but I'm trying. I want to do better.

With a sigh, I shake my head and pull out my cell phone, taking a quick picture of her confused face. "As long as you're good, I'm good. Now get out there and be the best hockey player ever so I can post videos on social media. I'm talking an obnoxious amount."

Max rolls her eyes, but it does nothing to diminish the excitement radiating from her. "Maybe only one or two videos, huh? Don't make it weird."

"I make no promises."

Well, except one.

I will not think about Gordon Maxwell Benson again this weekend.

21

GORDON

Me: So, what do you say to a woman you finger-fucked at a sex club three nights ago?

Ryan: I don't. One and done.

Gunner: Also, fucking rude of you to go to a sex club and not invite us.

Me: First of all, I'm not inviting you to go with me to a very exclusive and high-class fantasy club. And second, I was looking for Riley, not going to have a good time.

Ryan: Sure sounds like you had one anyway. <Winking Face Emoji>

Me: What if this woman was your assistant and you had to see her bright and early on Monday morning?

Gunner: Obviously, you pretend to be sick and avoid everyone.

Ryan: #accurate.

Me: I hate you both. Why are we friends?

Ryan: Because we are way cooler than any of the hockey guys you hang out with.

Ryan: Plus, we give great advice.

Me: Still waiting to hear some of this good advice.

Ryan: Is this the ex-girlfriend? The one you have unresolved feelings for?

Me: Irrelevant.

Gunner: Definitely yes.

Ryan: What's your end goal with this girl?

Me: Fuck if I know. I should keep my distance and fucking move on with my life.

Gunner: But?

Me: But I don't know how.

Ryan: Then you need to talk to her, and you might want to figure out where your head is. Do you want to date her? Or do you think you need to fuck her out of your system? If you don't know the answer here, you should.

Gunner: Wow. That's actually good advice.

Me: I'm quite surprised.

Ryan: I know things.

Gunner: Usually the things you know are limited to football and fucking.

Ryan: My two favorite things.

I BLOW OUT A BREATH, TURNING MY PHONE OVER IN MY hands as it continues to vibrate. Having the two of them in a group chat usually ends up with a string of messages I'll never read and a headache. This time is no different.

But I had to ask, and I guess there's a part of me that wanted to minimize what happened between us on Friday, and maybe exactly how much it affected me.

Fuck.

I know I need to move on from Riley, to figure out how to patch this gaping hole that's been in my chest for the past twelve years, but I don't know how. I've spent years punishing myself for being so damn unlovable that the only girl I ever gave a damn about dropped me like I was nothing. Without her, I was barely treading water in an ocean that wanted nothing more than to see me drown.

Or maybe it was simply my own thoughts.

Over time, I thought it was getting better—I thought *I* was getting better, but the second I saw her again, all the loss, the pain, the agony of losing her came crashing back. I've been drowning since.

They're right though. Regardless of how either of us feel, I definitely need to talk to her. Maybe hashing things out would give us some closure, a finality to that chapter of our lives, and maybe it wouldn't hurt so damn much to look at her.

Before I lose what little nerve I have, I push up from my desk and head out to the reception area, only to find her desk empty. Again. This conversation would be a whole lot easier if she were at her desk and not avoiding me like I suspect she's doing.

It's as annoying as it is inconvenient.

She wasn't at her desk when I got here this morning, and it was empty when I took the long way to get coffee a few hours later. And it was still empty when I came back from a lunch meeting. Logically, I know she's working and I know I'm not the only one here, but dammit, I need her to be at her desk.

With a long sigh, I rest my hand on the back of her chair and close my eyes. The lingering scent of peaches hits me hard and I take a deep breath, drinking her in... and then mutter a curse, realizing that I'm standing in the middle of the reception area sniffing my executive assistant's chair like some kind of deviant.

So, I do what any sensible man would do, I give her chair a shove and walk back down the hallway. I'm so lost in my own thoughts, I don't notice Dean's office door open, and I sure as fuck don't notice the stricken look on Riley's face until I almost run her over. I stop short, but not quick enough.

She lets out a small yelp, her eyes widening as all the papers in her hand flutter to the floor around us.

"Shit," I mumble, bending down to help her pick some of them up.

Riley slowly stands, pulling the last bit of paperwork from my hands and clutching it all to her chest. Her mouth opens, closes and then opens again. "Oh, hey, Mr. Benson, Sir."

Sir. Jesus Christ. I really need to get myself together or I'm going to be walking around the office with a damn hard-on for the rest of the day. Not that it hasn't been happening off and on through the last week, but it's not something that would be particularly helpful when her and I need to have an actual conversation.

I clear my throat and take a step back. "Can I see you in my office?"

She flinches, glancing behind me, to the ceiling, to the floor. Basically, anywhere but at me. "I'm a little busy right now. Can it wait?"

"No."

Her fingers curl around the papers, crinkling them as she holds them tighter to her chest. She still won't look at me, but gives me a curt nod.

"I'll try to be quick. I'd hate to keep you from your work."

That's a damn lie, and we both know it.

22

RILEY

Have I been avoiding Gordon today?

Yes, and I sure didn't plan on running into him in the hallway outside Dean's office. Which of course, immediately makes me think of the other hallway we met in, and my cheeks flame with so much embarrassment I really wish I hadn't come in today. Maybe I should have taken a page out of Max's book and pretended to be sick.

I follow Gordon to his office, trying really hard not to stare at the muscles bunching at his shoulders, but failing miserably. *Where is his damn suit jacket?* The last thing I need is to be caught ogling him when I'm really wanting to avoid anything and everything associated with Gordon Benson.

Especially anything that elicits any sort of sexual thoughts.

I don't know if he wants to talk about Friday night or

actual work stuff, but I am not mentally prepared for either of those things. Not when he's involved.

Yeah, I know, I promised myself I wouldn't think about him for the rest of the weekend, but that was short lived… and now I have yet to reinforce the walls around my defenses. When he touched me, whispered that old nickname for me, he systematically dismantled every brick I'd put up.

And I don't like it.

"Please have a seat." Gordon sweeps his hand in front of him, gesturing to the chairs in front of his desk.

He, however, doesn't sit. He walks over to his desk and instead of dropping his perfectly toned ass in the chair, paces behind it. So, I stand just inside the door, the papers still clutched to my chest. He said this will be quick, so I don't see a need to come in any more than a few inches.

"Or you can stand there by the door." He heaves a frustrated sigh, running his hands through his hair, making it look tousled in a way I'm trying to ignore. Which is no longer a problem as those damn hands continue to move. His fingers—the same fingers that were inside me—unbutton the cuffs at his wrists and he slowly rolls each sleeve up his forearms.

His thick, veiny forearms that make my mouth water and my thighs clench slowly come into view. Strike that, my entire body clenches which makes all the paper I'm holding crinkle loudly.

Gordon's eyes snap to mine, the heat churning in those emerald depths are enough to level me. When he speaks, his voice is rough, gravelly, like he's trying to hold himself together. "I need you to stop looking at me like that."

"Like what?" I manage to squeak, pulling in a breath of air, hoping like hell it'll steady me against Gordon. Against the one man who held my heart and fucking smashed it.

I need to remind myself why I hate him in the first place; of the pain and heartache he's caused not only me, but the daughter he's abandoned.

"Like you want me to touch you again." I stiffen at his words and briefly consider running back to Dean's office and hiding, but Gordon hangs his head, the sigh that escapes his lips full of defeat. "I wanted... I just... Why can't I get you out of my head?"

His question is laced with anguish and I don't know what to say, especially since it seems I'm having the same unwanted problem. Part of me wants to offer some comfort, a modicum of solace, but I don't dare move.

Gordon lifts his head, his gaze trailing up my body, and I can't help but take a small step back, putting myself a little closer to the door, a move that was clearly a mistake as his entire face hardens and he stomps toward me.

My eyes widen at this sudden shift and I take another step back. Dean's office is sounding better and better, but before I can tuck my tail between my legs and flee from his office, Gordon puts a hand on the door, slamming it behind me. He crowds me against the wood, his hands resting on either side of my head, and all the papers fall to the floor as my hands rest on his chest.

In this moment, I'm not sure if I want to push him away or pull him closer, I know what I should be doing, but that doesn't seem to matter when he's this close to me. Not when I can smell his spicy cologne, and definitely not when I can practically feel his entire body pressed against me.

My heart is beating a hundred miles a minute and I can't think, I can't talk, I can only stand here, captured in his orbit.

"Riley." My name is a desperate whisper tumbling from his lips, as his hand strokes the side of my face. "Why can't I escape you?"

My breath catches in my throat, and as tears prick at the corner of my eyes, I will myself to hold them in. "I don't know."

He rests his forehead against mine and sweeps his thumb along my lower lip. My legs tremble and my fingers sink into the front of his dress shirt to keep me from sliding down to the floor.

"I don't know if I want to escape you."

Another sweep of his thumb and I'm a damn mess. His gaze softens, and he leans forward. I'm frozen in place, and even though my brain is screaming at me to run away, I can't. My damn feet won't move, and my heart really wants one more kiss from this man, it doesn't matter if it's the last.

He whispers something I can't quite make out before his lips brush against mine, and I let out a soft moan. His touch is soft, delicate, and reminds me so much of how he used to kiss me, how he used to care.

Gordon's fingers trail across my cheek and wrap around the back of my neck. My eyes close and I can feel him getting closer, can feel his lips back on mine.

This shouldn't happen. I shouldn't want this. But dammit, I find myself shifting closer.

A ringing interrupts us and we both jump back, staring silently at each other. His cheeks are flushed and I'm struggling with each breath, but neither of us breaks eye contact. I'm not sure if I'm happy for the interruption or a little disappointed, but the answer is probably a mix of both.

The ring sounds again, barely breaking through my haze, and Gordon lifts a brow. "Are you going to answer that?"

Holy shit, my phone. My phone is ringing.

I dig in my pocket and as I pull out my phone, I see Harper's name on the screen. My first instinct is to send her to voicemail, but my stomach drops and there's a sudden weight on my chest. She wouldn't call me at work unless something was wrong, and by now she should be home with Max.

"Hello, Harper." My heart's about to bust out of my chest, and everything around me fades. I need to know everything is fine. I need to know I'm over thinking. Fuck. Fuck. Fuck. Here I am letting Gordon distract me again.

"Don't panic," Harper rushes out. "Everything is okay, but Max and I are at the hospital."

I nearly drop my phone as dread sinks its claws into me. "Hospital? What happened? Is it Max?"

Gordon raises a brow and frowns, leaning back on his desk and studying me. I couldn't give a flying fuck what he thinks right now.

"Max had a seizure when we got home from school. I think it caught her off guard and she lost her balance. She hit her head." The phone muffles and I can hear Harper talking to someone else. Every second that ticks by feels like hours, days. "Sorry about that. Max seems okay, but she was bleeding a bit so I took her to the ER."

I'm going to be sick. I'm going to throw up my turkey sandwich. The world turns on its axis and my insides twist. My mouth dries up and I can barely get out, "Where are you? What hospital?"

"We're at the children's hospital. They're looking to see if she needs stitches, but don't think she has a concussion."

Even though she can't see me, I nod. "I'll be right there."

By the time I hang up, my hands are shaking so bad,

I can barely get my phone back in my pocket. I meet Gordon's stoic gaze and swallow past the lump forming in my throat. "Hospital. I have to get to the hospital."

Before I can turn, Gordon's hands are on my shoulders and he leans down to study my face. He's talking to me, saying something I can't quite make out. It sounds like he's underwater, or maybe I am. *Why can't I hear him?* It doesn't matter. Nothing matters. I have to get to Max.

"I have to go." My words are mumbled as I try to brush past him, but he squeezes my shoulders and gives me a small shake.

"There's no way you can drive like this. I'll take you."

I shake my head. I don't need his help. I can get to the hospital. "I got it."

"Your entire body is shaking. I refuse to let you drive like this."

"We have to hurry."

Gordon nods, placing a hand on my lower back and guiding me out of his office. "I've got you." He pauses for a beat and takes a deep breath. "Riley, who's Max?"

"My daughter."

23

GORDON

A DAUGHTER.

Riley has a daughter, a daughter named Max, and I have so many damn questions spiraling in my brain but there's no way I can ask her a single one right now. Not when she's freaking out and can't seem to stop shaking.

And all I can focus on is that her daughter's name is so similar to my middle name. Is that super coincidental? Should I be reading more into this? Why would she have a kid with another man and name her after me? Or maybe I'm trying to make connections when there aren't any. Maybe I'm connecting dots that aren't there.

If I were a better man, maybe less broken, I'd offer her some comfort, but I'm not sure I know how. I'm nothing but rough and jagged edges, and she deserves someone better.

No wonder she looked so disappointed last week

when she asked me if I liked kids—cause she fucking has one. Or at least only one that I know of. Fuck. Is she married? *Did I finger-fuck a married woman?*

No.

There's no way.

She doesn't wear a ring, and she'd have mentioned it to someone. But it doesn't mean she wasn't married in the past. Is she divorced? Widowed? Did some asshole knock her up and leave?

Why do I suddenly want to maim every member of my own race?

I guide Riley through the parking lot and help her into the passenger seat of my car, doing my damnedest to keep my face impassive when I am so full of anger, I could rip the door from the hinges. And then there's this second emotion swirling with the first, making everything so much worse. Fucking jealousy—which, let me tell you, makes no sense. I was telling Riley the absolute truth when I said I never want kids, so why does my damned heart ache at the thought of someone else fathering Riley's daughter?

Why do I wish it was me?

I'm too fucked up.

I'd make a terrible dad, and her daughter is much better off with someone else's DNA. Yet that feels like the biggest lie I've ever told. If I let myself, I can imagine standing by Riley's bedside as she holds our child for the first time. Coming home after a day at the office to find a frazzled Riley and a little redheaded girl waiting for me with smiles. Her first tooth. Her first steps. Losing that same tooth. I can picture all of those things so clearly the pang of loneliness only gets stronger, but I need to push it down. Push it down and bury it in so deep it won't surface anytime soon.

Riley settles into the seat and instead of waiting for her to buckle her seatbelt, I grab it and lean across her to buckle it. She inhales sharply as my fingers brush across the top of her thighs, but once I have her buckled, I quickly get out of her side of the car and carefully close the door.

Before I get into the driver's seat of my Audi, I take several deep breaths. I need to get a grip on myself and fast.

Riley has already settled into my car, the purse we picked up from the desk wedged between her and the center console, and her phone is in her hand. Her fingers fly across the screen, and while they're still shaking slightly, it's not nearly as bad as it was.

I start the car and fasten my own seatbelt, glancing over at her. She's paler than usual, her brows drawn in concentration, and she's gnawing on her bottom lip.

"What hospital are we going to?"

"Nashville Children's Hospital. Do you know where it is?" She meets my gaze, a tear slipping down her cheek, and damn if I don't fight the urge to swipe it from her perfect face, to eliminate all her sadness, and let her know everything will be okay, even if I don't know if it's true.

I enter the hospital into my navigation and bring up directions. "I do now. Don't worry, we'll be there in twenty minutes. She'll be okay."

"I know, but please hurry."

Her voice is so small, so defeated, and I give her shoulder a gentle squeeze before pulling out of the parking lot and heading to the hospital.

We don't talk the entire way there; instead, we're surrounded by a tense silence. If I start talking, there's no way I'm not going to start pelting her with questions, and now isn't the time. We can talk tomorrow or later this week if she needs to stay home for a few days.

As I pull into the emergency room parking lot, I glance in her direction. She's still staring out the window. It's what she's done most of the trip, occasionally taking a reprieve to text on her phone. I'm assuming she's getting updates from her sister, but for all I know, she's also communicating with her daughter's father—a thought that leaves a bitter taste in my mouth.

She's out of the car as soon as I put the car in park, and I'm not really sure what to do. Do I follow her in? As her boss, that seems highly inappropriate, but as her ex-boyfriend... well, I guess that's even more inappropriate.

But then I notice she's left her purse, so the honorable thing would be to follow her. I grab the bag and turn off my car, slipping my keys in my pants' pocket.

Riley's not too far ahead of me, and I quickly close the distance between us. Her eyes widen slightly as she glances my way and then comes to a sudden stop as a woman who looks similar enough to Riley to be her sister, and a girl with bright red hair step out from behind an older car.

With a gasp, Riley pulls the little girl in for a hug.

This must be her daughter, Max. She's got a few white strips on the right side of her forehead and a little bit of dried blood in her hair, but otherwise, appears to be fine. She eyes me warily and I'm struck at how old she looks. In my head she was much younger, about five or six, but this girl looks like she could be anywhere between nine and thirteen.

Where the fuck is her dad? No, better question—who the fuck is her dad?

"Gordon Benson." Her sister crosses her arms and stares me down. Her eyes are the same bright blue as Riley's, and they flay me open. I don't know what I did to make her dislike me, but it's clear she's not a fan.

"Harper?" I ask hesitantly. Last time I saw her, she was about a foot shorter with braces.

"Sure am."

"You look different from the last time I saw you."

She laughs, uncrossing her arms and grabbing the

purse dangling from my fingers. "Well, duh. The last time you saw me I was a year younger than Max."

A year younger than Max?

My gaze swings to the girl in question, but before I can get another word out, Riley blocks her from my view and plasters on a fake smile. "Thanks for dropping me off. Harper can take me home. I'll see you at work."

She doesn't wait for a response, just turns and ushers the other two girls in the opposite direction. Harper gives me a small wave, and I can hear Max ask if I'm *the* Gordon Benson, but they're soon far enough away I don't hear Riley's answer.

I head back to my car, Harper's words tumbling around in my head on repeat. *I was only a year younger than Max.* If my memory is correct, she was about nine years younger than Riley, which would have made her about ten.

Does that mean Max is eleven?

No, it can't be.

It can't be him.

If my math and Max's age is correct, there's a good chance my old high school nemesis, Adrian Wylder, is her father. The same man she ran to after she dumped me.

So why the fuck did she name her after me?

Anger flows through me, my thoughts spiraling with every step I take to my car. My hands fist at my sides, and fuck, I'm going to murder him next time he comes to Nashville for a game.

I can't believe he got her pregnant, that he took that from me, that he took the life I didn't know I wanted until this very moment. He took my girl, my chance at a family. He took the damn life I should have had.

Jealousy really is a bitter pill to swallow, and this one just might choke me.

24

RILEY

"ARE YOU SURE YOU'RE OKAY?" I ASK AS I PULL MAX
in for another hug.

She's been tolerating my hovering since last night,
and even relented when I suggested she sleep in my bed.
And by relented, I mean she complained about it until
she fell asleep, but I felt so much better having her close
just in case something happened.

The doctors weren't concerned, and while I was
disappointed I didn't get to talk to them personally, I
understand. This was an anomaly, not a step back in her
treatment. She was exhausted and she forgot her meds.

It was my fault. She said she took them, and I didn't
double check.

"Yes, Mom." She uses that tone, the one that definitely says she's over me while simultaneously rolling

her eyes. "My headache is gone, and I barely notice the cut on my forehead."

Yeah, that's because she can't see it like I can. It's a beacon of my failure, and I can't not see it every time I look at her.

I give her a pointed look and purse my lips. "And we won't forget our meds again, right?"

"Nope."

I arch my brows. "Or stay up way past our bedtime?"

She groans, flopping herself down dramatically across the couch. "I was excited I made the hockey team. You can't blame me." She sits straight up, wincing slightly, but waves me off when she sees me moving her way. "You're still going to let me play, right?"

"I shouldn't." I really shouldn't, but her entire face falls, and yeah, I have to admit, this wasn't entirely to blame on hockey. "But I'm giving you one chance. You go to bed on time and you drink plenty of water. No exceptions."

She draws an x over her heart, a smile claiming her face. "I promise."

"Why aren't you dressed for work?" Harper asks as she comes out of her bedroom, her hair piled on top of her head in a messy bun, and a cup of coffee in her hands. "Don't think you're skipping work today."

I join Max on the couch, flopping down next to her a little less dramatically than she did, but dramatic all the same. "I don't want to go."

It's not a lie. I really don't want to see Gordon today. Not after he dropped everything to drive me to the hospital yesterday where he came face to face with Max. I didn't even think about him seeing her when he offered to drive me to the hospital. In hindsight, it's good that I didn't drive myself, but I should have found literally anyone else to take me.

Jesus. I couldn't get Max out of there fast enough. I couldn't let her talk to him, there's no way. Not after he bribed me and told me he wanted nothing to do with me and our baby.

And the worst part of all, he didn't look concerned. He didn't look sorry for abandoning us. He just looked confused.

Harper places her coffee on the side table and rests her hands on her hips, her eyes narrowing on me. "Max and I are playing hooky so you can go to work today. I'm not going to let you ruin our Kitchen Nightmare binge with all your complaining."

I cross my arms and stick out my bottom lip in a fake pout. "You guys are obsessed with Gordon Ramsey and I don't get it. Every episode is the same. He comes in and yells at everyone and then they get their shhh... crap together."

"His yelling is the best part," Max informs me and scoots over to the other side of the couch, grabbing the remote.

Harper sits down in the recliner and rolls her eyes at

me. "This is why you're not invited. Gordon Ramsey is a God among men. And yes, his yelling is the best part. So, go on. Get ready."

I push up from the couch, grumbling the entire time. The fact that I'm also going to see a grumpy Gordon who can also be considered a God among men isn't lost on me. Don't believe me? You should see that man roll up the sleeves of his dress shirt.

But dammit, she's right. I should go to work. They're fine. Harper will call me immediately if Max has even the smallest seizure, and I haven't been at the job long enough to accrue any time off or sick days.

Which means facing Gordon... and hoping he doesn't ask me about yesterday.

GORDON ISN'T in the office when I get there, and considering how late I am, it's surprising. Maybe he's sick, or maybe he was so embarrassed to see his daughter for the first time almost eleven-and-a-half years after she was born that he couldn't stand to face me. That seems likely, but I don't know anything anymore. Not when it comes to Gordon—and most certainly not when it comes to myself.

"If you need to leave at any point today, just let me

know. It's not a problem," Dean says and gives me a pointed look, grabbing several folders after I extend them his way. "Why didn't you tell me you had a daughter? I love kids."

I smooth down the front of my blouse, a simple black button up, and offer him a small smile. "My sister kicked me out of the apartment and told me I couldn't come back until her and Maxine were done watching Kitchen Nightmares." At his raised brow, I quickly add. "I'm sorry, but it never came up."

And you know, I didn't want to make things really fucking weird for everyone up here. Since Dean knows about Max, I'm assuming Jazz does too... which really has me wondering what she thinks of everything right now. Or is that why she's not here either?

"Do you have any pictures?"

I nod, pulling out my cell phone, watching Dean from the corner of my eye. I can't help but wonder if he's genuinely asking, or if Gordon admitted his big secret and he wants to see if they look alike. But his face doesn't give anything away, so I pull up a picture of Max, Harper, and I wearing matching moose pajamas, and show him.

He takes the phone from me, peering down at the screen. He studies the picture for several seconds and I wait, very impatiently. "I love the pjs. She's beautiful. Is this your sister?"

"Yep. She's finishing up her last year of college, and

then I'm sure she'll be off doing all sorts of brilliant things."

Dean returns the phone to me and I'm waiting for the questions, the comments, anything that would give me any indication he knows more than he's letting on, but nothing. "That's a whole lot of red hair and sass in one picture."

I'm as surprised by Dean's comments as I am by the laugh bubbling out of my chest. "You have no idea."

"If anything changes, let me know. Family comes first around here, and seeing that most of us are single or at least have no kids, that means you get special treatment." He winks, thanks me for the files, and heads back to his office.

That was nice. And weird.

His face gave nothing away, and either he knows nothing about Max's parentage, or he's a great actor.

The next hour crawls by as I dissect that interaction over and over and come up with no different conclusions. I text Harper and Max multiple times, and at this point, I'm sure they're both ignoring me. Not to mention, every damn time the elevator opens, I steel my spine and wait for Gordon to step off and into my space.

By the end of the hour, I was ready to fight with the mailman and two of the rookies.

I'm so annoyed with myself that the next time the elevator opens, I don't even look up. Probably another hockey player anyway.

But it's not.

Not that I notice until a shadow falls over me, forcing me to look up right into Gordon's scowling face.

I should greet him or at least thank him again for taking me to the hospital, but I don't want to say anything that reminds him of yesterday, of Max, so I remain silent and hope he gives me a little nod and walks off to his office. But no. He keeps staring, his eyes narrowed, his scowl so deep I think it might be permanently etched into his face.

"Can I help you with something?" I finally break as his continued glare has me squirming in my seat.

"No." His answer is simple yet his word is heavy, like there are a thousand things he's holding back.

There are several more questions I could ask, but instead, I bow my head and pull up my email, scrolling through my messages. None of them are important, but I need to look busy. Hell, I need to feel busy. Maybe then I'd have a chance at ignoring him until he goes back to his office.

"Why didn't you move to Vegas?"

When I look back at him, my eyes are wide and my mouth is hanging open as I mull over his words. Vegas? Why the hell would I be in Vegas? And why would this be the first question he'd ask me?

I close out my email, and very calmly place my hands on top of my desk, one folded over the other. "And what reason would I have to move to Vegas?"

"Oh, I don't know." He leans across the raised edge of the desk, his fingers dangling over the edge and gives me a sardonic grin that immediately has my hackles raising. "Just thought you might want to be closer to Wylder."

"What? Wylder?" I'm not even sure who he's talking about until it dawns on me a few seconds later. "Adrian Wylder from high school?"

He scoffs, raising up to his full height and straightens his suit jacket. "I hope he's paying you child support."

Without giving me time to respond, Gordon is gone, stomping down the hallway to his office.

I sit there for a moment, staring after him as my blood boils and anger rolls through me. How *dare* he. *How fucking dare he!* He's the one that said he wanted nothing to do with Max and I. He's the one that tried to pay me off with his father's money to disappear.

And now he wants to tell me his old high school rival should be paying me child support.

Something is clearly fucking wrong with his brain.

The longer I sit here, the madder I get, and before I can stop myself, I jump up and stomp down the hall after him. When I get to his office, I don't bother to knock, I march my ass right into his space, surprised to see him standing by the window, peering out into the city, most likely imagining himself lording over everyone in Nashville.

He's such a jerk. I can't imagine how I ever loved someone like this.

"What the fuck are you talking about?" I'm so mad I'm shaking, and I curl my fingers into fists at my sides hoping he doesn't notice.

He turns, slowly of course, no sign of surprise at all on his face. In fact, he looks indifferent to the entire situation, maybe even bored. "What part?"

"What do you mean, you hope he's paying me child support?" I grind out, crossing my arms tightly around my middle. It's the only way I can stop shaking, and maybe I need a little something to hold me together while I have this conversation.

His lip curls into a sneer, and this time when his gaze rakes over me, he looks at me like I'm nothing. Like I've never meant a damn thing to him ever. I don't like it. I may not be someone significant to him anymore, but I was. Rational? No, but I don't care right about now.

"I meant exactly what I said."

"Child support for what? Is he supposed to have fathered a child I don't know about?"

His brows draw together and I have to give it to him, he looks genuinely confused. "For Max. For your daughter. He's the father, isn't he?"

His question is so ridiculous all I can do is throw my head back and laugh like a fucking lunatic. I laugh until tears prick the corners of my eyes and Gordon has the good sense to look stricken.

I swipe my fingers under my eyes and straighten up, meeting his gaze head on. "No, Adrian Wylder is not Max's father. You are."

25

GORDON

"Excuse me?" The blood drains from my face and I'm frozen.

Riley huffs a laugh and shakes her head, pinching the bridge of her nose before she levels me with a look so full of disappointment I can't stand it. "You. Are. Maxine's. Dad."

I don't quite register the words at first, but as they permeate my brain, all the sounds around us die down and all I can hear is a low buzzing sound. Heat rushes through my body, it's suffocating, so suffocating I can barely breathe. All I can see is the storm brewing in the deep blue depths of her eyes, a storm so full of hate and disappointment.

My legs wobble and instead of trying to stand, a task that feels almost impossible this very second, I sink to the floor.

I heave a sigh, letting my head fall into my hands.

The brittle shell around my heart cracks and it feels as though the entire thing is breaking, shattering into millions of tiny pieces at Riley's feet.

After several long seconds, I raise my head and meet her hardened gaze. "Why? Why didn't you tell me?"

She makes a choking sound and looks at me like I have two heads. "What are you talking about? I told you. I called you time and time again after I found out, and you couldn't bother to call me back. You did your dirty work over text. You couldn't even…" Her voice breaks and she takes a shaky breath before continuing. "You didn't have the common decency to talk to me. It was like I was nothing. Like our baby and I meant nothing to you after being together for two years."

I don't even register what I'm doing until I'm across the room, wiping away the tears slipping down her cheeks. "I never got a message."

"Don't play with me, Gordon." She tries to turn away but I stop her, framing her face with my hands and forcing her to maintain my gaze.

"Look at me." I drop every mask, every fucking pretense I have to make sure she sees the hurt, the regret, and the goddamned agony written all over my face. "I didn't know."

My chest tightens. My heart races. I can't breathe, but it doesn't matter. Not now when I have Riley so close… when I have a daughter.

Riley and I have a daughter.

I have a daughter, and I had no idea she existed until now.

Another tear slides down Riley's cheeks, her voice wavering with every word. "You didn't tell me that I was the biggest mistake of your life? That you wished we'd never met? That our child meant nothing to you?"

I open my mouth to speak, but no words come out. I just… oh my God—no wonder she hated me. I can barely begin to imagine how much hurt my supposed words caused her over the years, how they poisoned her against me.

How they took away so much time with her and a daughter I've only seen once.

I missed out on so many moments with the both of them. Max's first birthday, her first tooth, her first smile, her first word, the first time she crawled, walked. I missed it all.

And for what?

There's only one person who could be responsible, and if he wasn't already dead, he would be after today. The same person who fed her that bullshit is the same one that kept me in the dark for so many years, tainting my heart, my very soul.

Max doesn't even know me. My damn father was so selfish, so self-serving, he took me from her. He stole my child's chance at having a dad.

And for what? Hockey?

My eyes burn with unshed tears and I drop my forehead to hers. "I would never. You're the only woman who's ever meant something to me. The only one I've ever loved. When I told you I never wanted kids, it was because if they weren't yours, I couldn't even imagine them existing."

Her breath stutters and her eyes well with more tears. "Then... how? Who said those things?"

Instead of answering right away, I close my eyes and pull her in for a hug, holding her tightly against my chest. I don't know if I'm holding myself together or her, but I need this. I need to know she doesn't think I could have ever said those things to her, that I couldn't have ever hurt her like that.

Her arms reluctantly wrap around me and she clings to me as tightly as I cling to her.

I let us enjoy this bit of solitude for a moment. A moment where the world falls away along with all the pain between us, and we can just be.

"I lost my phone right before I left for Boston," I whisper into her hair. "I didn't let you know because you had already ended things. You told me you didn't love me, and... I... I couldn't bring myself to face you, knowing I loved you so much and you didn't love me back."

She pulls back, tears now flowing freely down her cheeks, and this time she frames my face with her hands. "I lied."

26

RILEY

GORDON STIFFENS BENEATH MY TOUCH. "WHAT DO YOU mean, you lied?"

I take a deep breath, letting the air leave my lungs slowly as I walk over to one of the chairs in front of his desk and sit down. Gordon follows, sitting down in the chair next to me, giving me an expectant look.

I fidget with the hem of my skirt, refusing to meet his gaze. It'll be a whole lot easier to confess my truth if I didn't have to see the judgment on his face. "My mom had cancer." I take another deep breath, hoping it'll calm my rapidly beating heart. It doesn't. "It was bad. Terminal. I had to stay behind to help her and my sister, and if I told you, there was a chance you'd stay too. They needed me, and I needed you to let me go. You were meant to go into the NHL, Gordon. Hockey is in your blood. I knew you were meant for so much more than me."

Gordon slips down to his knees in front of me, stilling my hands with his own. "You're right. I would have given up everything for you."

My breath catches in my throat as his honesty catches me off guard, the raw intensity of his words breaking down some of the walls I've built between us. The Gordon I knew when we were eighteen would have given up his career for me, and hearing him say it now, after the animosity he's felt since then, levels me.

"You mean everything to me. You're my world. My light." Gordon pulls me against him, brushing his lips *across my temple. "I can't wait for you to come up to Boston. Two weeks without you is too much."*

"I... I..." The words are stuck in my throat and I pull *him closer, burying my face in his shoulder and losing myself in his woody scent for the last time. I let him hold me for a few minutes while I build up the strength to destroy us both. "I'm not going to Boston."*

He takes a step back, his arms falling to his sides, and his eyes already laced with hurt. "What do you mean?"

I swallow down all our good memories, all the love I feel for this man, and focus on my mom. On why I need to end this. Just because I'm stuck here, doesn't mean he has to be. He's on a straight path to the NHL, and I won't be the one to take those dreams from him. He's worked for this his entire life. "We need to break up."

The way he's looking at me now is nearly identical to how he looked at me the day I told him I didn't love him. The hurt, the agony, is written clear across his face, but this time we can make things right. Or at least we can try.

There's already been so many lies between us. I don't want anymore.

It's clear he's suffering, and I don't blame him. I can't imagine finding out you have a kid almost twelve years after she was born. I'd be absolutely devastated, destroyed.

And here he is, on his knees before me, flaying himself open even more.

"I know, which is why I couldn't let you." I give him a wobbly smile, ignoring the swell of emotion that always build up in my chest when I think of my mom. "She died right after Max was born, and then I had to raise my sister, and I had a brand-new baby. I barely knew which way was up, and you... I was so mad at you."

"And that's why you stopped figure skating, why you never went to the Olympics."

I nod as Gordon squeezes my hands, running his thumb back and forth over my knuckles. "It didn't seem important anymore. Without my mother, I had to start

working. It was on me to make sure everyone was taken care of."

Gordon doesn't say anything for a second, just keeps stroking the back of my hand. "And the show you did this month?"

"I was filling in after some of their girls were sick." It's only been a couple of weeks, but damn if it doesn't feel like it's been ages. And to think if the damn flu hadn't run through the figure skating show, we wouldn't have gotten to this moment. We'd still be barely more than strangers, and we'd still hate each other. "The woman who runs it is a good friend of mine. She's been trying to poach me for years, but I want Max to have a stable home, and my sister is still finishing college."

"I get it." He pauses for a minute, staring down at our joined hands. When he speaks again, his voice is hard. "The only person who had access to my old phone would've been my father. He didn't tell me you called or sent any messages. He'd only told me he'd seen you all over Wylder the weekend after we broke up. I'm assuming the two of you never dated."

"God, no. I was never interested in him." The laugh that leaves me is low, humorless. "It explains why you thought he was Max's dad."

"Yeah, I was a little pissed."

Somehow, I feel like that's the understatement of the century. Gordon and Adrian were enemies from the minute they both skated on the ice. There's no way I'd have considered dating him, especially not right after things ended. I don't think it would have been fair for me to start a relationship with anyone when I was in love with someone else.

I can't believe his dad told him that. I'm sure the news wrecked him. And then not to tell him about me? About the baby? I knew his dad despised me from the start, but hiding his own grandchild seems so fucking extreme.

But if I think about it, I guess it makes sense. After I broke things off and Gordon left for Boston, I'd never seen Mr. Benson so happy. The few times I saw him around town, he was all smiles instead of the usual scowl he reserved for me. He even asked me how I was doing after I thought I'd told Gordon I was pregnant.

Holy shit. *He knew.* He fucking knew I was pregnant and smiled right to my face after he told me all those nasty things and offered me money to lose that number.

What an asshole. He deserved everything he got in life. He deserved to die miserable and alone. Goddamn. Just thinking about him has my blood boiling.

It was no secret he didn't like me, and he was obsessed with the dream of Gordon following his foot-steps, but Jesus Christ. No dream is worth hurting so many innocent people. He's a monster, and Gordon is his biggest victim.

"I can't believe your dad did all that. It's not right." I shake my head, choking back a sob. "I'm so sorry he didn't tell you about me, about the pregnancy. If I'd have known, I'd have gone to Boston myself."

His eyes harden yet his tone remains gentle and laced with certainty. "If I'd known you were having my baby, nothing would have stopped me from being there. Nothing."

We fall into a tense silence, and Gordon gives my hand one last squeeze before returning to his chair. The loss of his warmth is immediate, and I cross my arms to keep from reaching out to him. While the stain from our past may be lifted, we can't go back in time and truly fix everything. There's been too much time, too much hurt, and miles between us.

We both need to move on.

It's for the best. Really.

I don't need a complicated relationship with him on top of the complicated mess this entire situation has become.

"Why did you name her Maxine?" Gordon's question pulls my gaze over to him. He's staring at his desk, loosening the tie from his neck, and I can't help but watch his fingers run over the silky material.

See? Everything is complicated, including me. "You were her dad and even though I thought you wanted nothing to do with her, I wanted her to have a piece of you. I thought you both deserved that."

"What's she like?"

But I manage to tuck away everything he makes me

feel and give him a genuine smile. "She's the best daughter I could've asked for—despite the sass and the impending teenage years. She's as smart as she is headstrong, and she has such a big heart. She's been through a lot, but she's tough, resilient."

He stiffens, his eyes meeting mine, full of trepidation. "What do you mean, she's been through a lot?"

"When Max was four, she started having epileptic seizures. The doctors aren't sure what caused the initial onset, but since we started medication, they've been few and far between. She's doing okay."

"And yesterday?"

"Yesterday she forgot her meds and stayed up late, even though she knows how important getting a good night's sleep is. She had a seizure when she got home, and was then lectured by both me and the neurologist on call about the importance of taking her medicine. She's at home with Harper today." I run a hand through my hair and scoff. "They're watching Kitchen Nightmares and I was not invited." When he quirks a brow, I add, "I'm not as big a Gordon Ramsey fan as they are. My sister said I would ruin their fun."

He looks at me for several beats before his other brow raises, and then he does something I don't expect. He laughs. Not only is it the first break in this tense situation, but the first laugh I think I've heard from him in over a decade. I didn't realize how much I missed it, and it doesn't take long for me to join in, laughing until my stomach aches and I'm wiping away more tears.

"How dare you. That poor guy." He shakes his head with a chuckle, and grins. "He's a national treasure." Gordon waits until my laughter dies down and then pins me in place with a look that breaks my heart. "I'd like to meet her, if that's okay. I know it might take a bit for everyone to get used to, but I want to be there. I don't want to miss out on anything else."

"Of course."

My answer is immediate. Before this conversation, I wouldn't have been as agreeable, but now that I see him clearly, free of the lies his own father painted around him, I can't keep them apart. It wouldn't be fair to anyone, and if Gordon is wanting to be involved with Max long-term, so be it.

Max deserves everything, including a father who loves her as much as I do.

"Do you want to see some pictures? Oh, and Max is obsessed with hockey. She's a lot like you, despite me trying to push her towards safer things like figure skating."

Gordon's smile is wide and cracks my damn chest right open. He nods, reaching out and pulling our chairs together. I let out a small yelp as they collide. He continues to smile, and I wonder if it's starting to hurt his face.

"No offense." The pointed look he sends my way

tells me he isn't the least bit sorry about what's about to come out of his mouth. "Figure skating is lame. Hockey is where it's at."

I laugh, pulling out my phone and going into my photos. "You didn't think it was so lame when you saw me in my competition outfits." I glance up when I realize he's not laughing, but looking at me with a hunger so intense my cheeks heat and I shift in my chair. Perhaps that wasn't the smartest thing to say. My eyes immediately go back to my phone. "Oh, look. I found some baby pictures."

He takes my phone, and I can practically see all the anger and tension leaking from his body as he stares at a picture of Max taken a few weeks after I came home from the hospital. She was sleeping in a muted pink bassinet my mom had bought for her.

"She's perfect." He strokes a finger down the screen and I melt. "Do you have more?"

"How much time do you have?"

"For my girls?" The smile he gives me about kills me. "All day."

I need to get a handle on myself, and fast.

27

GORDON

Me: Hey, we need to talk. Are you around tonight?

Jazz: Yeah, I just got to the house. I wanted to change before heading back to the arena for the game.

Jazz: Are you going?

Me: I don't think so.

Jazz: Why? What's going on?

Me: I'm heading over. I'll see you in a minute.

EACH STEP TOWARD THE HOUSE—MY FATHER'S HOUSE— sends dread slithering up my spine and settling like a lead weight in my gut. This isn't going to be an easy conversation to have. It's not like I can waltz in there and say, oh hey, you have a niece you didn't know about, but it's cool now, don't worry.

That would go over real fucking great.

Before I unlock the back door and go inside, I stop and stare up at the giant monstrosity. I'd love nothing more than to burn it to the ground—along with every last memory of him. He doesn't deserve a place in my past, or my future. What he deserves is to have everything he's ever owned, ever truly cherished, to end up just like him —in ash.

The legacy he left me is as brittle as his integrity.

He never loved me, that much is clear. He never loved anyone but himself. If he had, he wouldn't have hidden the fact that I have a child. His own grandchild. That's what gets me most of all; Max is his flesh and blood and he left her with no father, no grandfather, no aunt. Nothing.

He left Riley, a pregnant eighteen-year-old with a dying mom, with no support. She was all alone in the world, and it was all his fault.

With one last parting look at the window to the master suite, I head inside.

Jazz is waiting for me in the kitchen, shoving a handful of Goldfish crackers in her face.

"You need to talk?" she manages to get out between bites.

I nod, slipping my hands in my pockets and rocking back on my heels. She's staring at me expectantly, and I can't seem to find the words. So instead of just spitting them out like I should, I pour myself a double shot of Angel's Envy bourbon and toss it back.

She huffs a laugh and has a few more crackers. "That bad, huh?"

I nod stoically, pouring myself another shot, but this time, I leave it untouched. "You have no idea." I let out a sigh, running both hands through my hair. "Riley left early yesterday."

"Yeah, Dean said she had some kind of family emergency. I assumed it was her sister." She drops the fish and her eyes widen. "Is she okay?"

"She's fine, but Jazz, it wasn't her sister. Riley has a daughter." As soon as the words are out of my mouth, hers falls open. "My daughter."

She doesn't respond right away, and I'm assuming she doesn't know what to say, but she does pick up my glass of bourbon and drains it. Her face scrunches for a second and she slams the empty glass back on the counter. "And she was what? Hiding this from us for years? Was she ever planning on telling you?"

"Here's the thing." I sit down at the island and gesture to the chair next to mine. She shoots me an exasperated look, but sits down anyway. "She thought I knew."

"Why the hell would she think that?"

"She called, and when she couldn't get ahold of me, started texting. She told me everything, only it wasn't me on the other end. I don't know if you remember, but I lost my phone before I left for college, and Dad sent me a new one."

"Are you saying she talked to Dad?" she says slowly, looking around the kitchen like she's seeing everything in a different light. "That he knew?"

I nod, running a hand down my face and resting it on the countertop. "It seems that way. He pretended to be me, Jazz. He told her that I didn't give a fuck and tried to pay her to disappear."

"Holy fuck." Her voice cracks and she turns away, quickly swiping under her eyes. "How could he do that?"

"Your guess is as good as mine."

I don't realize I'm shaking until Jazz rests her hand over mine and gives me a tentative smile. "When do we get to meet her?"

As much as I'd love to introduce her to everyone right away, I'd like to be the first one to meet her and try to establish some sort of relationship.

"I'm not traveling with the team for the rest of the week so I'm hoping to spend as much time with them as possible. Maybe we can have everyone over for dinner Tuesday or Wednesday next week between away games."

Jazz hums her agreement, and I can tell she has so many more questions, but more than likely none I'd have an answer to. I can at least show her the pictures Riley sent me, so I pull out my phone and bring up our text thread.

"Here." I hand Jazz my phone and she stares at the first picture, the one from when Max was a baby, and this time she doesn't stop the tears. "Her name is Maxine Stella Adams and she's eleven. She's smart, tough as nails, and sounds like she has some of your sass. And she just started playing hockey. Apparently, she's pretty obsessed."

She puts a hand over her mouth to muffle her sobs and I put my arms around her, pulling her to my chest as my own tears threaten to fall. I've managed to hold myself together all day. Barely. I can feel myself right on the edge, and I can't afford to fall over and shatter.

I need to be strong for... well, everyone.

"She's... so... beautiful," Jazz manages to choke out, rubbing her nose on the front of my dress shirt. "We missed so much."

"I know."

"We're in the same... the same city, and she doesn't even know we're here."

My heart sinks, and I can't stop the tear that falls. "I know."

She suddenly pulls back, her bloodshot eyes locked on mine. "I'm sorry, I can't even begin to imagine how you feel. You've lost so much time with her. I feel fucking broken, and she's not even mine."

Another tear falls, and then a few more. I can feel myself nodding in response, but as I open my mouth to assure her I'm fine, nothing comes out. There have been so many lies already. "I'm not okay. I'm so fucking angry with our dad, and I can't yell at him. I can't ask him what the fuck he was thinking, I can't do shit cause he's already dead. And Riley…" My voice breaks on her name, and it takes me several beats before I can talk again. "Riley had to do everything by herself, and Max has no idea who I am." I take one shaky breath, and then another. "I feel like I let her down so much."

This right here is why it's so much easier to feel nothing. You can't fall apart if nothing gets to you, but right now, I feel every single thing. I feel like I'm being pulled in every direction at the same time. I don't just have one emotion leading me, I have all of them tumbling around inside me.

Jazz is the one who pulls me in for a hug this time. She holds me tight, and tells me everything will be okay, even though neither of us have a clue how. But she has faith, so maybe I should too.

Eventually she pulls away and I know it's getting late, so I send her the pictures I have of Max and usher her out the door.

I need some time to think, to be alone, so I end up pouring myself another drink, and after downing that one, I grab the bottle and take the stairs to the master suite—to my dad's old room.

It's just like he left it almost two years ago.

I couldn't bring myself to come up here and clean it out, or rather, I couldn't face him. His memory still haunts me from the grave. His voice is a constant in the back of my mind, telling me the things I'm doing wrong, how much of a disappointment I am, how I've thrown my life away.

Nothing I ever did was good enough for him. I could always do better, be better. He wanted me to be an emotionless machine like him. He wanted me to be his hockey prodigy, and until my knee was wrecked, I guess I was. His little dutiful soldier.

I walk around the room, and with every step I take, the more rage I feel.

He took my life away from me.

He took Riley.

He took Max.

He wanted me alone and miserable just like him. Well, I'm pretty fucking miserable now.

Are you happy, Dad? Are you fucking happy?

I'm sure that bastard is down in Hell, laughing his ass off. I'm sure he's loving the havoc he's wreaked on my life. He kept Jazz and Lincoln apart, and while I may not be Lincoln's number one fan, he makes my sister happy. He hated Riley because she distracted me from hockey, and he made sure Max grew up without a father because he wanted to be sure I made the NHL.

Lot of good that did me. Eight years in, and I fucking failed at the only thing I had.

My bitter laugh fills the room, and I bring the bottle to my lips to take a healthy sip… but I catch myself in the mirror standing in the corner of the room. My hair is sticking up in multiple places, my eyes are bloodshot, my dress shirt is half tucked in, and I'm about to drown my sorrows in alcohol.

I'm no better than he was.

He's turned me into a bitter, lonely man. He's turned me into his own fucking image.

Fuck him.

Instead of drinking the bourbon, I throw it across the room, shattering it and the mirror. Shards of glass fly everywhere, bourbon sloshes up the wall, and I'm very tempted to light the entire thing on fire and walk away.

I'm not his to control. I'm done letting him have any power over me.

I'm fucking *done*.

With a curse, I rip the drawers open on his dressers and scatter the contents around the room. His clothes go flying, and so does the junk he kept over the years. I move to the next dresser and send more of his crap to the floor. Piece by piece, it makes me feel better.

His favorite flask joins my broken bottle of bourbon, but as soon as I see the envelope that was hidden underneath, I freeze. It has my name on it. I don't know if I should rip it up, set it on fire, or read it.

But I can't bring myself to destroy it.

I stand in the middle of the wreckage and rip open the envelope.

Gordon,

I must have written this letter a hundred times, but I could never find the right thing to say, so I'm just going to come out with it. I'm a terrible father. I've done things I'm not proud of, but I would do them all again if it meant pushing you to accomplish our dreams.

You followed my footsteps into the NHL and were a far better player than I ever was. If I wasn't hard on you, if I wasn't so ruthless, you might not have made it.

You were my greatest accomplishment, but I never once told you I was proud of you.

I am.

As I'm nearing the end of my days, I've had a lot of time to think. No one wants to die alone, yet here I am, surrounded by vast emptiness. I don't want that for you. Find your happiness.

That's it? No apology? He's got one thing right—he

275

was a terrible father. He couldn't even tell me that I had a kid on his fucking death bed.

He's proud of me? That's a fucking laugh.

I couldn't hack it in the NHL, I'm probably going to lose this hockey team because of his fucking two-year playoff stipulation, and there's a good chance I'm going to be a terrible father.

I bet you're so fucking proud of me. *Fuck you.* Fuck you so hard.

With one last glance at the note, I tear it into shreds. I rip and I rip until I can't make the pieces any smaller and then toss them in the air. They flutter around me as they fall to the floor and as I step away from the destruction I caused, I lift both middle fingers in the air, and move to step out of his room.

And of course, that's when I see a framed picture sitting on his nightstand. It was taken right after I signed my first NHL contract. His arm is around me and we're both smiling at the camera. I was so happy that day and all I could think was how proud my dad must be because I finally did it. I finally made it.

His smile is nothing but a reminder of what he did, how shitty he was. He smiled right in my fucking face, knowing he was keeping such a monumental secret from me.

He knew about Riley, about Max, he knew I had a family somewhere and he pretended everything was normal. He could have told me then. He could have told me a thousand times, but he didn't.

I take that picture, the one and only picture of the two of us, and I smash the frame on the nightstand. Careful not to cut myself, I pull the picture from the broken glass, pick up the lighter he kept for his cigars, and I light that shit on fire.

I hope he rots in Hell.

28

GORDON

> Gordon: Are you home?

> Riley: It's ten-thirty on a Tuesday night, Gordon. Where else would I be?

> Gordon: Can I come up?

> Riley: What do you mean, up? Are you at my apartment complex?

> Riley: How do you know where I live?

> Gordon: Your employment paperwork. And yes.

I HOLD MY PHONE IN MY HAND AND I WAIT. I WAIT FOR the three little dots. I wait for the little vibration of an incoming message. Something. *Anything.*

But I get nothing.

I should have known better than to come here. After everything we went through today, and the wounds I ripped open between the both of us, I'm sure I'm the last person she wants to see. She can't know how much I need her tonight.

My entire life has been a fucking sham. Everything but her. We were the only thing that was ever real.

With one last look up at the dim second floor hallway, my shoulders slump, and I head back to my car. Maybe I'm more like my dad than I thought. Maybe I'm too damaged, too broken. Maybe I'm not worthy of love.

I make it about six steps when I hear soft footsteps behind me and I freeze, not daring to turn around. If it's not her, I want to live in this illusion for another few seconds.

"Gordon?" Her voice is tentative yet it runs down my body, soothing my opened wounds one by one. "What are you doing here?"

My voice clogs in my throat and I turn around, taking a moment to absorb Riley standing in front of me in one of my old high school hockey t-shirts and a pair of gray shorts. The air leaves my lungs in a whoosh. Seeing her dressed like that is like a punch to the gut. *Is she thinking about us? Is she remembering how good it used to be?*

Her hair is pulled on top of her head in a messy bun, with loose little wisps framing her face. She doesn't have any makeup on, but she's never looked more irresistible, or more like the version of herself I used to know.

Except for her eyes, those are bloodshot and a little puffy. It looks like she's been crying, not that I blame her. Today has been... fucking catastrophic.

"I had nowhere else to go." I take a step toward her. It's small, but I don't want to scare her off. "I didn't want to be alone."

She glances behind her shoulder, shifting back and forth, and her fingers toy with the edge of the t-shirt. "You shouldn't be here."

I take another step. "Is Max asleep?"

"Yeah."

"I'm not here to meet her now. I... I needed to be close to you. To both of you. I couldn't stay in his house for another minute." I hang my head, give it a shake, and blow out a heavy breath. "I'm sorry, this was a mistake."

She blinks a few times before swiping under her eyes, and just as I'm about to turn and head back to my car, she takes a step toward me. And then two more. "You'll have to be gone before Max gets up, but I'd like you to stay."

"You don't have to—"

"I don't want to be alone either."

She extends a hand to me, letting it hang between us like an olive branch. I'd be stupid to pass it up. I meet her halfway, grasping her hand and lacing our fingers together.

"Thank you." My voice cracks and I clear my throat. "I know this isn't exactly appropriate."

Riley huffs a quick laugh. "I'd say we crossed a few lines already. What's one more? Our history makes things complicated."

Complicated.

That's the oversimplification of a lifetime. Things were complicated before I put my hands all over her.

Before today, she was the one woman I couldn't get out of my head. Now, she's the mother of my child. She's so embedded in my past, and now my future, she'll never be just my executive assistant. The lines between us are so blurred, they may as well be nonexistent.

And here she is, holding my hand, wearing one of my old shirts, and sneaking me into her house like she used to back when we were in high school. I can almost imagine we're eighteen, her parents have already gone to bed, and she's waving me through the back door to her house. I'd press her against the sliding glass door, slide my hands around to her ass, and try to kiss her senseless while she'd giggle and try to get me to her room as quickly as possible.

Gordon, you're going to wake up my parents and get us both in trouble.

She opens the door to her apartment, closing and locking it behind us. "Shh. Harper and Max are sleeping, so we have to be quiet."

I take off my shoes, carrying them with me, and follow her to what I'm assuming is her bedroom. The lights are dim; only a few candles flickering along a dresser.

She'd pull me into her bedroom, quickly locking the door, and peeling off her pajamas. "I need you, Gordon. Please."

"Are you doing okay? Today was..." I trail off, running a hand up her arm. There's not a single word that seems like it holds the weight, that fully encompasses the multitude of what we unpacked.

"I don't know." She shrugs, glancing to the floor. "I think I'm still processing. What about you? I lived with a lie, but at least I had Max. But you..."

I nod and trail my hand along her jaw. "I've been alone. I have a kid I didn't know about for eleven years, and a dad who knew about her every single fucking day of her life and never said a word. He took that secret to his grave, and I'm not sure I know who I am anymore. Nothing makes sense. Nothing but you. When I left my dad's house, I didn't plan on coming here, but then I found myself in your parking lot."

After I tore up my dad's bedroom and found that picture from college, I tried to go back to the guest house. I really did. I was halfway across the back yard when I stopped and couldn't move another foot forward. There was something holding me back, keeping me from moving on, and no matter how badly I wanted to take another step, I couldn't.

It wasn't until I stepped backwards that I could move.

I drove around for an hour before I came here. It seemed stupid to get a hotel room when I had the guest-house and access to an entire mansion, but the thought of being alone, of staring into the abyss of my past, was a reality I couldn't face.

She's the only one who could possibly understand.

"We should try to get some sleep," Riley whispers as she blows out the candles and walks over to the left side of the bed, gesturing me to the right. "Max gets up at seven to get ready for school, so I can set an alarm for six."

I make my way to the right side—the side that used to be mine—the past warring with the present. She used to lay in the center, her hands coasting up and down the length of her body, teasing me. *"What are you waiting for?"*

"Yeah." My throat goes dry as she slides into bed.

I toss my shirt to the floor and reach for the button of my pants, fully intending to hold Riley against me and fall asleep. But then I see how she's watching me, and even in the dark I can see the hunger written all over her face. *What are you waiting for?*

She pulls her hair out of its bun and settles back against her pillows, the dark red strands fanning out around her. I can't tear my gaze away as I slide into bed and turn to my side.

"I'm not going anywhere," she smiles, turning to face me. "Or are you planning on watching me sleep all night?"

"Just making sure you're real."

Her breath catches, her bottom lip going between her teeth, and my eyes go straight to her mouth. I can't help it. I wonder if she tastes as sweet as she did in high school. I wonder if she'd still give me a soft sigh the first time our lips touched.

She scoots closer, closing some of the gap between us. "What are you waiting for?"

My eyes widen, and I'm pretty sure my tongue is stuck to the roof of my mouth. The line between memory and reality is thin, and I can't be sure if she said this in my head or out loud. If this is real, is she's saying this to me now... does that mean...?

Riley doesn't hesitate, leaning towards me and pressing her lips to mine. My brain short circuits for a second before it fully registers that Riley is kissing me.

Riley is kissing me.

It's like a homecoming, like a reawakening, like a cataclysmic event where the past and the present collide and create the perfect moment. My entire body sparks to life, and fuck, I didn't realize how absolutely fucking numb I've been to everything around me.

I've been living my life, going through the motions, but I haven't allowed myself to truly feel a thing.

But now?

I feel every little touch, I hear every little sigh and whimper, I smell the lingering scent of peaches, and I know I'm home. How did I live without her for so long?

She sighs and opens up to me as I run my tongue along the seam of her lips. Her hands run up my back and across my shoulders, her nails digging into my skin as I lick into her, stroking my tongue along hers at a deliberate pace, taking my time to explore every inch.

My heart hammers in my chest, and damn, my cock is rock hard.

With a whimper, she pulls back and shimmies out of the rest of her clothes before she yanks me back down for another soul searing kiss.

I sink into her, letting my hands explore her body, reuniting myself with each one of her curves. Her skin is so damn soft, and every touch, every caress, has her shifting against me, practically begging for more.

Every touch is like a connection to the past, a reminder that I never got over her. Being with her is ripping open all my wounds, exposing all of my insecurities. She flays me open until I'm nothing but a bleeding mess, but she still accepts me for who I am.

My tongue strokes hers again, and as her body arches up, I reach down, slipping two fingers inside her. She's so wet, so ready for me. She squeezes around my fingers and I growl, closing my eyes for a brief moment, just enough to take control of myself. I will not come until I'm inside her.

Fuck.

There's a part of me that's screaming in my head, telling me to slow down, to stop. It knows we shouldn't be doing this, that we're both so vulnerable and broken right now. But damn, her broken pieces fit with mine, and I can't stop. She reminds me of a time when things were good, when they were simple, and I want to do that for her.

"Please, Gordon," she whimpers, canting her hips and moving against me, forcing me to rub her faster, deeper. "More."

I groan, moving my hand along her collarbone and gliding up to her neck. I flex my fingers on her throat, tilting her chin up with my thumb, forcing her to look at me. "Are you sure? There's no going back."

"I'm sure."

With a nod, I grab a condom from my wallet, tossing it back to the floor with my pants. I rip open the condom wrapper, kick off my boxer briefs, and slide it over my cock. I settle back over her, and Riley wraps her arms around me as I sink between her thighs. I can't see much, but I find her gaze and keep it as I push into her. Her eyes soften, reflecting the love I feel, the love she's afraid of. She groans as she wraps her thighs around me, and I'm pretty sure this is exactly what heaven feels like.

God, it's been so long, I forgot what I was missing.

She's every good memory, every good piece of me.

I still, giving her time to adjust to my size. Her pussy

quivers around me, holding me in place, but then I take a deep breath and move.

As I fuck her in the darkness, there are no secrets, no lies, no bad memories. There's only the two of us, and I know without a doubt just how real this is.

Her soft whimpers and moans have me picking up the pace, and I bury my face in her neck, surrounding myself with her scent. I let her flip us over and she straddles my hips, leaning forward and maintaining eye contact. She fucks me slow and hard. She fucks me like she's missed me for twelve damn years.

If she wants control, I'll surrender it to her. As long as she wants me, I don't care what I have to do. I trust her more than I trust anyone.

Our breaths grow heavier, my heart rips open, and I bring a hand between us to circle her clit.

I keep the pressure light, my strokes slow but deep as I meet hers. Together, we build each other higher and higher, taking each other to the edge, and repairing the bond between us piece by piece. Her nails scratch down my abs as she lets out a silent scream, her body convulsing around me, and I can't hold back. With one last thrust, I empty inside her.

We don't move for a while, we just stay connected— physically, mentally, and emotionally. Something shifted in my chest and locked into place. For once, I'm not so disconnected, so completely and utterly alone.

Once we move, the moment will be broken and we'll

go back to our lives, but right now? Right now, we can stay lost in each other. We can ignore the outside world, if only for a few minutes.

As her breathing slows, Riley seems to come back to herself and she pulls away. "We should get some sleep."

I nod, rolling away from her, and cleaning up very quietly in her bathroom. Once my boxer briefs are back in place, I slide back into bed. "Thanks for letting me stay."

She rolls back on her side, resting her head on my chest, and I wrap my arms around her. "You're welcome. We can talk more in the morning. Goodnight, Gordon."

"Goodnight, Riley."

But I don't sleep, I can't. Not after something that cataclysmic. Reconnecting with Riley was life altering, and I can practically feel the tethers pulling between our souls.

I lay awake the rest of the night, holding Riley close and watching her sleep. When morning comes and the alarm goes off I know things will change, and I want to make sure I don't miss another precious second.

Especially if, with so many complications wrapped around us, this is the only night with her I'll get.

29

GORDON

Foster: I heard congratulations are in order.

Tag: You shall from here on be known as Daddy Gordon.

Me: Did you guys seriously put me in a group chat?

Foster: You're welcome!

Rhett: I just want everyone to know I was put here against my will.

Foster: Well, you are going to have a baby soon, so I think that gives you a solid place here in the Baby Daddy chat.

Rhett: Please don't call it that.

Me: That's the worst name ever.

Group chat name changed to The Baby Daddies

Me: I hate all of you. Can I leave the chat now? How did you all find out about this anyway?

Tag: Absolutely not, Daddy Gordon. Obviously, I overheard your sister and Linc talking about it after the game last night. She was a little upset still, but also very excited.

Foster: And then the rest of us were really excited.

Rhett: No offense, but I didn't care.

Foster: You're not fooling any of us. You shed a tear when you found out. Your impending fatherhood is turning you into a bit of a sap.

Rhett: I'm going to turn you into a bit of a sap next time I see you. Don't think sleeping with my sister is going to give you any special treatment.

Foster: That's not all I do with your sister.

Me: As lovely as it is to watch you all talk back and forth, I really have some work I've got to be doing. Shouldn't you all be enjoying the beach, or I don't know, getting a workout in before the game tomorrow?

Tag: I think that means he misses us. Not that I blame him—we are pretty awesome.

Tag: And you know, maybe give you some advice.

Me: You guys are going to give me advice? This oughta be good.

Tag: I mean, I did become a father last year to a nine-year-old girl.

Me: Fair.

Foster: I've got a baby in the house, although I don't expect you'll be elbow deep in diapers.

Me: She's eleven, so I'm pretty sure she's been out of that phase for a while now. But thanks.

Tag: Just remember that none of us know what we're doing.

Rhett: I don't think you ever know what you're doing.

Tag: <eye roll emoji> As parents, I mean. Most of the time we're scared shitless, and just when you think you have the hang of things, they get older and the game changes. You can't control them, no matter how much you want to.

Tag: You're not alone in this. You have us.

Foster: Between you and Dallas, now I know who the woman is.

Rhett: I always figured that was fairly obvious.

Me: I would have thought it was Lincoln.

Foster: That's because you don't like him.

Me: I don't not like him.

Tag: You did punch him in the face.

Me: <shrugging emoji> He deserved it at the time.

Foster: When do you get to meet your daughter?

Me: Tomorrow.

Tag: Good luck.

Foster: You're going to be a great dad.

Me: I sure hope so.

30

RILEY

"I**T'S SO COOL YOU WORK HERE.** H**OW DID YOU GET US A**
private tour?" Max looks up at me, her eyes shining with
excitement as she bounces back and forth on the balls of
her feet.

There are so many possible answers to this question.
The owner is my boss, my ex-boyfriend, your long-lost
dad. The safer answer is obviously the first one, but
instead of immediately answering her very easy question,
I stand there with my mouth hanging open.

"I… uh…" I shift the gear bag holding our skates
from one shoulder to the other and unlock the door to the
back of the arena. "I know the owner."

Nailed it. I'm not nervous at all, I'm as cool as a
cucumber. You know, if that cucumber were on fire and
everything around it was burning to the ground.

I'm fine. Everything is fine.

Max follows me inside, turning to ask me what I'm sure will be another simple question I can't answer, and stops short as Gordon rounds the corner. "Oh my gosh, Mom." She pulls me beside her, the words coming out of her mouth in a rush. "Do you know who that is?"

Oh, I know exactly who that is.

And clearly I was lying to myself, because everything is not fine.

For one, Gordon is wearing a pair of jeans and a tight-fitting sweater, and holy mother of God he looks good. Like too good. I don't know what happened to the suit he normally wears, but seeing him like this, dressed like a normal human being, does something to my insides and makes me forget all about the boundaries I've been trying to put up since he spent the night.

Two, I have no idea how to introduce him to Max. Literally none. Aside from noticing how nice his ass looks in a pair of jeans, my brain is empty.

Do we tell her now? Do we take her around the arena and tell her then?

What if she hates him for not being in her life? What if she hates me for not telling her who her dad is?

These questions have been running through my mind all day and I'm not any closer to being ready for this conversation than I was this morning. I blindsided Gordon with the news he had a daughter, but the biggest blow of all is how much time has passed; time neither of them will be able to get back.

It's why I agreed to introduce them so soon. I couldn't let another day go by without either of them knowing the other.

Max deserves to know who her dad is, just like Gordon deserves the chance at a real relationship with his only child.

Still, it doesn't make this any easier. I'm so on edge, I don't know what to say, how to act. So, I take the easy way out and stand back, holding the bag while Max runs forward to greet Gordon.

"You're Mr. Benson, owner of the Devils," Max gushes and extends her hand toward him with the biggest grin on her face. "I'm Max, and I'm a huge Devils fan. I love hockey."

"I am, but you can call me Gordon."

All the air sucks out of my lungs and the world seems to slow down as Gordon smiles and shakes Max's hand. It feels like I'm having an out of body experience, and I'm not sure if I should be happy or crying my eyes out... so I settle on gawking at them instead.

"My mom and I used to watch you play when you were in Chicago." Gordon's eyes widen and he glances away from Max, raising a brow as he watches me. My face heats, his smile widens, and Max remains completely unfazed. "Your last full season you had fifty-three goals, seventy-six assists, and your faceoff percentage was almost sixty percent. I think you could have beaten it if you didn't get injured."

A flash of regret crosses his face. It's quick, and if I hadn't been watching him, I'd have missed it. His injury was a bad one, and I remember watching the TV in horror as the trainers carried him off the ice. It was the only time since his father sent those texts that I wanted to reach out, but I didn't. I convinced myself that I was the last person he wanted to hear from, that I'd only make the situation worse.

"That was the plan before I got injured," he says and gives Max a small smile. "You're pretty good with stats. I'm also impressed that you remember all that from three-plus years ago."

Max shrugs before she replies, "I have a good memory. You were one of my favorite players."

I suck in a breath and rub a hand over my chest. I don't know how Gordon still has a smile on his face when I've almost cried twice now.

"Also, I had no idea your mom watched me play. She never mentioned it."

Max shrugs again, rolling her eyes in my general direction. She's completely oblivious to the heat crawling up my neck, threatening to consume my existence. "She wouldn't. Mom likes to pretend she doesn't like hockey, but I know she does. She'll hide in the kitchen and watch the games."

"So… you wanted to show us around?" I clap my hands and gesture toward the other end of the hallway. "I believe you said something about seeing the locker room and maybe getting on the ice."

They both turn toward me, piercing me with their near identical emerald eyes. Their heads tilt to the right as they stare at me, and that damn left eyebrow goes up.

I'm not going to survive this.

"Are you really staying with us the whole time?" Max asks, peering up at Gordon, adoration written all over her face, and I really hope this news doesn't destroy that.

Gordon freezes for a second, swallowing, and I'm momentarily distracted by his Adam's apple. Which of course brings me back to the other night, him looming over me in the dark. "Is that okay?"

"It's more than okay. This is so cool."

He sighs, his body visibly relaxing before he morphs into the best tour guide I've ever had. He shows us the gym, the family lounge, and finally, the actual player locker rooms, all while Max pelts him with question after question.

I keep waiting for the other shoe to drop, for Gordon to get frustrated, but he answers every single one with a smile on his face. He's hanging on her every word. He watches her when she looks away, and I can't help but wonder what he's thinking.

Does he notice how similar they are? Is she every-thing he expected?

And Max? She's completely enamored and giving him way more attention than she's given me in the past couple of years. She's hanging on his every word, and the more I see them together, the more I know we need to clear the air.

"And this is the tunnel that will take you to the bench." Before Gordon can finish his sentence Max is gone, taking off down the tunnel and shouting for us about two seconds later.

I laugh, nudging him with my shoulder. "What do you think? Are you ready to tell her?"

"I'm ready if you are." Gordon stares after Max for several beats before shifting his gaze to mine. "She's got my eyes." He pauses, taking a deep breath. "I didn't think it was possible, but I love her already. Is that weird?"

"No," I comfort and shake my head with a smile. "She's the best parts of us."

"She's perfect, and I… I wasn't sure I was ready to be a dad. I'm still not sure I'll be good at it, but I'd like to try."

This time I can't hold back the tears and a few fall down my cheeks, but I'm quick to swipe them away. I'm not sure If I'm ready to share Max with anyone else, or if I can even let someone into our lives after being alone for so long, but I need to try.

31

GORDON

"ARE YOU READY?" RILEY LOOKS UP AT ME WITH AS much trepidation as I feel. At least I'm not the only one scared shitless.

I nod, not really knowing what else to do or say. I've played hockey my whole life, I've won two Stanley Cups, but this? This isn't like anything I've done before, and to be honest, I don't think anything can prepare you for one of these conversations. It's not like Max is still a baby, or even five or six. She's almost twelve, and according to Riley, full of opinions.

It's not like we're just having to tell her something benign, like your favorite pizza place is closing. The fact that she hasn't had a dad—or knew who I was—for over a decade is a big deal, and she has every right to be pretty damn bitter about it. Her mom kept her in the dark about who I was, and it might not have been my fault, but I was very absent from her life.

There's a good chance she's going to be pissed at the both of us because the one person who's truly responsible, the one who owes everyone an explanation—and a fucking apology—is dead.

May he rot in Hell.

As we head down the tunnel, Riley's hand brushes against mine and I curl my fingers around hers for a moment, just enough to remind myself I'm not alone.

Max is waiting for us in the player's box, leaning halfway out of it as she takes in the entirety of the arena. Her eyes are wide, and I swear I hear her mutter, *holy shit this place is huge!* I'm pretty sure I should say something about her swearing, but I don't really think anything I say matters yet. But you know, she's not wrong—this place is fucking huge.

Riley sits down on the bench and I follow suit, sitting down next to her and reaching my hand up to fiddle with my tie before realizing I'm not wearing one.

Dammit.

Now I have no idea what to do with my hands, so I settle on pulling at the collar of my shirt. It keeps them from shaking, but only for a moment, so I clasp them together in my lap.

With a heavy sigh, I glance at Riley. She's watching Max with watery eyes, and the way she's gnawing on her lower lip tells me just how nervous she is.

There's a small space between us, and I have the urge to close the gap and pull her close. I want to offer her what little comfort I have, but it's not the time. Even after spending the night with her, I have no idea where we stand. After we reunited, she closed herself back off. I don't know if it was as soul shattering for her. And the last thing any of us need is to force that conversation right now.

"Hey, Max? We need to talk to you for a few before we get out on the ice." Riley's doing her best to hold it together, but her voice cracks on the last part of the sentence.

Max turns around, and after her gaze volleys between her mom and me, she crosses her arms. "What's going on?"

I open my mouth, but quickly snap it shut when I realize I'm not sure what to say. Or rather *how* to say it. I've never even considered being a dad before, and I'd be lying if I said this wasn't a bit surreal.

Of course, I'm relieved Riley didn't have a love child with that asshole Adrian Wylder, but I'm completely out of my comfort zone. I don't know how to talk to kids. They don't typically like me, and until very recently, I didn't typically like them. But this is my daughter, and I want her to like me.

But what if she doesn't? What if I say the wrong thing? What if I hurt her feelings?

I have a feeling being a parent is going to be like running through a minefield.

"We haven't talked much about your dad over the years, and I'm sorry for that. I was under some misconceptions and I thought he knew about you and chose not to be involved in our lives." She reaches out and grabs Max's hand, giving it a squeeze. "I found out recently that's not true. He never knew about you, and only found out a couple of days ago."

"Okaaaay," Max says slowly, drawing out the word for several beats. "So my dad had no idea I even existed?"

"He didn't."

Her brows draw together and she takes a step away from Riley, her lower lip quivering. "But you knew who he was the whole time and didn't tell me?"

"I did, and I'm sorry." Riley hangs her head for a moment, wiping a few tears from her face. "I thought I was making the right decision, that I was protecting you from a deadbeat dad like mine. I just... I didn't want you to hurt like I did growing up. I wanted to protect you."

Max rolls her eyes and scoffs. She uncrosses her arms, but after leaving them hanging at her sides for several seconds, crosses them and levels her mom with a frown she clearly got from my side of the family. "You always want to protect me instead of letting me live my life. I'm almost a teenager, Mom. At some point, you need to realize I can make my own decisions."

"You're right." Riley takes a deep breath and glances toward me. Her eyes are rimmed with tears, and fuck if I don't want to take her face in my hands and wipe away all her pain. I never hated my father more than I do at this moment. He caused this. He's the reason Riley is breaking before my eyes, and Max is upset and probably confused.

"Well, yeah. That happens sometimes."

Riley gives me a small smile and my heart races as I strain to hear her over the blood whooshing in my ears. "Would you like to meet your dad now?"

"I would." Max's tone is strained, and I don't blame her one bit for being upset. I only wish my dad were here to see what he did. To see how he broke apart an entire family for fucking hockey.

It might have taken up a huge part of my life, but it's just a fucking game. It's not living, breathing, and it's certainly not made from my flesh and blood.

I look between my two girls, my fingers gripping each other so tightly my knuckles ache. I'm on the edge of my seat, and I need to hear those words. I need Riley to tell her who I am.

"Gordon is your dad," Riley says softly. "I'm sorry I didn't tell you sooner."

Max's gaze locks on mine, her eyes shining with unshed tears as emotion after emotion crosses her face. Hurt, anger, resentment, sadness... and finally nervousness. "Are you really?"

I nod my head, forcing down the swell of emotion bubbling up my throat. "I'm sorry I wasn't there for you growing up, but if I knew you were born, if you were mine, nothing would have kept me from being in your life. Your mom and I were young when we were together, and my own father thought he knew what was best for me and kept you a secret. He kept us all in the dark." I pause and take a deep breath, dispelling some of the anger coursing through me. "I'd really like to get to know you, if that's okay."

She studies my face for several seconds, and the world seems to stop. I stop breathing, Riley stills next to me, and I don't know what I'll do if she says no. Probably go cry in my office, but I wouldn't give up.

"We have the same eyes. Oh, and your middle name is Maxwell, kind of like Maxine." Max's head tilts to the side and she cracks a smile. It's small, but lights up my entire world. "Are you also weirdly good at math?"

The question is so unexpected that I can't help but laugh. "Actually, yes. I hated it, but it was my best subject."

Silence settles around us, the air thickening with tension, and Riley remains quiet so I follow her lead. Max looks off to the side of the arena, her brows crashing together, and she bites on her bottom lip—just like her mom. "So does this mean you didn't want me? Was I a mistake?"

Riley and I jump up at the same time, and the gear bag falls off the bench with a loud thud.

"Absolutely not," Riley says at the same time I spit out, "No fucking way."

Now they're both staring at me, but at least Max looks thoroughly amused. Riley, however, does not. "I think we're going to have to talk about appropriate language around the eleven-year-old."

"I'm almost twelve," Max says, her tone full of amusement as she sits down on the bench and pulls out her skates. "I've heard everything."

I don't want to know what that means or why eleven-year-olds are using that kind of language. Shit. I mean fuck. Fudge. *This is going to be hard.*

"I have one more question." She toes off her shoes and shoves them into the large duffel bag. "Well, since you're my dad and you, you know, own the Nashville Devils... do I get to come to every home game?"

"You can come to every game—" Riley clears her throat, and I toss her an exasperated look. "So long as it's not a school night and your mom says it's okay."

Riley sits down next to Max and pulls her in for a hug, whispering to her for a moment before pulling out her own skates. "Are you going to skate with us?"

I freeze, my hands raking through my hair several times.

It's a simple question, with such a complicated answer. I'd love to say I'm over my injury, that the

311

moment I crumpled down to the ice doesn't play on repeat in my head day after day, but I can't. Those few seconds changed my life, took away the only good thing I had left.

After the accident, I could barely walk, let alone skate. The season was almost over, and by the time off-season rolled around, the doctors and trainers agreed that it would take a miracle to get me back on the ice. I knew they meant being ready for a high-level NHL game, but I took it to heart.

I haven't been on the ice since. At least not on skates. And it's the one thing that scares the shit out of me. I grew up on skates. I played in the fucking NHL for eight years. Who am I if I can't skate?

But as Max looks up at me, her eyes so full of hope, I might be something better. I might be a dad to a little girl, and that beats hockey any day of the week.

Maybe as long as I have my family, I'm not alone. I'm not nothing.

Max stands, resting her small hand on my arm, and the look she gives me fills my heart with so much love, so much encouragement. "If you're nervous, you can hold my hand for a few laps."

"I'd like that." This time all the emotions crash over me, and I do everything I can not to cry on the spot.

Being a dad for five minutes is better than any goal I ever made. It's better than winning the Cup. It's everything I never knew I needed.

Lucky for me, I had a pair of skates stashed in the back of the locker room. I always told myself they'd be there when I got strong enough, when I was ready. I thought owning a hockey team and watching them skate almost every day would inspire me to get back out there. I thought they'd give me the strength I needed to push through, to regain that part of my life, to reconnect with something that was so important to me.

I've been waiting for so long to get my life back. Or I guess, start living it. Fuck. I've been waiting for so long.

Who knew all I needed was my ex-girlfriend to skate back into my life?

I grab my skates and go back to the player's bench, but instead of sitting down and immediately putting them on, I stand there for a second and watch my girls out there on the ice.

Riley and Max are skating circles around each other, both of them laughing, and both clearly in their element. Max skates like a hockey player; she's aggressive in her movements, alternating between bursts of power and coasting on her skates. Riley is the exact opposite. Every move she makes is elegant; as effortless as it is refined. She skates cause she loves it, cause it's who she is. Because it's in her blood, like I thought it was in mine.

She's so fucking beautiful.

Her red hair flutters around her shoulders, her cheeks are pink from the cool air, and even in a sweater and a tight-fitting pair of jeans, she's radiant. She always has been. I could watch her all night.

And I'm tempted, but they see me around the same time and skate over to the bench.

Max holds out her hand, gesturing for me to come join them. "Do you have your skates on yet, Gordon? We've been waiting for you. I hope it's okay I call you that for now."

"It's just fine," I reply with a nod, sitting down to quickly exchange my dress shoes for skates. "You can call me Dad if or when you're ready... I mean, if you want to."

I push myself up from the bench and walk to the edge of the rink. I stand there for several seconds... minutes, staring down at the ice while my heart races, and every breath I take feels like thousands of tiny razor blades cutting up my throat. I stand there waiting for what, I'm not sure. An epiphany? The crushing sense of dread?

Max and Riley wait by the boards, only skating over to me as soon as I raise my head. Max is the first to extend her hand and I slide mine into hers, letting her guide me out onto the ice.

Riley falls in next to me, taking my other hand and lacing her fingers with mine.

I move my right leg and then my left. I'm not going to lie, I half expected my right leg to give out, leaving me crumpled on the ice, but everything is fine. I glide forward one foot at a time, and holy shit, the cool air blowing through my hair is like a welcome home.

"You're not quite as good as Mom," Max says with a grin, squeezing my hand before letting go and skating backwards in front of me, "but maybe with some practice, you'll get there."

I throw my head back and laugh, gripping Riley's hand tightly as I let her lead me to the middle of the rink. "No one is as good as your mom."

Which isn't a lie. Riley is everything good and perfect, and I'll do anything in my power to show that I'm worthy of her. That I'm worthy of both of them.

32

RILEY

"I CAN'T BELIEVE YOU INVITED US BACK TO GORDON'S house." I glance at Max as I pull into a very long driveway, following Gordon's expensive looking Audi with the same car I had in high school. Nothing like a stark reminder that we've lived completely different lives, and aside from Maxine, have nothing in common.

I mean, look at how freaking big his house is. It looks like it's the biggest on the block, and the only thing running through my brain is, *who cleans this thing?* I'm sure he's never worried about cleaning a house a single day in his life.

We drive along the side of the house, and it just feels massive. Is this Gordon's house? I mean, I may have thought he was a bit of a pretentious prick, but this seems a bit excessive.

"Wow! This place is huge." Max jumps out of the car

—thankfully it was in park—and runs up to Gordon. "Do you live here all by yourself?"

I slide out of the SUV and hightail it over to them before Max has the opportunity to invite us to live with him too. She was real slick once we finished skating. He may not know, but she already has him wrapped around her little finger.

All it took was one look and her asking if we could come back to his house, and it was over. He looked slightly surprised, but almost immediately agreed. Still, I can't help but wonder if he had any plans. Beyond seeing him at work and knowing he goes to a sex club, I don't know much about his life.

What if he was going back there tonight? The thought of him going back there, of being with someone else, has jealousy gnawing at my insides. But you know, he's a grown ass man. What he does shouldn't be any of my business. So, why does it have my insides twisting?

"My sister lives in the main house. She's traveling with the team right now, but you should be able to meet her soon." Gordon points to the monstrosity to our left, and then to the two-story home we parked in front of. "I live in the guesthouse."

I have several questions.

He unlocks the door and ushers us inside. "Why don't I go ahead and order a pizza? I know you've got school tomorrow, and your mom and I have a full day at the office."

A fact I may have forgotten as soon as he slipped his hand in mine and didn't let go, even though he was skating just fine. Part of me wants to dissect everything and read between every line there is, while the more rational part knows he was simply holding onto me so he didn't fall flat on his face.

It was his own trepidation, not any feelings he may still have.

Right?

Max groans, flopping herself down on his couch like she's been here hundreds of times. "I don't want to go to school tomorrow." She covers her eyes and sighs dramatically, but suddenly sits straight up. "You have the new hockey all-star video game."

"Oh, yeah." Gordon rubs a hand along his jawline, studying his big ass TV, new game console, and finally, all the games stacked across his entertainment center. He can look at that while I note how good he looks with a little stubble. "I get all the games early. The guys come over and play sometimes. You're welcome to check it out."

Max squeals, jumping up from the couch, but before she takes over his entire TV set up, turns and looks at me. "Is it okay, Mom?"

Oh look, she remembers I'm here. "I don't know. Gordon was going to order food and give us a tour. Don't you want to see his place?"

She shrugs, quickly glancing around the living room

to the dining area and the kitchen. "You guys can tour the house. I'm fine here, besides, I can see the important parts, and you know I like pepperoni and sausage."

"It's fine," Gordon says, laying a light hand on my shoulder, his fingers brushing the side of my neck, and I ignore the shiver that crawls down my spine. "I can show you around. You know, if you want."

Do I want that?

Do I want to be alone with him? And more importantly, do I want to see his bedroom?

That thought has butterflies flapping around in my stomach, and my damn brain remembering exactly how it felt to have his fingers curled inside me. The roughness of his touch. The way I wanted more.

The night at the club, an absolute contrast to how he touched me earlier this week. When he moved against me in the dark, he was gentle and loving. It brought me back to a time when we were young, to when things were simple. Our times together couldn't have been more different, yet I love them both the same.

He looks so vulnerable, so open as he watches me, and right now, I don't know if I can deny him anything— which is dangerous for so many reasons. Still, I find myself nodding and standing here awkwardly as he orders dinner, and Max settles in with a video game.

While he's on the phone, I let my gaze wander, taking in everything from his dark leather couch to the small but nice galley kitchen. Not surprising, it's very clean, but also not very homey. He has no photographs, no knickknacks... really nothing beyond a few lamps.

This is where he lives, but it isn't home.

I don't know why, but I figured he'd live a much more extravagant lifestyle. I had always pictured some fancy penthouse with all this modern décor, and some big piece of art that cost more than years' worth of rent hanging from a wall. I imagined him with floor to ceiling windows, looking out over the city, with a glass of bourbon in one hand while his other was curled around a lingerie model. But no, here he is, living in a guest house behind his father's mansion. It's the total opposite of a swanky penthouse.

As soon as Gordon slips his phone into his back pocket, he gives me a smile that has my heart skipping a beat. "Are you ready?"

For a moment I stare at him, not exactly sure what I should be ready for. Gordon's green eyes are soft, and he's looking at me like I'm someone important, like I matter to him, and I find myself getting lost in his emerald gaze. There's something about him that draws me to him. He's familiar, yet different. Refined yet rugged. Hard and jaded, burned by his past, but maybe there's a chance we can both find some sort of solace, some kind of happiness.

I'm not sure if I stepped closer, or if Gordon closed the distance between us, but we're so close we're almost chest to chest. He reaches up, his hand pausing beside my face, but before he can run his hand through my hair or stroke my cheek or just put his hand down and call it a day, Max hollers at something on TV and breaks us both out of the moment.

"Yeah," I stammer, giving myself a little mental and physical shake, "let's go."

Gordon's hand finds my lower back, and even though we're both fully clothed, it feels so intimate. I can practically feel his skin gliding against mine, and I lean into his touch.

"Kitchen is over there, and there's a guest room and a full bath down that hallway to the side." He leads me the opposite direction, towards the stairs. "This is uh, the upstairs. It's nothing fancy. Another guest room, a bathroom, and a little sitting area."

Step by step we make our way upstairs, and by the time we reach the landing at the top of the stairs, I'm afraid my heart is going to burst out of my chest.

"Where do you sleep?" I didn't mean to ask him that question, but it popped out of my mouth before I could stop myself.

His fingers flex against my back and he exhales a choppy breath. "My room is up here too. It's nothing fancy like in the main house, but it has a great view."

As soon as I walk into his space, I do see a great view, but I don't think it's the one he's talking about. A king size bed is in the center of the room, complete with slightly rumpled sheets. I can imagine waking up in this bed, Gordon's legs tangled with mine, and his lips at my neck. I can see myself holding onto his wooden headboard, riding his face until I come all over it. I can picture him tying me up to all four corners, blindfolding me, and edging us both for hours. And then there would be the lazy Sundays and late nights were he would make love to me for hours. His touches would be unhurried, and we would take our time exploring—

"Riley?" Gordon has crossed the room and is staring at me, brow raised, as he holds open the door to the balcony.

Oh, yes. The view that is not his bed.

My face heats as I turn away from the bed and head his way. I swear it feels like it's getting redder with every step I take, and I keep my eyes on the floor. Definitely not on the bed. Maybe he didn't notice? Except when I get close enough to the door, I look up and see the smirk on his face. I'm so busted.

"Maybe you won't like this view as much as I thought." His fingers skate down my spine as I take a step outside, and while it's a little chilly, that's not the reason I wrap my arms around myself. If I don't, I may touch him, and that wouldn't be good for either of us.

He's so distracting, I don't notice how nice it is out here until I take a few steps away from him. Until he's no longer touching me.

There's a wooden gazebo running the length of the balcony with white lights wrapped around each individual plank, and beyond that is an unobstructed view of the Tennessee sky. We're in the backyard of the main house, but with the lights, it feels intimate.

"It's beautiful out here." I run a hand along one of the wooden posts.

"It is."

When I turn around, Gordon is staring at me and I freeze.

The air around us becomes electric, drawing us together, and before I know it, we're inches apart. My breath catches in my throat and my stomach flip-flops.

"Thank you for giving me tonight." Gordon lifts his hand, and this time, strokes a hand down the side of my face. "You've done a fantastic job with Max. She's great. Thank you for allowing me to be a part of her life."

"Of course. It's not your fault your dad's a dick."

"It probably is." His hand runs down my throat and wraps around the back of my neck. "I have no idea what I'm doing or what it takes to be a good parent."

My legs tremble and I let out a low moan as his fingers tighten. "I don't always know what I'm doing either."

He huffs a small laugh, tilting his face down toward mine. "That's what I heard parenting is supposed to be about. I don't know what I'm doing with you either."

He strokes a hand through my hair, and when I open my mouth to respond, I realize what he said. Like it truly sinks in and I take a step back, letting his hands fall back to his side.

"I'm so sorry." I take another step back, putting more much needed distance between us. "We're lost in the moment. You don't want this. Me. You're feeling good after the day with Max, and it's only natural to want to try to fix what's broken, but Gordon, despite what we did the other night, we've been done for a long time. We work together, we have a kid together. There doesn't need to be anything more between us."

Before he can respond, a car pulls up the driveway and I make my way back inside, leaving him out on the balcony.

It's better to put distance between us.

It's safe.

Practical.

I can do this. I can put one foot in front of the other and walk away.

33

GORDON

I SPENT THE ENTIRE NIGHT TOSSING AND TURNING AND barely slept at all. I kept hearing Riley's broken voice. *You don't want me. We've been done for a long time.* I get where she's coming from, I really do. *There doesn't need to be anything more between us.* But you know what, fuck all that.

We haven't been done for a long time, well, maybe she has, but I haven't. She ended things, but I never got closure, and you know, I don't think I want it.

I never forgot the little sigh she made when my hands coasted down her back, or how she opened up beneath me when I pressed my lips to hers, or how she used to say my name like a sigh—like it was a prayer, like it was *everything*.

I want that back. I want *her* back.

I want someone to actually give a shit about the real

me, who sees me for who I am and not the paycheck or the notoriety I earned when I was in the NHL. Someone who can soften my rough edges and maybe, just maybe, someone whose broken pieces line up with mine.

Yeah, it would be great for Max to have her whole family together, but that's not why I want Riley. I want Riley because I haven't been able to get her out of my mind—or out of my heart—for twelve damn years. She's the first person I think of with every high, every low. She's who I dream about at night.

She's the reason I've had a bleeding hole in my heart for over a decade.

I'll never be able to find anyone else, because Riley has always been it for me. I fell in love with her in English class our sophomore year when she gave an impressive analysis of The Great Gatsby, and I've never fallen out.

Her pushing me away when things get a little complicated isn't going to deter me one single fucking bit.

With a huge smile on my face, I pull up my email. We're the only two in the executive suites today, and she won't be able to avoid me for long.

To: RAdams@NashvilleDevils.com
From: GBenson@NashvilleDevils.com
Subject: Lunch Meeting
Miss Adams,

I know I expressed my previous displeasure at the length of your skirts, but I have since amended my opinion and would like to point out that they are no longer short enough. I'd also like to request a lunch meeting with sushi, and the contracts for the new trades coming in. And as my executive assistant, I could use your opinion and your help organizing an open skate day for the low-income children I'm helping with my charity, as well as ideas on getting businesses to donate the money to provide skates and hockey gear for the kids.

Best,

Gordon Benson

To: GBenson@NashvilleDevils.com

From: RAdams@NashvilleDevils.com

Subject: Re: Lunch Meeting

Mr. Benson,

You will be displeased to know that I will no longer be wearing any skirts to the office. Also, I don't mind emailing that information over to you, but I think a lunch meeting between the two of us is a bad idea.

Please let me know if you need anything else,

Riley

. . .

To: RAdams@NashvilleDevils.com

From: GBenson@NashvilleDevils.com

Subject: Re: Re: Lunch Meeting

Miss Adams,

But it's for the children. You wouldn't want to disappoint them, would you?

Best,

Gordon Benson

To: GBenson@NashvilleDevils.com

From: RAdams@NashvilleDevils.com

Subject: Re: Re: Re: Lunch Meeting

I'll be there at noon.

Riley

34

RILEY

IT'S 12:05 AND I HAVE THE SUSHI, THE CONTRACTS FROM the four new trades—which yes, could have been emailed—my laptop, a notepad, and more butterflies in my stomach than I know what to do with.

I'm not sure how I'm supposed to eat... Or look at him... Or do my job... Or basically do anything that passes as a functional human being. Not when he looks at me, and certainly not when all I can think of is Gordon putting his hands on me.

Clearly, I need more time before I go in for this meeting.

Time I don't have, because I'm already six minutes late.

Dammit.

We'd better be doing things for the children, or I'm going to be mad.

I gather everything and very slowly make my way down the hallway. There may be a point where I literally drag my feet, but nevertheless, I find myself standing in front of Gordon's office only one-and-a-half minutes later.

We haven't seen each other since last night, since he and Max peppered each other with questions over pizza while I avoided all eye contact. Not sure how I'm going to manage avoiding it today, in his office, where there will only be the two of us. Maybe I can focus on my laptop the whole time.

His door is open and I hesitate outside, completely distracted as Gordon leans over his desk, inspecting something that doesn't matter. His jacket is off and his sleeves are rolled up to his elbows. I'm really not sure when forearms became so damn delicious, but this is the world I live in. And the best thing? Or wait, maybe the worst. It's his black tie falling forward and brushing the desk. It's completely innocent and shouldn't be flipping my stomach and tying my insides in knots, but I just want to grab that tie and pull him to me. I want him to take it off and tie me up... I want... I want to get back to a life where I'm not fantasizing about my ex-boyfriend every time I see him.

Of course, that's when he looks up, his gaze working it's way from my heels to my skirt—an appropriate length one—lingering on my chest, and finally meeting mine. His eyes darken with a hunger I'm going to assume is for the sushi, and as he pushes his sleeves over his elbows, I think my mouth drops open—but only for a moment and then I recover, snapping it shut. Except Gordon caught the whole thing, if the smirk on his face is any indication.

I duck my head, my cheeks flaming, as I make my way over to his desk. The opposite side of where he's standing. I do my best not to make any more eye contact as I put down all of my things and unpack our food.

"Are you going to avoid looking at me this entire lunch meeting?" he asks, grabbing the container with his shrimp tempura roll and popping one in his mouth.

"No," I mumble, opening up my Diet Coke and taking a large sip. "Just most of it."

His laugh rumbles right through me and I take another sip, pretending it doesn't affect me in the slightest. "You have those contracts?"

"Sure do." I hand him the stack of papers before adding, "I could have emailed them to you, you know."

"Oh, yeah. I know." He eats another piece of sushi, his smirk widening. "But what fun would that be?"

I grumble to myself, snatching my sushi and eating a large piece, waiting somewhat patiently for him to read through the contracts on our newest acquisitions. "With these new players, you have a good shot at the playoffs." Gordon grunts, reading through the next page. "I mean, that is still the goal, right. Making the playoffs?"

He glances at me and winks. "Was that hockey pun intentional?"

"No."

He eats a few more pieces of sushi, shuffling through the papers, and taking a large drink of his water before looking directly in my eyes and simply saying, "No."

My brows draw together as I stare at him, waiting for some sort of explanation, but he remains silent. "No, what?"

"I mean making the playoffs isn't the main goal." He says this so casually, like he's not talking about the fate of his team. "Or at least it's not mine. Not anymore."

I rear back, nearly choking on a piece of tuna. "What? How is that not the main goal? Isn't that what we've all been working for?"

"Yes, but also no." He pops another piece of sushi in his mouth and smiles. I want to slap it right off his face.

"You're impossible," I groan, taking out my laptop and the notepad. "If you're not going to give me any actual answers, I'm not sure if we're going to get anything done. Didn't you want to talk about the charity?"

"We will."

I groan again, louder this time, and violently spear a piece of sushi with my chopsticks. "Again, you're impossible."

"So, you said." Gordon leans forward and smiles. "You're not asking the right questions, Firefly."

I huff a breath and sit back, crossing my arms and pinning him with a glare. He's lucky I'm not tossing a piece of fish at his forehead. He's five seconds away from being slapped with a piece of salmon. "We're here to work, Gordon, not play games."

"You know, for the first time in pretty much forever, I really don't feel like working. Can you pass me a miso soup? Let's talk about your skirt instead." He grabs the container of soup from me and looks at me expectantly. "It seems a bit long."

Does Gordon really think I'm going to sit here and have a conversation with him about my skirt? There are literally hundreds of things we can talk about, and the length of my skirt is not one of them.

I'm not sure what the hell was in that shrimp roll he ate, but he seems to be having a severe reaction. A severe personality reaction. I should really get back to my desk, get on the old Google search, and see if it's something permanent.

"Well, this was a great chat and I hate to leave you to it, but I'm going to. I've got so much work to do at my desk, or you know, anywhere but here. I'll see you at dinner on Sunday. Max is really looking forward to meeting your sister." I'm sure he still has that stupid ass smile on his face, and you know what? He can smile in here all by himself where I don't have to see it.

I pack up my unused notepad, laptop, and grab what's left of my Diet Coke. He can have the rest of our lunch; I seem to have lost my appetite. He makes some kind of protesting grumble, followed by an exaggerated sigh, both of which I ignore as I get up and head for the door.

Except that he's here, right behind me, placing a light hand on my shoulder to stop me.

I close my eyes for a brief moment and say a silent prayer for anyone who's willing to listen. "Please let me go."

"Never," he says softly, spinning me around, taking the stuff from my hands and putting it on the floor next to us. "Riley, I—"

"Gordon." I take a small step back and put my hands up between us, doing my best to keep my voice from wavering. "You're my boss and Max's dad. Things are already complicated as it is. Last night—"

"Last night you said some stuff, and I'd like to set a few things straight." He closes the distance between us, grabbing my hands and holding them to his chest. "You assumed I don't actually want you outside of the fact you're Max's mom. You said we've been done for a long time. You said there doesn't need to be anything more between us, but there already is."

"Gordon…" I try to pull away, but he holds my palms over his heart.

His voice is raspy, raw, and when he speaks, it has *my* heart beating rapidly in my chest. "Tell me you don't feel anything for me."

I open my mouth, but I'm not sure what to say. We've already had so many lies pulling us apart throughout the years, and denying that I feel anything would just be another one on the list. Gordon makes me feel so many things. He makes my heart race, my stomach flutter, and my insides twist into knots. He makes me feel like I'm right back in high school, like I'm a sixteen-year-old girl with a crush. He makes me have hope, makes me think I could be happy, and dammit, he makes me dare to want more than I already have.

"That's what I thought." He brushes his lips across my forehead and links his fingers with mine. "I've never been done with you. You might have moved on, but I never did. I fell in love with you our sophomore year, and you buried yourself so deep in my heart, I've never been able to get you out."

"Gordon..."

His name is barely a whisper, and before I can take another step back, he does. My hands tremble as they fall and I clasp them in front of me, my feet frozen to the floor.

He never moved on?

I really should turn back, but Gordon pins me in place with the emotion swimming in his green eyes, and I have to know what he's going to say. If this is true. I watch him, both confused and fascinated as he loosens his tie, pulling it from his neck and tossing it behind him.

This is so out of character for him. He's not the kind of guy who strips in his office for no reason, yet here we are. He doesn't break eye contact, nor say another word as he unbuttons his shirt, his fingers starting at the top button and working their way down his torso.

My breath catches in my throat as a bit of ink is revealed on the left side of his well-defined chest. My fingers itch to trace the bold yet intricate pattern circling his pec.

This is just another stark reminder of all the time that's passed us by, of the things I missed out on—the things we don't know about each other.

He shrugs out of his shirt, and tosses it haphazardly behind him. It falls to the floor in a heap, but that's not what has my attention. This time my breath doesn't just catch in my throat, I can't breathe *at all*. I can't think. I definitely can't move. Holy shit. *Holy shit.*

"Is that…?" I point a shaky finger at his chest, at the black and gray tattoo directly over his heart.

A small smile plays across his lips as he runs a hand over the ink and across his chest. "A firefly."

"When… when did you get that?" My voice wavers and cracks, my eyes burning with unshed tears. *Has he had that the whole time?*

"Right after I won the Stanley Cup. Well, the first time."

I gasp, my eyes widening as I stare at the firefly directly over his heart; the one thing that symbolizes me permanently on his body. And yes, it's been on his chest the whole time, and he never said a thing. And Tuesday night, it was dark. I couldn't see a thing. "But that was…"

"Four and a half years after we broke up. I never stopped loving you, Riley, never stopped thinking about you. You were there for all my highs, all my lows. You were my last thought before I went to sleep every night, and my first when I woke up."

My head spins, or maybe it's the room around us.

He frames my face with his hands, grounding me, keeping me in the present. "I've loved you for fourteen years, and I don't see myself stopping anytime soon."

"But, Max?"

"Max is the best thing that ever happened to me. But you? Riley, you're a part of me, you're the other piece of my soul. You're the light in all the darkness that surrounds me." Gordon leans his forehead against mine, his eyes almost pleading. "You own me, and you always will. The other night with you was like a reawakening. It cemented how much we belong together."

I have no idea what to say, but I can't go any longer without touching him, so I push to my tiptoes and press my lips to his.

35

GORDON

Holy fuck.

I feel like I've been waiting for this for days...years. Things between us have shifted, deepened. And maybe, just maybe, there's a chance we can make things right. That she'll let me try to mend the pieces of our broken hearts.

With a groan, I take over the kiss, licking along the seam of her lips until she opens beneath me. I tilt her face, changing the angle to deepen it, sliding my tongue against hers, and I swear it's like fireworks are going off around us.

It's like my entire life has done nothing but bring me to this moment.

The past—all the pain, the suffering, all the goddamned agony I felt over the years was worth it, because it brought me here. It brought Riley back to me.

I pull her to me, pressing her body against mine, and I can't get close enough. I need more of her, more of this. Riley has absolutely destroyed me in the best way, and I love this woman. I love every single thing about her, everything from her smart mouth to the dedication she has to those around her. But I can't tell her, not yet. She's not ready. Instead, I pour every emotion—all the love, the longing, the devotion—all the things I feel for her into the kiss.

I fuck her mouth, and it's not nearly enough.

She answers my kiss with her own, so full of passion, of desire, and I know she hasn't let me go either. Not completely. She meets me stroke for stroke, her nails digging into my shoulders. She holds me in place, but I'm not going anywhere. Not when she's driving us both into a frenzy neither one of us will be able to come back from.

Even if there's a small part of her that still loves me, I can work with that. I can show her how well our bleeding hearts beat together, how we're each other's missing half.

I wrap her hair around my fist and pull, forcing her heated gaze to mine as I break the kiss. "There's no one in the office to hear your screams, Firefly. It's just you and me." I run my other hand down her body, loving the little sighs and whimpers that escape her lips. "I only got a little taste of this pussy, and I'm fucking starving."

"Oh, yes," she groans, her hands moving to the front

of my pants, but I bat them away. Right now, it's not about me, and she'll understand soon that she may own me completely, but she's not the one in charge here.

I may have been gentle the night I showed up at her doorstep, but I can't be tonight.

It doesn't matter how hard I try to fight it, the dominant side of me is fighting to get out. Her brightness calls to that darker side of me. A side that wasn't there when we were younger, a side that came out shortly after I joined the NHL and needed a healthy outlet for my aggression. I'm not sure how she'll react, although if her reactions to me at the club are any indication, she'll be on her knees the second I tell her to drop.

I will hear the words, *yes, sir*, coming from her pretty lips before the night is out.

She lets out a disgruntled curse and I smirk, releasing her hair to yank her skirt above her waist. "As much as I'd love to slide into your tight little cunt and fuck us both into oblivion, it'll have to wait." I lean forward and kiss down the length of her throat. "It's been way too long since I tasted heaven, and I can't go another second without tasting your pussy."

"Gordon—"

"Be a good girl and hold on to the doorframe."

Her answer is a whimper that dies on her lips as I fall to my knees, gripping her hips and holding her in place as I press a light kiss on the inside of her thigh. I move to her other leg, gently dragging my tongue up and down her soft skin, moving close to the black lace covering her dripping pussy, but not touching it. It's where we both want me to be, and I know I'm torturing us, but between the noises clawing their way out of her throat and the way her legs tremble, it's worth it.

She groans, rocking her hips, trying to get me to move higher, press harder, but I resist, teasing the edge of the black lace with my fingers. Her hands sink into my hair, her nails raking against my scalp, and she pants my name.

Fuck. She's so desperate for my touch I almost come undone, but I can't lose control, not yet.

I press one last kiss on her upper thigh, right along the edge of her thong, before I pull the damn thing from her body and toss it behind me. Riley cries out, her hands tightening in my hair as I lick the length of her slit. Just as good as I remember. I could eat her pussy for fucking days, and when we get a chance, I just might.

I flick her clit with my tongue a few times before sucking it into my mouth and raking it with my teeth.

My name is a pretty prayer on her lips as she bucks against my face.

Her legs tremble, and she's pulling my hair so hard she might rip it out, but nothing is going to stop me from eating my goddamn meal until she comes all over my face.

"Fuck. Gordon. Oh, God."

I hike one of her legs over my shoulder, working her

clit at a relentless pace. With a growl that vibrates right through her, I slide two fingers inside her tight pussy, fucking her fast and hard. Fucking her like she's mine.

Riley is fucking drenched, and I can't wait to feel her choking my cock.

She whimpers and moans, cries out my name, and begs for release. I increase my pace, thrusting my fingers in and out of her slick cunt. She leans back, her hands leaving my hair, and slam on the doorframe.

Her thighs shake, but I don't let up. I alternate short licks and suction, I increase the pressure so hard she can barely stand, and then I let off just for a moment, just enough to keep her on that edge without going over.

It's been so long, too long, and I want everything from her. I want her pleasure, her cries, her orgasms. I want her damn heart, and I have no intention of giving anything back.

"Please. *Please.* Fuck, Gordon." She's not screaming my name yet, so it's not enough. But fuck, she's so pretty when she begs. I can't wait to see her on her knees, begging for my cock.

I suck her clit into my mouth and curl my fingers, rubbing against the spot I know will tip her right over the edge into oblivion. Her leg gives out, but I keep her against me. I don't stop, I don't let up, and seconds later, her entire body spasms and she screams my name.

It's music to my ears.

Her pussy squeezes around my fingers, and the high

heel she's wearing is digging into my back, but I don't dare move. I'm not ready to let her go. I circle her clit, the movements light, and slowly pump my fingers into her as her body trembles and then stills.

With a groan she collapses against me and I catch her, maneuvering her so she's sitting in my lap. Her cheeks are flushed, her eyes, more green than blue today, are clouded with lust, and she lets out a low moan, resting her head against my chest.

"Fuck, Gordon, I…" she trails off on a sigh, her hand brushing across the tattoo I got for her.

I press a kiss to the top of her head. "I know. It's always been you, Firefly."

36

RILEY

FIREFLY.

His light in the dark.

When we were in high school, Gordon used to say I was his light, the one bright spot in his life, his beacon of hope that there was something more out of life, something I had to destroy when I ended things with him.

But four years after I broke us apart, he got a firefly tattooed right above his heart. *It's always been you, Firefly.* He never moved on. He never stopped loving me. Like me, he put on a mask, he pretended he was fine, even though living every single fucking day without him, thinking he'd dismissed me, was agony.

Something inside me died the day I walked away from him, but now it's wide awake, ready to give him another chance.

"Gordon?" I lift my head from his chest, brushing my lips across his. "I want you."

I want to feel him inside me. Fuck, I want to feel him everywhere. I want him to burrow under my skin and brand himself on my body. He owns me, and if I'm being perfectly honest with myself, he always has.

Even when I told myself to forget about him.

My nickname might be tattooed on his chest, but his name has been seared on my soul since we were sixteen.

"Are you done running from me?" he asks softly, his hands running down my back, and I lean into his touch.

"I'm not running anymore, Gordon."

He nods, rising from the floor and helping me stand. I take a moment to drink him in. His hair is perfectly disheveled, despite being pulled in multiple directions. Oh, and did I mention he's shirtless? I was so distracted by the tattoo, I didn't notice how broad his chest is, how defined his abs are. His shoulders are divine, and then there's the perfectly distinguished V that disappears into his dress pants.

He looks like a living, breathing hockey God.

Not that he didn't look good all those years ago, but he's so much bigger than he was back then, and I want to explore every ridge of muscle. I want to peel off all the clothing from his body and lick every single inch of skin, to reacquaint myself with his body.

I can't believe I left the lights off last time. *What was I thinking?*

"Strip."

My gaze shifts to his at the drastic shift in his tone, and it's like my entire body snaps to attention. It's also when I realize I'm standing here in his lap with my skirt bunched around my hips and my panties nowhere to be seen. Despite having his face buried between my legs only moments ago, my cheeks heat and I quickly straighten my skirt.

He doesn't move or say anything further, but as I sit here studying him, his eyes harden and his lips press together in a flat line.

"When I tell you to strip, I expect you to do it." His words demand obedience, and there's something about the intensity of his voice and the way he watches me that has me spurring to action, unbuttoning the front of my blouse.

It seems his physique isn't the only thing that's changed.

This is a whole new side to Gordon, and good lord, I'm not upset by it. I want to comply. I want to please him.

And I'm not sure I can explain why, considering I've never wanted to please anyone.

He moves to lean back against his desk, watching me as I shrug off my shirt and drop it beside me. I move to take a step toward him, to help him get out of those uncomfortable looking pants, but he lifts a brow and pins me with a glare. "Did I tell you to come over here?"

I freeze, reaching behind my back, undoing my bra, and dropping it to the floor with my blouse. My skirt quickly follows, and I stand in front of him completely naked. He hasn't moved a muscle, unless you count the one clenching in his jaw.

His feral gaze doesn't leave mine as he stalks toward me, and I hold my breath as he circles me.

"You're a goddamn dream come true, firefly." His voice is raw, heavy with emotion. "I didn't think it was possible for you to be more beautiful than you were before."

I huff a quick laugh. "I don't know about that. I have stretch marks now."

His hands settle on my stomach as he peers down at me. "The imperfections make you perfect. Fucking look at what you do to me." Gordon toes off his dress shoes, and in what seems like one swift movement, takes everything else off. "Look at how hard you make me."

He takes his dick in hand, giving it a hard squeeze, and I nearly swoon. I wasn't ready, and damn, I can't help the wobble in my legs. He doesn't need to tell me to drop to my knees, I'll do it willingly. It's been way too long since I've felt him, had him in my mouth.

Fuck me. I almost forgot how long and girthy his cock is.

And holy shit… is he pierced?

Oh. My. God. Gordon Maxwell Benson, my ex-boyfriend, my boss, has piercings going through his cock.

We are never having sex with the lights off again. *How did I not notice those?*

There's a metal barbell running from the tip of his dick to the top of his shaft, a second one running across the underside just below his head, and a third one at his pubis. I've never seen anything like this in person, and I want to know how they feel running along my tongue.

His fingers caress the metal as a smirk spreads across his face. "Don't worry, Firefly, you'll get a chance to suck my dick, just not right now."

"I said that out loud?" I bite my lower lip, my gaze moving back to his gorgeous cock.

"You sure did. Now, I'm going to need you to lean over my desk. I can't wait another second to bury myself inside you."

I rush to comply, leaning over his desk, and wait for him to impale me. Only he doesn't. Instead, his hands coast up my back and around to my breasts. He gives them a hard squeeze, twisting my nipples between his fingers, and I cry out. The heady mixture of pleasure and pain has my thighs clenching together and my nails digging into his desk. He circles them before giving the buds another pinch, running his hands down my stomach.

"Fuck, Riley," he groans as his finger sweeps through me, and I arch my back against him. "You're so wet."

His fingers work my clit, and my legs are already trembling with need. "I want to feel you inside me."

"You better hold onto something, Firefly." Gordon drags his teeth over my neck, right where my pulse is going crazy, and bites down. "I've been thinking about you every second of every day. It's been twelve years since you truly surrendered yourself to me and I can't promise I'll be gentle." My thighs clench again, and as a shiver works down my spine, he smiles against the curve of my shoulder. "But you don't want me to be gentle, do you?"

Fuck, I don't. I want to be used, to be fucked so hard I can't stand, to feel him with every single step I take tomorrow. I want to know he's destroyed me.

He grips the back of my neck, pushing my face to the desk as he thrusts forward, burying himself inside me.

He feels so damn good, the bite of pain with every deep stroke only intensifies the pleasure I feel. The piercing on the underside of his shaft rubs against this spot that has me whimpering and clutching at the desk. It's too much and not enough at the same time. I need more of him; I need him to move faster. Fuck me deeper.

"Riley…" The way he growls my name has me pushing back against him, meeting every thrust with one of my own. "Why does it feel like it's been so damn long?"

His head falls to the middle of my back and he places a gentle kiss along my spine, a stark contrast to his hips as they piston in and out of me.

With another growl he pulls my hair back, forcing my head to lift slightly, just enough to watch our reflection in the window, to see him lose control. He quickens his pace, fucking me so hard papers go flying off the desk. As do multiple pens. And the lamp. But he doesn't let up. He doesn't stop. His other hand digs into my hip as he holds me in place.

His piercings are so deep inside of me, dragging against spots I didn't even know existed, and I can't help the cry that echoes through the room.

This isn't just another reconnection, it's a claiming.

There's no way I can go back to a life where this, *him,* doesn't exist. For the first time in forever, I let go of all my worries and I just feel.

Only Gordon has made me feel so good. So full. So used. So absolutely shattered.

His gaze meets mine in the window's reflection as he destroys me in the best way. His eyes are absolutely savage, yet they remain focused on me.

His hips snap forward, his hand tightens in my hair, and he fucks me at a furious pace. He groans and growls as I whimper beneath him. My legs quiver and shake, my pussy flutters around him, and I know I'm close.

I cry out his name, and fuck, he runs his tongue along

his bottom lip and releases my hair to grip my throat. He squeezes tight enough that I see stars around the periphery of my vision, and changes his angle so his piercings drag against that spot that drives me fucking wild.

I can't hold back and neither does he, fucking me with wild abandon.

My entire body trembles, and I clamp down around him as he gives my throat another squeeze. An orgasm rips through me, tearing my soul from my body, and I swear I black out for just a moment. I buck against him. I scream his name. I come completely undone.

Gordon curses, biting down on my shoulder as he thrusts deep inside me and stills.

I let my head fall back to the desk, my breath heaving, and his hands come down on either side of me, no doubt supporting his weight so he doesn't crush me to the wood. He rests his head on my shoulder, and we stay like this for several minutes.

With a heavy sigh, he bands his arms around my waist, and we both collapse in his chair. His cock is still half hard inside me, and that's when I realize we didn't use a condom.

"Gordon," I mutter and crane my neck to peer up at him, "we didn't use a condom. I'm on the pill, but—"

"I'm clean. I haven't been with anyone since moving to Nashville," he says quietly, letting the words fall between us.

My brows draw together and I turn toward him, or at least as much as I can with him still seated inside me. "You haven't had sex in over three years? But the club— Onyx?"

He sighs again, his arms wrapping around me, and he kisses the top of my head. "I just go to watch. Pathetic, I know. But I just… you were the first person I was with at the club."

My heart stutters in my chest and I relax against him. "I was tested last year, but I haven't been with anyone in a while."

"Good. I like the idea of you dripping with my cum."

He must really like the idea because his cock hardens inside me. I arch against him and swivel my hips, but his arms tighten around me, holding me in place.

"I'll fuck you in a minute, just let me enjoy the moment." His lips brush along the shell of my ear, and his hands trail up to cup my breasts.

I let out a low moan, letting my eyes flutter closed. "I think we broke your lamp."

His laugh rumbles through me, and he brushes his thumbs across my nipples. "We could break everything in my office and I wouldn't give a fuck."

"I could get used to this."

"Good. I'm going to make sure to add an addendum to your contract. Fuck your boss Fridays. It'll be mandatory."

I laugh, but it quickly turns into a groan as he shifts beneath me. "Just don't send it out in an email."

"Firefly," he begins and nips my ear, his hips shifting again and I moan, that damn piercing doing things to me. "I don't give a fuck who knows about us. You're mine, and I don't plan on letting you go ever again."

37

GORDON

F OR THE FIRST TIME IN A VERY LONG TIME, I FINALLY feel like my life means something. Like I'm more than just some guy who plays hockey, or some rigid jerk who happens to own a hockey team.

I'm a dad, and that means more to me than anything in the world.

Sure, I don't want to lose the Devils to some unknown asshole, but at the end of the day, the team is my dad's legacy, not mine. Now that I have Max and Riley, I could walk away and be happy for the rest of my life.

But I don't want to give up my connection to the game, and I don't want to make that decision for my sister, so I'll still fight for it. If anything, I don't want to be forced to sell because my father is a dick and wants to dictate my life from the grave.

As of now, I've made my peace with him. His ghost and I had a long one-way conversation after I trashed his room, and while he might not be able to respond, I don't care. He used to chew my ass off and never gave me a chance to speak up or defend myself. It's about time the tables are turned.

After I went home last night, I cleaned up what was left of his room and dropped everything viable off for donations. The pieces of the letter he wrote me went in the trash—along with all the alcohol in the house.

I refuse to be like him.

He may have had a big ass fancy house, an expensive car, and an even more expensive drinking habit, but he had no one.

He died alone.

Really, that's his legacy, but it won't be mine.

I walk into the small community arena and make my way over to the ice. There are so many medium-sized kids out there on the rink, all wearing helmets, that it's almost impossible to pick out Max.

The kids look like they're running through serpentine type drills, winding around a cone in the corner of the rink, another one toward the center and then shooting toward an empty net. They're not terrible, but it's the first practice of the spring league, so I'm not expecting anything stellar. But before I can turn around and look for Riley, one of the players rounds the second cone at an impressive speed and sends the puck flying into the back of the net.

That was a good shot.

And the red hair sticking out of the back of her helmet tells me I've just found Max. My chest swells with pride, and it's this exact second I know I'm not like my dad. I don't think he felt that for me once. Max could be the worst player out there and I'd be proud.

She spots me as she gets back in line and waves my way before sending another quick wave to someone in the bleachers.

Riley.

I spot her almost immediately, a few rows back from the ice. Her hair is pulled up in a messy bun, her cheeks are slightly pink, and she's wearing a faded Devils hoodie and jeans. She's a fucking knockout.

She gives me a shy smile, and I head her way.

This is my legacy—my girls.

Not a hockey team. And certainly not an alcoholic, abusive father.

I smile at a few of the other moms as I sit down next to Riley, brushing my leg against hers. "Fancy meeting you here."

"Small world," Riley muses. She glances at me for a brief moment before her gaze swings back to Max. That bottom lip is between her teeth and she wrings her hands in her lap, her nervous energy almost palpable.

"We should meet up more often." I reach over,

stilling her hands with mine and link our fingers together.

It's a little different being on this side of the glass, so close to the ice.

Normally when I'm in the owner's box, there's a certain level of separation between me and the team. I'm watching them, yes, but the distance doesn't make me feel as connected. But here, I'm invested. I'm not an owner, I'm a father.

"I wasn't expecting to see you until Sunday dinner." She glances between me and our entwined fingers and promptly adds, "Not that I mind having you here."

I nod toward the ice. "Max said it was her first practice and I've missed so much, I didn't want to miss any other firsts."

Her eyes widen and she mutters a curse. "I didn't think…I'm so sorry I forgot to tell you about practice today. Wait, Max told you?"

"Yeah, I gave her my phone number after our dinner the other night. I hope you don't mind."

"Oh no, of course not," she replies quickly, the words running together before she takes a deep breath. "I'm sorry, this is going to take a little getting used to. I'm not used to sharing Max with anyone. It's a little weird. Not bad weird, just weird."

"I understand. It's going to be an adjustment for the both of us." I pull my gaze from Riley, back to the ice just in time to see Max fly through the cones and bounce the puck off the crossbar, right into the net. "Our daughter is excellent. She clearly takes after her dad." I huff a laugh, bringing our hands into my lap and pulling her close—or as close as I can get without being indecent. "You've done this by yourself for a long time, and you know, I've been doing some thinking, and I want to apologize."

Her brows draw together. "Apologize?" Her voice rises, earning us a couple of looks from the other parents. I give them a small wave and a look that tells them to mind their own fucking business. This time when she talks, she leans in closer and whisper-yells, "For what? You didn't do anything."

"I know, but my father did, and unfortunately, he's a part of me, just like Max is. For years I let that man run my life, and I should've known better than to believe him when he told me you jumped into bed with Wylder." I hang my head, stemming the irrational anger at the thought of him laying a finger on my girl. "I should have fought for you."

Riley doesn't respond right away. She pulls her bottom lip back between her teeth, and the two of us fall into a comfortable silence. We watch practice for a few minutes, the coach running them through the cones one last time before they work on puck passing.

Max is great out there, and even though this is her first time officially running through any of these drills, she's a natural. She excels at everything out there on the ice. I can't wait to get her in the rink with some of the players and see how she likes running through our drills. I'm sure Riley won't be a fan initially, but after talking with her neurologist, hockey isn't a limitation. So long as she's taking her medicine, getting plenty of rest, and not overdoing it with carbs, he's not concerned.

I know Riley is, and fuck, I'm scared shitless at the thought of her having a seizure in my care, but I don't want to keep her from living her life.

"I'm sorry too," Riley says softly, resting her head on my shoulder. "I should've fought harder. I should have known you wouldn't have said those things, and you'd never use your dad's money to pay me off. I wish I had trusted my gut and flown my ass all the way to Boston to demand an explanation."

"I would have begged you to take me back."

She laughs, brushing back a lock of hair that fell from her bun, and I itch to take the whole thing down and run my fingers through it. "So... what now? If we're going to be together, should I find a new job?"

"No," I grunt, using my free hand to tip her gaze to mine. "Despite my previous protests, I enjoy seeing you every day. And if you quit, there's a chance Dean might kill me."

Which isn't a lie. Dean will kill me; he told me so earlier this week.

"So, you're not going to get sick of seeing me every day?"

"Nope."

"You sure?" She's trying to keep her tone light, but I can hear the hesitation underneath.

I turn to face her, running a hand along her cheek and tracing her bottom lip with my thumb. "I went twelve years without you in my life, Firefly. I'd be happy to not go another day without you in it. And it would be great to have you by my side as the season comes to an end."

Riley nods, nipping at my thumb, and I can't stop myself from giving her a very quick and very chaste kiss. "I'm assuming you have a plan there."

"I'm going to let Dean, Mick, and the other coaches do their jobs. My dad was a big micromanager, and I don't want to be like that. I have good people in place, and staying back from the games this week has given me some perspective." That, and trashing my dad's room. "I don't need to be involved in every little decision. If they need me, they know where to find me."

"Wow." She blinks a few times, staring at me, and I'm going to pretend not to be offended that she's this surprised. "That's very adult of you."

"I am a dad now," I wink, a smirk spreading across my face. "I may even leave the office by five."

She gasps, putting a hand over her heart, and laughs. "Dean's not going to know what to do if you leave the office before he does."

"I feel like that's a Dean problem, not a Gordon problem."

Practice winds down and Riley jumps up, pulling me after her to greet Max by the locker rooms as the kids shuffle off the ice. We're a little slow to get there—a few of the other dads recognize me and pull me aside to introduce themselves, and, of course, give me their opinion on the new trades, and how the rest of the season will shape up.

By the time I get to my girls, Max runs up and gives me a tight hug.

"You made it!" she beams up at me, nudging the blonde girl next to her. "I told you he was really my dad." Her eyes widen and she slaps a hand over her mouth. "I hope it's okay to call you that."

I want to rejoice, high five all the other parents, light up a cigar, and tell everyone I'm a new dad, but I refrain. Barely. I manage a nod even though the rest of me is screaming, *yes*. "Of course you can." A couple of the kids do give me a high five, which I return enthusiastically. "How do you girls feel about going out to dinner tonight?"

Riley leans over Max and sniffs. "If we can get this one to a shower first, then I'm in."

Max scoffs, rolling her eyes at Riley and giving me another hug after I take her gear bag. "Thanks, Dad. I'm so glad you came to practice. It was so fun." She tosses her head back and groans. "I can't believe I've waited this long to play hockey. I can't wait to meet Aunt Jazz. I watched some of her old games last week."

"She's super excited to meet you too." Funny enough, she also threatened to kill me if I don't set up a dinner or somewhere where they can meet. "How about Monday after school? She'll be home between away games. You can meet Lincoln Dallas then, too."

"He's so dreamy."

I barely contain the growl rumbling in my chest. "He's something."

And now I guess I need to play nice with my sister's boyfriend.

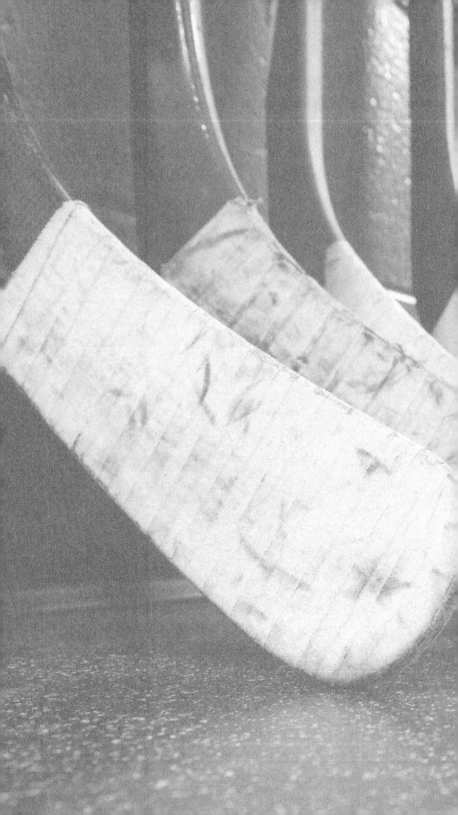

38

Ryan: Wellness check. Please respond if you're alive.

> Gordon: Have you seen anything about my death on the news?

Ryan: Uh... No

> Gordon: So you're just being dramatic. I wanted to make sure.

Gunner: <face with tears of joy emoji> <face with tears of joy emoji> Hey Ryan, need some cream for that burn?

Ryan: I hate the both of you.

Gunner: Oh, look. Now you're turning into the grumpy one.

Ryan: I stand firm in my statement.

Ryan: Also, where have you been lately? You ask for advice with your fantasy sex club fiasco—still bullshit we haven't been invited—and you've given us no update on where things are with your ex. You have no other friends, so I'm not sure who you've been talking to, but it's very hurtful.

Gunner: I get it. It's not that he's grumpy, it's his time of the month.

Ryan: Let's not bring up how mopey you were at practice today.

Gordon: Yes, let's not.

Gordon: So, uh, things here have been busy. Found out I'm a dad. Surprise. Her name is Maxine, she's named after me, even though I didn't know she existed. She's eleven, is obsessed with hockey (sorry), and way smarter than I was at her age.

Gunner: You have a kid?

Ryan: She's eleven? And you just found out?

Gunner: Fucking brutal.

Ryan: Is the ex-girlfriend the mom? Are you pissed?

Gordon: Yes and no. Look, it's a lot to go over, too much to text. How about a poker game soon?

Ryan: My house. I'll look at the game calendars and let you know when.

Ryan: And Gordon?

Gordon: Yes?

Ryan: Congrats, man. Seriously.

Gunner: Maybe you can bring her to a football game and we'll try to sway her to the good side. She's clearly been sheltered.

Gordon: LOL. My sister gets to meet her first, and then I'll think about it.

Gunner: Tell your sister I said hello.

Gordon: I will tell her nothing.

Gordon: But you can go fuck yourself.

Ryan: There's our old Gordon. <rolling on the floor laughing emoji> <rolling on the floor laughing emoji> See you soon.

39

RILEY

"HOW ARE YOU FEELING ABOUT EVERYTHING?" I ASK, meeting Max's gaze in the rearview mirror and giving her what I hope is a reassuring smile.

Except she's not the one to answer. Harper lays a light hand on my shoulder, her smile practically taking over her entire face. "I feel fine, thanks for asking. Should I be concerned? Anxious? Excited?"

I shrug her hand off and toss her one of those looks that just says, *really*? "I don't think I was talking to you. Max?"

Max glances up from her cell phone momentarily and sighs. "I'm fine, Mom."

"Are you sure?" I glance down at my GPS, taking the left turn the British man instructs me to take. "There have been a lot of changes here recently, and we haven't had a chance to talk about everything."

"I have a cool dad, and yeah, I wish I'd have known about him sooner, but it is what it is. I've got an aunt who played hockey in the Olympics. We've had Mexican food twice in one week, and I kind of own a hockey team."

Jesus. I laugh, taking the next turn, this one bringing me back into a very fancy and very expensive looking neighborhood. I've been here once, but when you're not used to it, it's a little disarming. "Your dad kind of owns a hockey team."

"Duh." Pretty sure she rolled her eyes in my general direction. "And I'm his only child." She pauses for a moment, ditching us for her phone, but then her head shoots up. "I am, right? He doesn't have any more illegit-imate children?"

"Illegitimate, now that's a word," I scoff, trying to ignore the burning jealousy coursing through my veins at the thought of Gordon literally touching anyone else. "And no."

"Then I'm good." She says this so matter-of-factly that Harper covers her mouth, muffling her laughter. "Oh, and Dad said he'd pick me up from school tomorrow and take me to practice so you don't have to worry about it."

"Is that your nice way of telling me you prefer having him there?"

"No offense, Mom, but he did play in the NHL for like, eight years."

Alright, I'll give her that. I played in the NHL for zero years, and when I show up to practice, no parents pull me aside to talk to me. Well, to be fair, since Gordon showed up both Saturday and Sunday, I've had several moms go out of their way to say hello. I just hope I don't have to remember their names, or I'm not expected to be handing out hockey tickets like they're candy.

I don't own the team. Apparently, Max does.

Harper mumbles a few choice curse words as we pull into the Benson's driveway and instead of pulling around back, I stop out front, behind what I'm hoping is Lincoln's SUV. "Seriously? This is his actual house?"

"Technically it's his dad's house," I reply and turn off the car, grabbing my purse and locking the door behind me, more out of habit than anything, because seriously, if someone wants this car, they can have it. "He lives in that guesthouse."

"It must be some guesthouse," she mutters, smoothing down her dress and joining me on my side of the car.

Max shrugs, slipping her phone into the back pocket of her jeans. "It's nothing too special. He has a pool, but it's not like one of those houses with a bowling alley or anything."

"Good to know that's what makes a house," I laugh, but it dies a slow death as I make my way up the couple of steps to the front door. "Everyone ready?"

Harper nods, clasping her hands in front of her, and

Max gives me another shrug. I guess that's as good as I'm going to get.

I raise my hand to knock, but before I can bang my hand against the wood, the door pulls open and I have to restrain myself so I don't hit Jazz in the face. That would be a poor way to start a dinner party—especially when she's the host, and even more so because this is the first time her and I have seen each other since Gordon found out about Maxine. Punching her in the face after it looks like I've been keeping Max to myself for eleven years would probably send the wrong message.

"Riley." She stares at me, tears rimming her eyes, and pulls me in for the tight hug. "I'm so sorry my dad was such a dick. I hate that he did this to all of us." She pauses and then whispers, "You're not alone anymore."

The breath stutters in my throat, and I wrap my arms around her as tears prick the corners of my eyes, and I struggle not to let them fall. But then I hear her broken sob, and I can't hold back anymore. We cling to each other, blocking the entire doorway for several minutes while her words tumble around in my head. *You're not alone anymore.*

Sure, I have Harper, but for a long time I was her caretaker, and I guess in some ways, I still am. I've been alone since I was eighteen. After my mom died, it was me. I had no one to depend on. No one to talk to. No to who would be there to help.

And now I've got Gordon. And Jazz.

I don't know why, but this is the first time it's hit me. I'm not alone.

As Jazz pulls back, I wipe the tears from my eyes and she leans down. "Hi, I'm Jazlyn."

I look into the foyer, and time seems to stand still as I lay my eyes on Gordon. He's wearing jeans and a light sweater with his hands shoved in his front pockets. He's watching us, and a tear tracks down his cheek. It's the most surreal and beautiful thing I've seen.

These are my people. My family.

"I'm Maxine, but everyone calls me Max. And this is my other aunt, Harper."

I take a step toward Gordon at the same time he takes one toward me. The air is charged, and it feels like there's a force, something bigger than us, pulling us together. His arms slide around me and he lifts me up, burying his face in my neck. I'm pretty sure one of my heels flips off, but I couldn't care less.

"Gordon, I…" My throat tightens and I trail off.

He kisses my neck, winding his fingers through my hair. "I know."

"I still love you, you know," I whisper as another tear tracks down my face. "No one could ever come close to replacing you."

He holds me closer, squeezing me tighter. "I've loved you since we were sixteen, and I'll love you until the day I die… maybe even longer."

"You guys didn't tell me I'd be ruining my makeup,"

Harper sniffs, and I feel Gordon's laugh rumbling through his chest before I hear it.

What Harper said wasn't even amongst her most clever lines, but I find myself joining in, laughing as Gordon lets me down and I find my shoe. Jazz closes the front door, and her and Max come to join us, watery smiles on both their faces.

Gordon nods toward Harper, a smirk growing on his face. "I'm sorry you didn't get the proper warning. Next time, I'll have tissues waiting at the door."

"Was that a joke?" Jazz gasps loudly, wiping away the last of her tears.

"Did Mr. Grumpy Pants just make a joke and I missed it?" Lincoln asks as he steps into the foyer wearing a frilly pink apron, and wraps his arms around Jazz.

Gordon slides an assessing gaze from his head to his toes "I'm pretty sure the joke is what you're wearing."

"Wait until you see the one I picked out for you."

"Great."

Lincoln laughs, his easygoing smile infectious as we make introductions and head into the large kitchen. Gordon comes up behind me, draping his arms around my shoulders as we stand off to the side, watching the other four fall into an easy and animated conversation.

"This house is beautiful," Harper says as she waves a hand around her. "I'd love to have a kitchen like this— and don't you go agreeing." She gives me a healthy dose of side-eye. "This would be a waste on you. You'd still burn everything."

"Rude," I mutter, pinning her with a glare. "Most of my food is edible."

Max makes a gagging sound that has everyone laughing. Again, rude.

"So…" Jazz begins and turns my way, and suddenly everyone is looking at me, and I'm not sure how I feel about it. I push back against Gordon and he merely chuckles, kissing my cheek. Nice, but it feels unhelpful. "What are your intentions with my brother? Are you guys dating?"

My gaze cuts to Max, who seems to be watching us with curious intent. "Yeah, Mom. What are your intentions with my dad?"

I swallow past the lump in my throat and twine my fingers with his. "I think I'd like a chance to be happy, and Gordon makes me happy. Is that okay?"

Max shrugs, and I swear one day that is going to be the death of me. I guess it's better than an eye roll. "I guess that's fine," she smirks before adding, "just don't do any nasty kissing in front of me."

"You got it. No nasty kissing."

Max seems content with my answer and turns back to Jazz. "Do you live here too?"

"Kinda," Jazz answers slowly, sharing a look with Lincoln, "although I think I spend most of my time at Lincoln's apartment."

"So you have this huge house that no one lives in?"

This time it's Jazz and Gordon who share a look. Gordon sighs, pulling away from me and pulls a bottle of water from the fridge, offering one to the rest of us. "This was your grandfather's house, and after he died, we just kind of moved in."

"Have you thought about selling it?" Harper asks, resting her elbows on the island and opening up a water.

Everyone seems to fall silent. The Bensons are looking at each other, and Lincoln shifts back and forth on his stool. Something tells me that if it weren't for Gordon, the house would already be on the market.

Finally, Gordon nods. "I should have sold it the day my father died, but this house became a purgatory of sorts, and I don't think I was ready to move on. I think it's time though. It's too big, and it's filled with nothing but bad memories."

He smiles at his sister, and it's like a weight has been lifted from the two of them. Their shoulders are straighter, and it seems like they can breathe a little easier.

Lincoln whispers something to Harper and excuses himself to check on the grill. Jazz swivels around, smirking at Max. "I have a few questions for you."

Her brows raise and she crosses her arms. "Go on."

"Favorite color?"

"Black."

"Music?"

"Alternative rock and nineties grunge."

Jazz nods, tapping a finger against her lips. "Hockey or football?"

"Hockey, duh." Max doesn't roll her eyes, and I'm a little surprised. "I just started playing. What was it like playing in the Olympics?"

"Epic. Did you know Lincoln played too?

"Which is why he's the best. What did you study in college?"

"Business. What do you want to be when you grow up?"

Max hums, glancing at me quickly before answering. "I think I want to be a doctor. I want to help sick kids."

My eyes widen and I swear my jaw hits the floor. I never knew Max wanted to go into medicine or work with kids. My kid is fantastic. Sure, she's only eleven and has years to change her mind, but the fact she's even thinking like this is mind blowing. And yes, this is why parents brag about how smart their kids are, this feeling right here.

The two of them exchange more rapid-fire questions and answers, and Jazz invites her to the upcoming game against Vegas, which of course, Max is ecstatic about. I'm not going to ruin the fun and tell her we were already planning on going.

Gordon makes his way back over to me, shielding his face as he kisses me on the lips. He pulls back with a smirk. "I wouldn't want to get in trouble for any of this gross kissing nonsense."

"So about that." I glance down at the floor before leaning in to whisper, "Do you think we could go to the club again? I can't stop thinking about it."

"Depends." He tucks a lock of hair behind my ear. "Are you going to sneak me in your apartment tonight for a little sleepover?"

"Maybe," I shrug, trying to act casual.

His lips graze my ear and I close my eyes as my thighs clench. There's no chance I'm not inviting him over tonight. "I'll make you a deal, Firefly. You let me fuck your face tonight and I'll fuck you in a viewing room Thursday night." I shiver and he shifts closer. "That's what you want right? You want me to fuck you where there's a chance someone might see?"

I nod, not daring to speak right now.

"Don't worry, this time I'll be prepared."

Do I even want to know what that means?

40

GORDON

THERE'S NO WAY IN HELL I'M GOING TO LET ANYONE SEE Riley's naked body, and they're certainly not going to see the face she makes when she comes.

Those belong to me, and me alone.

If my little Firefly wants to think anyone can walk in that voyeur hallway and watch as she chokes on my dick, that's what she'll think.

She doesn't need to know the hallway is conveniently closed for maintenance, and yes, I bribed the owner to make sure the door was securely locked so there wasn't a chance anyone would get to see what's mine.

Riley's been buzzing with anticipation all day, especially after we went over her limits and picked a safe word, and while I seem calm and collected on the outside, I'm anything but.

We've obviously seen each other at work all week,

but I haven't been able to fuck her as thoroughly as I want. Work has been busy, it always is after the trade deadline, and while I've spent the night at her place a few times, that's all it's been—just sleeping, and I'm eager to get back in her tight cunt.

Right now, she should be on her way here. I dropped her and Max off at their apartment about an hour ago after hockey practice. That gave me plenty of time to shower and pack a bag full of my newly acquired purchases before heading to Onyx and getting everything set up.

Almost time.

I shrug off my suit jacket, loosen my tie, and roll up my sleeves.

And then I wait.

And I wait some more. Each second that passes by sends another wave of irritation through me. Where the fuck is she? She was supposed to be here fifteen minutes ago. I give her another five, but as I get up to stomp my way through the club, there's a soft knock at the door.

I open it and nearly swallow my tongue.

Riley is in the tightest black dress ever, and I don't know if I want to rip it from her body or cover her up so no one can see her perfect curves. Her dark red hair is falling down her back in soft waves, but it's the matching deep red lipstick that snags my attention.

I hope that shit smudges.

"You're late." I cross my arms, doing my best to act insulted.

She hums, tapping her index finger against those stained lips. "Sorry, I must have lost track of time. I ran into Ian and Owen. We had a few things to catch up on."

I close the distance between us in seconds, wrapping my hand around her throat, and slamming the door shut behind her. Her eyes widen and she takes a small step back, one I match with a step toward her.

"Mention another man tonight and your pretty lips won't be the only thing that shade of red." Her mouth falls open and I take advantage of the situation, sweeping my thumb into her mouth and gagging her with it. I drag it from her mouth seconds later, swiping it from her bottom lip to her chin.

A grin stretches across my face. Smudgeable.

"You're going to ruin my lipstick," she pouts, sticking out that bottom lip, completely oblivious to the red trail underneath.

I lean in, licking the length of her throat, nipping the underside of her chin. "Nice dress. Now take it off. Do you remember what to do if you don't like something?"

"Yes," she nods. "I say peaches, and if I can't talk, I tap you twice."

I take a step back, my eyes never leaving hers as I unbutton my dress shirt and pull off my tie, tossing it on a small stack of towels. She reaches to her side, unzipping the dress, and lets it fall to the floor.

My mouth dries, and fuck, my jaw is so tight I might break my teeth.

"Where did you get that?"

"Oh, this?" She raises her brows, running her hands along the black lace covering her chest before dropping them to the matching thong and garter made from several crisscrossing straps, and finally brushing them across a pair of sheer black thigh highs. "Just something I had in my closet."

I'm definitely fucking that smart mouth of hers.

"Something in your closet, huh?" I pull off my dress shirt, toss it next to my bag, and grab a pair of leather wrist cuffs. "Turn around."

Her breath shudders and her thighs clench, but she complies. I fasten the cuffs around her, tugging on the links between them and dragging a finger down the center of her back. Riley lets out a low groan and tests the cuffs, that groan turning into a frustrated huff as she realizes how little movement she now has in her arms.

I turn her back toward me and walk to the center of the room. "Come here." She nods, stopping directly in front of me. I run the back of my hand down the side of her face. "Now, drop to your knees."

Her lashes flutter as she peers up at me and I steady her as she obeys. She glances to the mirror several feet away before her eyes flit back to me. "Is that where they're watching?"

They would be if I allowed it.

I nod, sweeping my thumb back between her lips and hooking my fingers around her chin, keeping her facing me. "Your sassy little mouth needs to be fucked. Do you want to show them how pretty you look with my cock sliding down your throat?" I move my thumb in and out of her mouth, groaning as her lips close around it and she sucks. "That's a good girl."

Biting back another groan, I pull my thumb from her mouth and damn if it doesn't make a little popping sound that has my dick twitching against my zipper, eager to get into the warm heat of her mouth.

Despite the red-hot need coursing through my entire body, I take my time unzipping my pants, loving how her little pink tongue darts out and licks along her lips as I pull my dick from my boxer briefs. A little tongue that flicks the barbells at the tip of my cock as she leans forward.

I growl, plunging my hands into her hair and wrapping it around my fist. She continues toying with my piercings, and I'm ready to leap out of my skin. She gives me one more lick, her tongue running around the head, and I can't take it anymore. With my free hand, I pull her chin down and slide my dick into her mouth.

And I don't fucking stop until I hit the back of her throat and she gags around me.

I take a deep breath, pulling halfway out before pushing back in. Tears fall from the corners of her eyes, and her dark red lipstick is smeared all around her swollen lips.

I've never seen someone more beautiful.

She swallows me down, her gaze trained on me as I tighten my grip on her hair and fuck her mouth like I've wanted to do for years.

This is both heaven and hell, a purgatory of my own making. She feels so good, almost too good, and I find myself having to hold back. I'll be damned if I'm going to cum down her throat. Right now, I want nothing more than to fill up her cunt to the brim. I want to know I'm dripping down her thighs as she puts on her tight dress and walks out of here.

I want all these motherfuckers, including the Bruiser Brothers, to know exactly who she belongs to.

She's fucking *mine*, always has been and always will be.

I wipe the tears from her face, my fingers gently brushing against her cheek, a stark contrast to how vigorously I'm fucking her mouth. She groans, and I feel it all the way to my toes. I growl, I curse, and as I feel a little zip of electricity along my balls, I pull out.

"Fuck," I groan, releasing her hair and helping Riley to her feet.

She stumbles a little but I steady her, giving her a second to catch her breath before leading her over to the bed.

"Have you ever had something in your ass?"

Her light gasp tells me she hasn't, and the flush that creeps across her cheeks tells me that she'd like to.

"But you're…" She glances down to my cock, still rock hard and coated with her spit. "You're huge."

I chuckle, pulling a small plug and a bottle of lube from my bag. "Not me—at least not yet. Trust me, I intend to fuck all your holes eventually."

A blush creeps up her neck as she eyes the plug and eventually gives a small nod.

"Be a good girl and bend over the bed for me." She quickly turns and I run a hand down her spine as she bends, tugging on the straps of her garter and the cuffs at her wrists.

I take my time, running my fingers along the cheeks of her ass, the tops of her stockings, and the straps of the garter. She sighs, leaning back into my touch, and once my patience wanes, I rip the lacy fabric of the thong.

"These were expensive!" she grunts in protest, starting to stand, but I push her back down.

"I'll buy you a hundred pairs if I get to rip them off your body." I pop open the top of the lube and drip it down the crack of her ass and coat the flared end of the plug. Leaning forward, I circle her clit with my fingers while lightly pressing the plug to her asshole. She jumps slightly, but as I increase the pressure on her clit, she relaxes. "That's a good girl, just relax."

The plug is small and slides into her easily. She pushes back against me with a strangled moan, and fuck, if I don't get inside her right now, my dick will never forgive me.

I unfasten the cuffs and flip her over on the bed. Riley shifts, most likely getting used to the small jeweled plug before watching me with rapt attention as I take off the rest of my clothes. I press a kiss to her knee, the thigh on her other leg, her stomach, and nip at the curve of her shoulder.

"Gordon, I need you." She wraps her legs around my waist, the soft silk of her stockings driving me just as mad as her whimpers. "Please, fuck me."

I tilt her face toward the mirror, sucking her earlobe into my mouth and flicking it with my tongue. "I want them to see your face as I slide my cock into your tight cunt, knowing how full you are with the plug in your ass."

We both groan as I slide into her, plunging my tongue into her mouth at the same time I thrust into her pussy. She quivers around me, her legs tightening around my hips, and don't hold back. She's so tight, so wet, and so fucking *mine*.

I fuck her into the goddamn mattress like a man possessed, like I can't get enough, and in truth, I'll never have enough of her.

I'm not just her first love, I'll be her last. Her only.

And that thought drives me to fuck her hard, fuck her deep, fuck her like I've never fucked anyone before.

Her hands are clawing up my back, they're pulling

my hair, they're clutching my shoulders. She's consuming me, my soul, and I never want it to stop.

She cries out, her entire body trembling, her cunt squeezing me so hard, and I can't hold back anymore. Her nails dig into my back as she screams my name. My balls tighten, and a tremor crawls down my spine. With one final thrust, I still, draping my body over her as I fill her with my cum.

I bury my head against the curve of her neck and wait for my breathing to slow down. When it does, I work my way up and down her throat, kissing every inch of it. "How was that for a show?"

Riley chuckles, brushing her lips across my cheek. "Show, huh? Are you saying you actually allowed people into the voyeur hall?"

"Maybe I did." I shift, pressing my lips to hers. "And maybe I didn't."

"I knew it."

"Firefly, I'd give you anything in the world, but I'm not going to share you with anyone."

Her eyes soften as she runs her fingers through my hair and down the side of my face. "Maybe I don't want to share you either."

"You'll never have to worry about that."

41

GORDON

Me: I have an emergency. Or rather a situation.

Foster: Daddy chat activated.

Tag: What is it? What do you need, Big Daddy?

Me: Jesus, please don't call me that.

Rhett: Why am I still in this chat? <meh face emoji>

Foster: I saw the size of Lucy's baby belly, and you are going to need us sooner or later.

Me: Dare I ask how Lucy is doing?

Rhett: Are you asking because you're still interested… Or because you're genuinely concerned?

Me: The second one, you asshole.

Rhett: In that case she's slightly miserable but doing well. She's happy. Excited. We've got another three and a half weeks left.

Tag: I can't wait to meet baby Remington. Hope he doesn't have your attitude.

Foster: So, boss, you had a question?

Me: I regret texting this chat. But Max is coming over and spending the night with me for the first time. By herself. Riley will be at home doing her nails with her sister.

Rhett: I don't see the emergency.

Tag: So you let her pick out a couple of movies, or since she's into hockey, you can watch one of the games tonight. You know her favorite food?

Me: Yeah, she likes Mexican food.

Tag: So have dinner ready to go, and maybe some games you can play with two people, just in case. Nothing for super young kids, and nothing that requires multiple players.

> Tag: I also have a snake you can borrow.

> Rhett: Pretty sure he has his own snake.

> Tag: You know what I meant, dick.

> Rhett: Did I, Rag? Or was it Bag? I think that was your favorite.

WITH A CHUCKLE, I SHAKE MY HEAD AND TOSS MY phone down on the couch. These guys are idiots, but they're my idiots.

I've got dinner ordered, the sports channel ready to go, a deck of cards, and a few boardgames I'm sure I'll suck at. I've also called Riley no less than three times, and might have checked with my sister twice to make sure they're on their way. Her and Lincoln took Max out for some kind of shopping expedition earlier, and I wasn't invited.

Very rude of them, I know.

I'm about to call Riley for the fourth time when there's a knock on my door. But on the other side isn't Max. It's not Jazz or Lincoln.

"What the fuck are you doing here?" I fill up the doorway, puffing out my chest, and frown.

"That's hardly a hello." David Carlisle, an old team-mate of my dad's and all-around prick smiles at me. Of course it's not friendly, it's entirely condescending. Typical.

He used to come around some when I was a kid, and when I first started playing in the NHL, I'd see him occasionally. He always had something snide to say, and I'm pretty sure he was drunk eighty-five percent of the time.

So you can imagine him and my dad got along swimmingly.

I cross my arms, doing my best to look down on him, even though we're about the same height. "I don't remember inviting you to my home."

"You mean the guesthouse in your dad's backyard?" He makes a point to look back to the main house, and when he turns around, his expression is full of disgust. "I spent twenty minutes knocking on the front door. Figures you'd want to live back here."

I don't know what this guy wants, but at this point, I don't give a flying fuck. All I want is for him to get off my fucking property as soon as humanly possible.

"As pleasant as this conversation is, I'm afraid I'm going to have to ask you to leave." I start to shut the door, but he reaches out, slamming a giant hand against the wood.

His eyes narrow on me, and he has the audacity to fucking snarl. "You don't even want to know why I'm here?"

"No."

He looks at me for a second, a smirk spreading across his face. "You sure?"

I lean forward, making sure to get right in his face.

"If you've come to pay your respects, I don't need them."

In fact, I don't need anything from this asshole. I wouldn't call him if I were destitute. He had a piss-poor attitude when he was a player, and it obviously didn't get better with age.

"The only one who will need to be paying respect is you—especially when I take that team off your hands."

No. No fucking way.

This Douchebag? This is the fucking guy my dad picked to get the team? He's selfish, arrogant, and there's no way he's getting shit from me.

I uncross my arms, my hands clenching into fists at my sides. I'd love nothing more than to punch that fucking smug smile right off his face, but I'm not sure that would be wise. "Listen, David, the team isn't for sale. And even if it were, I would never sell it to you."

"I don't really see that you have a choice." He rocks back on his heels, that damn smile covering his face. "If you don't make the playoffs, you'll be legally obligated to offer me the team."

"If." I take a step toward him, forcing him to take one back. "If we don't make the playoffs."

He laughs, it's dark, sardonic, and that smirk falls right off his face. "I'm not sure if luck is on your side, Benson. There's a chance you'll get a wildcard slot, but you and I both know it's slim."

"What I do know is that you've worn out your welcome."

David flaps his button-down jacket and opens his mouth, but whatever he's going to say, dies on his lips. Because of course, Jazz and Lincoln are right behind him, Max nestled between them. "Well, isn't this a cozy family reunion."

"Mr. Carlisle." Jazz eyes him warily, putting her arm around Max. "This is a surprise."

"A pleasant one, I'm sure."

I narrow my eyes, barely restraining a growl. "He's the asshole who's waiting to buy the team if we don't make the playoffs."

Everyone freezes, and the air thickens around us. The tension is palpable, and one thing is for sure—David Carlisle has absolutely worn out his welcome.

Too bad he hasn't gotten the memo. He reaches out toward Jazz, and I'm not sure what his intention is, but Lincoln intercepts, grabbing his hand and twisting it at a painful looking angle.

"Touch her, and you'll lose this hand," Lincoln grits out, giving his hand another little twist.

David grimaces but quickly recovers, pulling his hand from Lincoln's grasp and shaking it out slightly. "You'll be the first one I trade, Dallas. I've always been a firm believer in a strict no fraternization policy, something you clearly have zero regard for. I hope you like it out West."

Lincoln takes a step toward him, going toe to toe, nose to nose. "I hope you like disappointment. Now get the fuck off my lawn before I embarrass you in front of everyone."

David scoffs, stepping around Lincoln and smiling at all of us like he didn't just get his ass kicked outta here. I'm ready to let him walk away quietly, until he leans down looking at Max, his head tilted. He has two seconds to get away from her before I snap. "Next generation loser, I presume. Good luck with this gene pool."

Thinking he has the upper hand he jingles his keys and takes off down the driveway. I move to follow him, not quite sure if I'm going to stab him with his own keys or just tell him off, but Jazz stops me with a hand on my chest.

Except he doesn't get the last word. Max turns around and calls out after him, "Better a loser than a douche-canoe like you."

I'm not sure if that's something she's allowed to say, but it wasn't any of the major swear words, so I'm prepared to let it slide. And also, not tell her mother—especially when Lincoln and Jazz give her a high-five and she beams as she shoulders her backpack and skips past me into the guesthouse.

"Nice use of, 'get off my lawn', Dallas." I clap him on the back with a laugh. "Very grumpy old man of you."

He shrugs, giving me a lopsided smile I'm sure my

sister loves. "Thought I'd take a page out of your play-book. Although, maybe you're not as grumpy anymore."

"That's what happens when you take our advice and go after the girl you're still pining for." Jazz puts her hands on her hips, and one of those damned eyebrows raises at me. "You're welcome, by the way."

Max must be rubbing off on me because I almost roll my eyes at her. "Oh, thank you so much for hiring my ex-girlfriend, even though I told you not to, and meddled in my life."

"You're welcome." She surprises me by pulling me in for a hug. "Although you would have found your way to her eventually. I just like to think I sped up the process."

"Thank you." This time when I say it, it's not drip-ping with sarcasm. I even clap a friendly hand on Lincoln's shoulder and meet his unwavering gaze. "Thank you for taking care of my family. I know you always have their back when I can't be there. I guess you'd make an okay brother-in-law one of these days."

I wasn't expecting him to start crying and hugging me or anything, but I kind of figured he'd do more than just stare at me. But then he smiles and pulls me in for one of those manly, back-clapping hugs.

"They're my family too," he nods toward the door-way, "Max, Riley, and yes, even you."

"Don't go getting all mushy on me, Dallas."

"Wouldn't dream of it, Benson." He shoots me a grin,

puts his arm around my sister, and after they both say their goodbyes to Max, head toward the house. By the time I make it inside, Max is sitting on the couch, feet propped up on the coffee table, and watching the hockey game.

Looks perfect to me. I grab us a couple of waters, kick off my shoes, and join her.

"Are you going to tell Mom I said douche-canoe?" she turns toward me and asks during the next commercial.

I laugh, opening my water and taking a sip. "Nope. Also, he is one."

"And if you don't make the playoffs, he gets the team? That doesn't seem right."

"I know." I nod toward the TV. "I think hockey was the only thing my dad actually cared about. It sure wasn't me, or anyone else in this family for that matter. But don't worry, we're going to do everything we can to make sure we keep the team."

She hums her approval, crossing her legs at the ankles. "I'm not worried. I know you've got it."

I put my feet up on the table beside her, settling in until dinner gets here. Or at least I was until Max leans forward, and I get a good glimpse of the long- sleeved Devils shirt she's wearing. Of course, it has Dallas' name and number on the back.

"Did he buy you that shirt?" I ask and point at it with a frown.

Her brows crash together and she purses her lips, looking at me like I've lost my mind. "No. I've had this shirt. You don't like it?"

"It's great," I say quickly and nearly choke on my own spit when I add, "Lincoln is a great player and I don't know, I guess he's a good guy." I add with a grumble, "If you like that sort of thing."

"Aunt Jazz offered to buy me a Dallas jersey too."

"Of course, she did."

Too bad they don't have Benson jerseys. Although, that doesn't mean I can't get them made. I am the fucking owner after all, and I should be able to do something simple like that.

But what if you're not the owner for very long?

I shove that voice back and choose to ignore it. Too bad we can't ignore David Carlisle. I have a feeling deep in the pit of my stomach that this asshole isn't going anywhere anytime soon. He was never one to back down from a fight when he played in the NHL, but I have news for him—neither was I.

And I'm sure as fuck not backing down from this one.

42

GORDON

I SIT DOWN AT THE CONFERENCE TABLE AND EXCHANGE A concerned look with Jazz before clearing my throat. "Guys, we have a bit of a problem."

Dean eyes me warily, and Mick steeples his hands, waiting for me to continue, but before I can get another word out, David barrels into the conference room, Riley hot on his heels.

"I assume you're talking about me," he states as he smooths a hand down his Devil red tie. There's a good chance I'm going to choke him with it.

"I'm so sorry," Riley apologizes and looks around the table, her frazzled gaze resting on me. "He was rather insistent, and I couldn't stop him from coming back here."

I put up a hand and sigh. "It's not your fault. This

man doesn't seem to understand what the word 'no' means. Please have security on standby."

"Yes, sir." She gives me one last apologetic look and practically flees from the room. Not that I can blame her. David Carlisle is as unpleasant as he is unwelcome, and the way he turns and leers at her as she leaves has my blood boiling. *Fucking lecherous bastard.*

He chuckles, and I sure as hell hope he doesn't think he's getting any brownie points with anyone here. "I'd hate to have to fire that one. She looks like she's a feisty little thing."

I slam my hand down on the desk making Jazz jump beside me. "What are you doing here?"

"Oh, man." He smiles smugly, sitting himself at the other end of the tables. "Not you too, Gordon. You and your sister need to get out more. I know this arena is large, but there are plenty of single people out there in Nashville."

I stare at him, my eyes narrowing, and I'm pretty sure my entire face just twitched.

"I don't know who you think you are, but this is a private meeting," Dean grits and stands, shrugging off his suit jacket. "If you don't leave willingly, I'm afraid I'll have to escort you."

David laughs, making no attempt to move. Not surprising. "I like your gumption, Prescott. I just wanted to stop by and introduce myself to my future team."

"Future team?"

All heads swivel toward me and I rake my hands through my hair, heaving a substantial breath. "This is David Carlisle. He used to play with my dad up in Toronto. Apparently, he's the third party waiting to buy the team should we fail to make the playoffs this year."

"And I'm very impressed with how buttoned up everyone's been about it. When I talked to Channel Eight, they had no idea," he says casually, propping his dirty dress shoes up on my conference table and giving us all a lazy smile. "You might want to turn on the TV."

Jazz shoots him a glare before standing and taking the long way around the room to grab the remote, making sure to bump into his chair hard enough to knock his feet down. "My bad."

"I'm sure." That sly smile falls off his face momentarily, but he's quick to slip his mask back in place.

She turns on the TV, and it's not even Channel Eight, but sure as shit, here we are, front and center. Our story, along with a candid interview from our *esteemed* guest, is being highlighted on several channels, including the sports network.

I'm going to jail for murder, that's all there is to it, and if the hardened look on Jazz's face is any indication, she's thinking the same thing. As I look around the table, I'm a little shocked to find matching expressions on Dean and Mick's faces, too.

They can't arrest us all, can they?

I'm about to throw him out of the building myself

when Mick stands up, pointing a finger at David. "I remember you from your days in the NHL. You were selfish and volatile, the very definition of *not a team player*. Now, I think it's about time you leave before I have your ass tossed out of this building. You don't own shit around here yet, and if I have my way, I'll never see you again."

David's smirk never falters as he stands, adjusts his tie, and looks around the room. "Just remember how replaceable you are, Coach."

With one last glance in my direction, he's gone.

I don't quite realize how much I'm shaking or how tight my jaw is until Jazz lays a hand on my shoulder. I don't relax completely, but at least I'm not going to break any teeth.

"Thanks, guys." Jazz turns off the television and pats Mick on the back. "The guy is a menace. He showed up at the house Saturday night."

Dean scoffs. "He needs his ass kicked. He just single-handedly created a media shitshow. I'm going to get on the phone with PR and see how we can get ahead of this before it turns into a circus. You guys might want to think about talking with the team. I'm sure Mick can get the entire team and all the coaching staff in for a meeting this afternoon."

Mick nods, shooting to his feet. "I can hold them after practice if you want to wait. I fucking hate that guy."

"Why don't you shorten practice today?" I run a hand down my face and blow out a breath. I really didn't want the entire team to know about this will stipulation because it could affect their play, and their dedication to this entire organization. But now that the news is out, there's no way I can't not address it. "If you get everyone together in the locker room in about an hour, we'll be down."

The three of them chatter amongst themselves as they leave to get shit handled. Not me. I let my head fall into my hands and I mutter every single swear word I know.

There's no way I'm handing the team over to Carlisle. He has no regard for anyone, and would only use this organization for his own self-serving agenda. The good people will quit, and eventually the players will get traded. He will single-handedly drive the Devils into the ground. I'll be okay, but the thousands of people who either work here or have contracts with us... they won't be.

I push to my feet, getting ready to head to my office, but the second Riley comes in, I stop and pull her into my arms. I close my eyes and surround myself with her warmth, her comfort, and sweet peach scent. She hugs me tightly, her head resting on my chest, and we stay like this for what feels like hours.

Eventually I pull back, brushing my lips against hers. "Thanks. I needed you."

"I figured." She gives me a playful wink and tries to

turn around, presumably to go back to her desk, but I pull her back to me, frame her face with my hands, and kiss her like she deserves.

She lets out a soft moan as I sweep my tongue into her mouth, sliding it against hers. She wraps one hand around my tie as the other curls around my neck, and fuck if I don't kiss her like this is our last. I take my time exploring her mouth, and when I'm seconds away from pushing her on the desk and ripping off her clothes, I pull back.

Dean pokes his head back in the room, a huge smile on his face, and despite all the bullshit going on, I find myself smiling back. "About damn time."

MICK DID his thing and got everyone piled in the locker room. Jazz and Lincoln are talking quietly right outside the room while I pace the hall. My insides twist, and even though I know most of these guys, I'm nervous. I'd like to think they'll have my back and won't let this get in their head come game time, but I just don't know.

"You ready?" Lincoln asks as he stops in front of me, head cocked, watching me.

I stop about a foot from him and adjust my tie. "Are you escorting me to the prom?"

Lincoln chuckles, shaking his head, and the look he shoots me is amused. "You should be so lucky." He pauses, has some sort of silent conversation with my sister, and nods toward the locker room. "She thinks you and I should address the team. Her, Mick and Dean will be behind us, but she thinks having the captain on your side might help."

"What do you think?" I raise a brow.

"I think they know I'm sleeping with one of the owners, but it couldn't hurt." At my growl, he puts both hands up and laughs. "I'm trying to loosen you up. It's gonna be fine."

With a shake of my head, I follow him into the locker room. Almost immediately, the conversations around us die, and that damned sense of dread is back. But the further I walk into the room, the more it lightens. I get a nod from Tag. Another one from Rhett, and one from Foster. A few more from Ian, Owen, and Dimitri.

I know these guys.

They're hard working, loyal, and even though a few of them like being pains in my ass, they're my friends.

I make my way to the front of the locker room, taking my place in front of my sister, my head coach, and my GM, feeling much more confident and determined than I did just minutes ago. Lincoln steps up next to me, his hand firm on my shoulder, and a look of under-standing passes between us.

"Over the past two years, we've faced different challenges, some big, and some small. The team went under new ownership, management, and to shake things up, we brought in a new coach." I glance at the guys behind me before turning back to the team. "I'm sure most of you have heard by now that there is a clause in my father's will; a clause that requires us to sell the team to someone of his choosing if we don't make the playoffs this year, and up until two nights ago, we had no idea who it was. This is just another challenge, one I'm confident we'll overcome."

"And if we don't?" This comes from West, one of the rookies, and it's a fair question.

"If we don't, we're sure as hell going to go down fighting. Legally, there doesn't seem to be anything we can do, but I have lawyers looking into it anyway." I take a deep breath and look around, moving from player to player, making sure to make direct eye contact with everyone. "I'm sorry I haven't been more open about this, but I didn't want it in the back of your minds every time you stepped out on the ice. There are enough distractions out there, and I didn't want this to be a heavy one resting on your shoulders."

Rhett stands up, thumping a fist over his heart. "This is my home, my family. Carlisle is a fucking prick, and there's no way he's getting his fucking fingers on any of this. You want to fight? We'll fight with you."

Tag is next, mimicking Rhett's movements. "Let's fight for the playoffs, for each other... and for Gordon and Jazlyn fucking Benson, because without them, this isn't a team I want to be on."

"Fuck that bloody wanker," Foster chimes in and is the next one to stand, thumping his chest, except he's grinning. "We're the fucking Nashville Devils, and this is our year. We're going to demolish everyone, starting with Detroit tomorrow."

The rest of the guys stand one by one, even the rookies and the brand-new trades. They pledge their allegiance to me and Jazz, and to this team. By the time the meeting is up, everyone is hyped and ready to kick ass at the game tomorrow, and every game after that.

I just hope that between the players, Mick, and his excellent team of coaches, they can pull it off.

Because Remington is right—they are family, and I'm not losing this one.

43

RILEY

It's been a long four weeks.

Gordon and Jazz haven't missed a game since the day all hell broke loose and Gordon talked to the team. They've been behind him every day since, and I'm not sure what he said, but they've been on one hell of a winning streak. We still have a few more games, but if we beat Vegas tonight, we make the playoffs.

Max and I have been to a few home games, but there's been nothing that compares to the energy surrounding tonight's game.

Gordon is already in the owner's box when we get there, and while he greets us with a smile, it quickly morphs into a frown when he sees our jerseys.

"What are those?" he asks, pointing between us, his lip curling up like he walked into a fart cloud, and for all I know, he did.

421

"Gloria made these for all of us." Max and I turn around, showing him the very sparkly Dallas on the back. "They're bedazzled."

"I can see that." The muscle in his jaw tics as he scoops up Max for a hug. "Are you excited for the game?"

"Excited to kick some Vegas butt!" She replies and lets out some sort of war cry, followed by her and Gordon doing this secret handshake thing I haven't been invited to learn—and then she promptly ditches us for some nachos and Chloe, Tag and Elle's daughter, who she's recently befriended.

"Still salty about the handshake?" Gordon asks as he wraps his arms around me, skimming my lips with his and leaning in to deepen the kiss.

I nip his bottom lip as I pull back, asking, "Still salty about the jersey?"

He retaliates, running his lips around the shell of my ear. "I don't particularly like seeing you with another man's name on your back."

"I could have worn a Wylder jersey."

He growls, biting down on the side of my throat. "I would have made you change and then taken you to my office to turn your ass a shade of red that would match your hair."

"Tempting," I smirk, knowing full well how that would end up. He'd spank me a few times before pushing me under his desk and having me show him how good I can be. Ask me how I know. "But wait until tonight—I got some special panties with your name across the front."

"I swear to every hockey god that if you're joking, I'm going to write my name across your stomach with my cum."

"You'll just have to wait and find out." He growls, but before he can respond, I pull Ryan and Gunner into a quick hug. "You guys made it."

Gunner nudges Gordon. "I was told it was kind of a big deal."

"Besides—" Ryan starts, but is quickly interrupted by Dean.

"What the hell are you two doing here?" he asks as he greets Ryan with a hug, but instead of saying anything to Gunner, he completely ignores him. Seems like there might be a story there. "I thought I told security that no football meatheads allowed."

"That was until Gunner wowed them with his dazzling personality."

"Doubtful," Dean replies before adding, "how's Dad?"

"Dad?" Gordon looks between the two of them, brows raised. "Are you two related?"

Dean shrugs, his gaze momentarily following Gunner as he excuses himself to get a drink from the bar. "Half-brothers. Not a lot of people know. We were raised by different moms."

Gordon leans in, almost like he's scrutinizing the two of them. Hell, I think he is. "You have the same mouths. Chin too. And you both get on my nerves."

Interesting. I'm sure there's a story there too, but it doesn't seem like now is the time to ask.

As the three of them fall into easy conversation, I hear Max call my name and I slip away, finding an empty seat next to Jazz. She's got Max and Chloe on her other side, with Elle and Lucy next to them. I give everyone a small wave, and then the lights go down.

44

GORDON

MY GIRLS ARE WATCHING THE GAME ALONG WITH THE other wives and girlfriends, and I can't seem to settle down. My hands are shaking, my knee aches, my insides are twisted into all these tiny knots, and this is the first time since I quit that I'd really like a drink.

But I refuse to be my father, so I chug the rest of my soda and throw the can as hard as humanly possible into the garbage can.

Of course, that's when David *fucking* Carlisle walks up, clinking the ice around in his bourbon. His amused expression has my hands clenching, and I have to remind myself he's losing. He didn't get the rise out of us he wanted with the media, and instead of his empty threats getting inside everyone's heads, they've motivated us.

The city is on our side which is why this game is sold out, and there is a sea of red in the seats. It's surreal, and

I'm finally starting to see how this can be part of my legacy, not just my dad's leftovers.

"I don't believe I invited you to the box," I growl as I button up my suit jacket, my jaw automatically clenching.

He raises his glass, slowly taking a sip of his bourbon, making sure to keep eye contact with me over the glass. "I wouldn't want to miss out on your fine collection of whiskey and bourbon. Don't worry, after you lose tonight, I'll keep a seat up here for you. It's the least I can do for your old man."

My teeth grind and my fingers flex. This guy is a complete bag of dicks. I know he's trying to get a rise out of me, and I can't help but give him exactly what he wants. He knows exactly what buttons to push—and how hard.

"Old man? You talking about yourself?" Gloria chimes in, stopping next to us and passing me a glass of water with a wink. "You know, guys with attitudes like this are usually so angry because they have small peckers." She leans down, inspecting the crotch of his dress pants over the top of her glasses, and it takes everything I've got to keep from laughing out loud. Especially when David shifts and tries to cover himself up with his glass. "Yep, just as I thought. It's a micro."

His face turns a very lovely bright shade of red. It's not quite Devils' red, but still, I'll take it.

"It's... it's not... it's not small!" he stutters, giving

me one last glare—one that loses all potency with his red, blotchy face—and scurries off. He's probably gone to terrorize some small children.

And then I do something I never in a million years thought I would do—I pull Gloria in for a hug and lay a kiss on her weathered cheek. "Gloria, you're a beautiful human being."

She chuckles, patting me on the chest, something that started out innocently, but now I'm pretty sure I've just been felt up. "He's just jealous of the BDE that surrounds you."

"Do I dare ask what that is?" I raise a brow and go to take a sip of my water, but think better of it. Whatever she's about to say will probably have me choking on it.

"Big Dick Energy, duh," she says as casually as if she were talking about the weather. "And you have it in spades. Your girlfriend is a lucky girl."

"I'm the one that's lucky. She gave me a family."

"You've always had one." This time when she pats me it's lower, and I have to take a step back before she full on grabs my dick. "You just needed someone to open your eyes."

"Thanks, Gloria." I'm tempted to pull her in for another hug, but I think I've reached my groping limit.

Instead, she pulls my arm toward the seats. "Come on, sir, you're missing a good game. Let's watch your team wipe their asses with Vegas."

"You mean wipe the floors?"

"Sure," she shrugs, leading us to a few empty spots close to the ice.

As soon as we sit down, Max sits on my other side and gives us a running commentary of the game, including what we missed—a great slap shot by Foster close to center ice that gave us our first goal, another goal by Lincoln after he snagged the puck from a Vegas player, and a hit by Rhett that had Wylder crumpling to the ice like an accordion. That one made me chuckle.

He's playing, so he's clearly fine. I'm not that much of an asshole, but still. There was a brief period of time I thought he was Max's dad, and for lots of years, I thought he dated Riley. None of it may be true, but it doesn't mean I like the guy. He's still a dick.

We're down to the third period. Five minutes left in the game, and while we're ahead by one, I've seen the score swing dramatically in the other direction in a matter of seconds—especially when the guys are playing like they are tonight.

Both teams want this win.

Wylder has the puck, and damn he looks confident as he skirts by Tag. My fingers are digging into the armrest when I feel Max's hand on mine. I turn mine over and she laces our fingers together.

"We got this." Her smile is easy, and her confidence in me and my team levels me.

I nod, glancing down the row of chairs at Dean, who's unusually calm and collected. He meets my gaze and smiles, giving me a thumbs up that has me questioning his judgment.

"Don't mind him," Gloria whispers. "He's too busy trying to ignore the football player to give the game his full attention."

"Ryan?"

"The other one."

Weird, but I quickly write it off. I'm pretty sure half the stuff that flies out of Gloria's mouth is nonsense.

But it doesn't matter. I'm drawn back to the game as the crowd cheers, chanting for a goal, just as fucking Wylder misses the shot and Lincoln takes control of the puck. He passes it to Tag, who passes it to Foster, and the three of them skate down to the other end of the ice, keeping up this elegant dance between them. The Bruiser brothers are out there doing what they do best, and I'm on the edge of my seat as Tag circles their net with the puck.

I lose sight of it for a second as it goes back and forth between him and Lincoln. The Vegas goalie surges to the right side of the net and Lincoln shoots. I hold my breath, Max clutches my hand, I even think Gloria pitches forward to watch.

The puck sails over the goalie's shoulder and sinks right into the left side of the net. There are two minutes and ten seconds left of the third period. The crowd goes wild, everyone standing to catch the last bit of the game.

With a two-goal lead, we just have to keep them from catching up.

The shifts change. The puck goes up and down the ice. The time counts down, and I swear this is the slowest hundred-and-thirty seconds of my life.

It gets down to sixty seconds, and no one else has scored. Forty-five. Thirty. Twenty.

There's no way they can catch up now. We've won the game. We're going to the playoffs.

The Nashville Devils are going to the fucking playoffs!

Every single bit of tension I've been carrying for the past two years flits away with the cheering of the crowd.

We fucking did it.

Fuck my dad. Fuck him so hard.

Max jumps up and I lift her in my arms, hugging her as her arms pump in the air. She's screaming in my ear, and I couldn't give two fucks if I can't hear tomorrow. When I put her down, we run through our secret hand-shake and she says something I can't hear before running to meet Chloe.

Riley finds me in the crowd, and despite Max's no kissing rule, I pull her to me, sweeping my tongue into her mouth and bending her backwards. Somewhere around us a camera goes off. They could put this on the Jumbotron and I wouldn't care.

I pull back and reluctantly let Riley stand on her own. "I love you," I shout over the crowd.

She smiles, grabbing my hand. "I love you, too."

I'm searching for my sister when David steps in front of me, this time his face is Devil red.

"Carlisle, do me a favor and get the fuck out of my arena. This is my team, and I don't want to see you or your small penis ever again." I push past him, linking my free hand with Max and holding tight to my girls as we all make our way out of the box and down to the ice.

I was hoping to see Jazz before we got there, but she's several yards ahead, chatting with Dean. Most of the time the arena is packed with people leaving the game, but it looked like most everyone was still out there, watching the team take their victory laps and listening to the announcer wrap up the regular season.

Rhett is the first one to skate over to us, finding his wife and keeping her from strutting on the ice while she's almost nine months pregnant. Tag lifts up Chloe and kisses Elle. Foster grabs Mason, Avery's son, and skates around her.

Lincoln gets to Max first. She gives him a strong fist bump before he pulls her and Riley in for a quick hug.

He looks at me, brows raised. "What's it gonna be, big guy?"

I huff a laugh, patting him on the back and he takes that as his clue to wrap me up in a bear hug. "That was a good game. I'm glad to have you on my team."

"I'll always be on your team." He gives me one more

pat on the back and grabs something from Coach Weller. "Now excuse me while I propose to your sister."

The smile he gives me is nothing but pure bliss as he skates a circle around Jazz before sinking down to one knee. "Jazz, I love you more than anything—even hockey. You're the best thing in my life, and I would be humbled to have you by my side for the rest of it. I want to grow old with you. I want to see you pregnant with my babies, and I never want to let you go. Jazlyn Rose Benson, will you marry me?"

Riley and Max squeal beside me as Jazz shouts out a resounding yes and kneels down to kiss him. It gets a little more graphic than that, but I'm refusing to see it for anything other than chaste.

"Dad!" Max pulls on my hand, tugging my attention away from my sister and my soon to be brother-in-law. "Adrian Wylder."

The smile falls off my face as Wylder stops in front of me. We played against each other when I was in the NHL, but we haven't said two words to each other since high school.

"Good game, Benson," Wylder says, pulling off his glove and extending his hand to me.

It takes me a second to register what's happening, and then shake his hand, making sure my grip is nice and strong. "Thanks."

"I mean, if you were playing, we would've won." He

smirks and waves at Riley. "Nice to see you, Adams. You look good. Happy."

She slides closer, tucking herself under my arm. "I am."

He nods, mumbling something to himself before meeting my eyes. "Not surprising. You two were always grossly in love."

"You should see them kiss," Max says as she scrunches up her nose and makes a gagging sound, but Adrian just smiles.

"I have. It's bad for everyone." He shoves my shoulder playfully. "I'll leave you to it. Believe it or not, I was rooting for you. It wouldn't be as much fun beating your team without you at the helm."

"Thanks," I huff out a laugh, wrapping my arms around Riley. "Max, look away. I'm going to kiss your mom."

She makes more gagging sounds, but I couldn't be happier.

I've got my girls. My team.

I've got everything I need.

Epilogue

Three months later-Gordon

"HEY THERE, MR. BENSON," RILEY GREETS AND TUGS on my apron, a manly grilling one, not the pink frilly thing Lincoln likes to wear.

I slide my arm around her shoulders, kissing her in a way that might seem indecent for a family BBQ. "Hello, future Mrs. Benson."

She sighs, glancing at the engagement ring I gave her last week at our beach getaway. "I can't believe you spent so much money on a ring."

"Wait until you see the houses I have lined up for us to look at." I smirk down at her, and she lets out an exasperated sigh.

"I'm glad you and Jazz are finally selling this giant

monstrosity of a house, but you know I don't need anything extravagant."

"I'm obviously the high maintenance one here." I kiss the tip of her nose before flipping the burgers.

"Wyatt Patrick Remington!" Rhett semi-yells and holds his three-month-old at arm's length. "Lucy, he pissed all over me."

Foster doubles over with laughter. "Mate, you have to point it down."

"Don't you think I know that?" Rhett snaps, grabbing Wyatt's diaper bag and heading toward the house, but before he heads inside, he glances at me over his shoulder. "I'm going to borrow your bathroom for a second."

"Have fun," I call after him, shaking my head. I never thought I'd see Rhett Remington carrying around a pink diaper bag with a fuzzy blue bear on the front, but here we are.

"Don't worry about him," Foster says, stopping by the grill and hovering over the hamburgers and bratwurst, but I have news for him—they're not ready yet. "He's just pissed I knocked up his sister."

I chuckle, running a hand through my hair. "That would do it. Did you at least break the news gently?"

"Nope," he chuckles and leans toward me, the biggest smile growing across his face. "I called him while we were in England last month. Told him I knocked her up and to have a nice summer. And then I hung up on him."

"I'm sure he was pissed," I say at the same time Riley replies, "Ouch."

"Oh, yeah. He's a big softy though. He got over it when Avery gave him a copy of her newest book, because she dedicated it to him." He shakes his head and glances back toward the house. "Bloody twat though, he didn't deserve the whole book."

Riley laughs, grabbing my ass before walking away. "I'm going to mingle. Have fun with your meat."

"Is this where the cool guys are hanging out?" Lincoln asks, replacing Riley on my other side.

"It was," Foster points out with a smile.

Lincoln mutters, *asshole*, under his breath and nudges me. "Hey, have you heard from Carlisle?"

"Nope." I pull some of the burgers off the grill and load them up on a plate. "The fucker vanished back into whatever hole he crawled out of. Last I heard, he was getting divorced by wife number four. Not sure how he tricked one woman into marrying his ass, let alone multiple."

"No shit."

"Next year is going to be fun though," Foster starts while grabbing one of the peppers from the grill and promptly dropping it in the grass. "That's bloody hot! Despite you lot trading out the Bruiser brothers." He pins me with an unhappy look. "I want the cup. I like how we look."

"Me, too." I glance around the backyard, taking in

the team and their families. One last hurrah before this house is sold, and my dad's ghost can finally be laid to rest.

We played a hell of a season this year. We got knocked out of the playoffs at the end of the second round, but there's always next year.

Trading Ian and Owen wasn't my first choice, but Dean knows what he's doing, and they'll fit in nicely in Vegas. Ian was the most excited to leave. He kept chanting 'showgirls', and I feel like he might have some unrealistic expectations.

I wouldn't be at all surprised if he decided to moonlight as a Chippendale dancer. He showed me some of his moves the last time he was in the office, and while Riley seemed to enjoy them, they needed work.

I'm going to miss them, but we'll see each other several times a year. Between them and Wylder, playing Vegas is going to be fun.

Especially when we beat them.

Everyone seems to realize there's food at the same time and floods the table set up with all the side dishes Riley—under Harper and Jazz's supervision—made this morning, and I add the finished hamburgers and brats.

I'm content hanging back and watching everyone smiling, laughing, and eating. That's when Lucy finds me.

"Happy looks good on you," she says and nudges me with her elbow.

I nod to Rhett as he comes out of the house, carrying his now clean baby. "You, too. Who knew you'd find it with Mr. Grumpy?"

She laughs, giving me a little side eye. "Funny, that's what he calls you."

"Ha. Ha. Ha."

"I thought so."

"Still happy with the football players?" I ask, even though I know the answer. I've tried to get Lucy to come back and work for me countless times, but the answer is always the same.

She raises a brow. "You mean your best friends? Yep. I can't wait until the season starts. This year is going to be a good one."

I know she's talking about the football season, but it's going to be a good year all around.

I glance to Max, who's still swimming in the pool with Chloe, Tag, and his now wife, Elle, and then to Riley. My life is perfect.

And now that I no longer have the clause from my father's will hanging over my head, I can try to relax and enjoy myself

Because this—family—is what makes life worth living.

It took me a long time to figure that out.

I know what I was missing all those years... love, support. And Riley and Max. Now I have my girls, my team, and my fucking freedom.

That's my legacy.

THANK you so much for reading BOSSY DEVIL!! I really hope you loved seeing Gordon and Riley fall back in love the second time around. Gordon surprised me in so many ways and I really hope his story came across as beautifully broken as I intended.

This story is the end of the Devils, but we will still see them along with the players in other books.

I APPRECIATE each and every one of you for taking this journey with me.

As an Indie Author, I would love your help spreading the word about BOSSY DEVIL. If you enjoyed the story, please consider leaving a review on Amazon, Goodreads, or even referring it to a friend. Even a sentence or two makes a huge difference.

Thank you for taking this journey with me.

Melissa

Also by Melissa Ivers

<u>DEVILS HOCKEY</u>

FORBIDDEN DEVIL

UNTAMED DEVIL

BROODY DEVIL

DIRTY DEVIL

BOSSY DEVIL

JINGLE DEVIL (A Devils Holiday Novella)

<u>ACES FOOTBALL</u>

FALSE START

LOOSE END (COMING SOON)

TIGHT END (COMING SOON)

<u>LOVE IN ASPEN</u>

MISTLETOE AND MISCHIEF

Acknowledgments

Damn, I thought Foster was tough, but then Gordon looked at me and said, *hold my beer.*

Christiana. I think it goes without saying how much you mean to me, and how much you contribute to everything I do. Even if all I need is a pat on the head, you're there to do it. You helped make this the masterpiece it is. We took a grumpy, broken hero, and we made him beautiful.

Angel, you were with me every step of the way. You were my cheerleader, you cursed at me when I left you hanging, and you encouraged me to keep going when I thought things were looking grim.

Echo, you came in at the last minute and made me throw something in the book, but it came out so much stronger.

To all my alpha readers, you guys are always invaluable. I wouldn't be where I am without your support.

A HUGE thank you to all the reviewers and bloggers for reading the story and helping me spread the word about it.

And I especially want to thank YOU! Thank you for reading. Thank you for making it to the end. And hopefully, thank you for loving it.

Melissa

About the Author

Lover of all things romance and hockey, she also loves to bake extra delicious treats. Melissa Ivers loves to write steamy stories with all those hot, alpha men and women who can bring them to their knees, literally and figuratively. Melissa lives in Kentucky with her eye-rolling teenage son and two of the laziest dogs known to man. She has numerous fictional boyfriends, but—shhhh—they don't know about each other.

When she isn't writing or working, you'll find her under a blanket on the couch reading a book on her Kindle, binge watching shows off Netflix, such as the *Office* and *Vampire Diaries* and being an all-around joy.

To keep current with what Melissa is doing stalk her on social media or check out her website.

https://iversdare.store/

facebook.com/Melissa-Ivers-101656934932663

instagram.com/melissa_ivers_author

amazon.com/stores/Melissa-Ivers/author/B08LP6G625

tiktok.com/@melissa_ivers

Printed in Great Britain
by Amazon